THE
DEVIL'S WHISPER

THE
DEVIL'S
WHISPER

MIYUKI MIYABE

TRANSLATED BY
Deborah Stuhr Iwabuchi

FIC
MIYABE

KODANSHA INTERNATIONAL
Tokyo · New York · London

Originally published in Japanese in 1989 by Shinchosha, Tokyo, under the title *Majutsu wa sasayaku.*

Distributed in the United States by Kodansha America, Inc., and in the United Kingdom and continental Europe by Kodansha Europe Ltd.

Published by Kodansha International Ltd., 17–14 Otowa 1-chome, Bunkyo-ku, Tokyo 112–8652, and Kodansha America, Inc.

ISBN 978–4–7700–3053–5

First edition, 2007
15 14 13 12 11 10 09 08 07   10 9 8 7 6 5 4 3 2 1

Library of Congress Cataloging-in-Publication Data

Miyabe, Miyuki
   [Majutsu wa sasayaku. English]
   The devil's whisper / Miyuki Miyabe; translated by Deborah Iwabuchi.
       p. cm.
   "First published in Japanese as Majutsu wa sasayaku by Shinchosa"—
T.p. verso.
   ISBN 978–4–7700–3053–5
   I. Iwabuchi, Deborah Stuhr. II. Title.
   PL856.I856M3513 2007
   895.6'35—dc22
                            2007008659

www.kodansha-intl.com

CONTENTS

Prologue

Tokyo Daily News, September 2, page 14:

Wedding Jitters? Woman Leaps from High-rise

A young woman jumped to her death from the roof of the six-story Palace Okura apartment block in Miyoshi, Tokyo, at 3:10 PM yesterday. According to the Ayase precinct police, the woman was Fumie Kato (24), a resident of the building. Kato was seen climbing over the 1.5-meter guardrail on the roof and jumping 15 meters, to the street below. Kato was due to marry next week. She left no suicide note, and police are trying to establish a motive.

From the evening tabloid *Arrow*, October 9:

At Tokyo's Takadanobaba Station today at 14:45, a young woman jumped from the platform into the path of a Tozai Line limited express train bound for Nakano, and was declared dead at the scene. The woman was identified as Atsuko Mita (20), a company employee residing at Co-op Kawaguchi in Sengoku, K—— City, Saitama prefecture. A man waiting for the train noticed Mita behaving strangely and tried to stop her, but was too late. There was no suicide note, but the police are tentatively labeling it a suicide.

You never get the full picture of an incident or accident when reading about it in the newspaper, nor can you ever appreciate the shock of those who happened to be on the scene. Readers find out what happened, but not what was left behind.

The readers didn't know that when Fumie Kato jumped off the roof a woman had been up there airing out her futons. They didn't know that the woman heard Fumie running up the stairs to the roof. She saw Fumie looking back—it was as if she were being chased—and watched as she ran across the rooftop, scrambled frantically over the guardrail, and fell. Nor did the readers know that the woman went over to the spot at the guardrail, touched the cold metal, and just as quickly let go.

The readers did not watch the police officers on the scene scooping up pieces of Fumie's brain and putting it in plastic bags. The building caretaker came out and hosed the blood off the street, then sprinkled the area with salt to purify it against similar misfortune. Fumie Kato herself had had no recollection of talking to someone on the phone immediately before her death.

The readers didn't know about the businessman who tried to save Atsuko Mita. He had been standing on the platform hoping that his plans to refinance his housing loan would go smoothly. Atsuko had walked unsteadily past him, glancing back several times as if suspecting that something or someone were following her. That's what she was doing when her foot went over the edge.

The readers will never know that the businessman reached out to grab the collar of Atsuko's thin jacket, and that she might have been saved if only she had buttoned it all the way up to the neck. When the train blew into the station with a high-pitched metal-on-metal screech and snatched her off the platform, the man was left standing dumbfounded, the feel of the jacket's fabric still on his hands. The readers hadn't seen Atsuko earlier, when she read the train schedule out loud for an old man standing on the same platform. They hadn't seen him doff his hat in thanks and head up the stairs.

It took a while to clean up the scene because her body had been splattered in all directions. They couldn't find her head until they slowly backed up the train and it fell with a moist thud onto the tracks from the coupling between the first and second cars. The readers didn't see Atsuko Mita's eyes, both darkly open.

All these details remained buried between the printed lines.

And now—

Something else was taking place of which the newspaper readers were unaware. Another young woman was getting out of a taxi and waving good-bye to her two friends in the back seat. She had wanted the driver to let her off in front of her apartment and she wished now that she had insisted, but she told her friends that she would be fine; they could let her off on the main road from where it was just a short walk home. There in the deserted road under the bluish streetlights, she repeated those same words to herself. There was nothing to be afraid of—she only had to turn a corner and cross a single street no more than a hundred meters away. She began to walk.

Just before she turned the corner, her wristwatch alarm went off. It was as loudly out of place as a sound during a pause in a concert.

It was at that moment that she was sure she heard someone stealing up behind her. She walked faster, and she could hear the steps behind her speed up, too. She looked back. The street was empty, but she knew she had to escape before something dreadful happened. She mustn't be caught!

She began to shake and broke into a run. Stumbling along with her hair in her eyes and her shoes clacking on the road, she was too scared to scream. Her only thoughts were to run; to escape. *I've got to get home . . . to safety! Help me!*

She didn't slow down when she reached the intersection with its red light. Help came abruptly and in the worst possible form as she was blinded by a set of headlights.

On that same night, under the same sky, a pair of pale hands opened up a scrapbook. On the right-hand page were the articles about the deaths of the two women, neatly cut out and positioned. Fingers so white they might have been bleached reached out to lightly tap the newsprint.

Fumie Kato and Atsuko Mita.

On the left-hand page was a single color photograph of a young man wearing heavy black-framed spectacles and a smile that revealed a set of straight white teeth.

A clock somewhere struck twelve midnight.

The white hands closed the scrapbook and turned out the light.

How It All Started

In his dream, Mamoru Kusaka had gone back twelve years to when he was four years old. He was in the house where he had been born, and his mother, Keiko, was there, too. She was standing next to the shoe rack by the front door, the telephone in her hand. Slightly hunched over, she was twisting the black cord in her fingers as she listened, nodding and interjecting an "Uh-huh" or "I see" every ten seconds or so.

This scene was not something Mamoru was recalling from memory. He hadn't actually heard the conversation when his father's boss called to say his father hadn't reported in to work that day. It wasn't until much later that Mamoru learned his father was missing. But in the haze of his dream, Mamoru was sitting against a wall, hugging his knees and watching his mother go pale as she spoke quietly into the phone.

Mamoru woke up and stared at the rafters in the ceiling, wondering why he was having a dream like this all these years later.

He often dreamed of his special friend, Gramps. These dreams were usually memories of the last days they had spent together. The old man must have known his time had come because he had given Mamoru a brand new set of tools. Then there had been the safe with the triple lock, really tough. It had been the boy's final test.

Mamoru pulled himself up so he could see his bedside clock. It was only two in the morning. He sighed and pulled the covers over his head again, but in the quiet of night he could hear his Aunt Yoriko's soft voice coming from downstairs.

She was on the phone.

Mamoru kicked off his futon and swung his legs over the edge of the bed. The floor was cold as he stepped out into the hallway. At almost the same moment Maki, looking sleepy and with a cardigan over her pajamas, came out of her room on the other side of the hall.

"It's the phone," she mumbled and started down the stairs ahead of Mamoru.

Mamoru could see that his cousin was worried. Her father was a taxi driver and she knew full well what a midnight telephone call could mean. Mamoru tensed.

Yoriko set the receiver back on the hook as the two came downstairs and stood barefoot in front of her.

"What's the matter?" asked Maki.

Yoriko frowned. "Well, it happened."

"An accident?"

Yoriko nodded.

"What hospital is he in? Dad's been hurt, hasn't he?"

"It's not your father."

"So what happened?"

"He had an accident all right." Yoriko licked her lips, hesitating to go on. "He hit someone."

The November cold ran through Mamoru's feet and straight up to his heart.

"It was a young woman. She died instantly. That call was from the police."

"Police?"

"Your father's been arrested."

Mamoru was awake for the rest of the night. Only nine months had passed since he had come to live with Yoriko Asano, his mother's elder sister, and he was finally getting used to his new family and life in Tokyo.

The Asanos lived in the old Tokyo downtown area, below sea level. The rivers and canals that ran through the area were higher than the rooftops. Yoriko's husband, Taizo, had driven a taxi for almost twenty years. Maki, their only child, had just graduated from junior college the spring before and was in her first job.

Mamoru had been born and raised in the city of Hirakawa, north of Tokyo, where the cherry trees bloomed a little later than they did in the capital. It was an old castle town and boasted a small but good quality natural hot spring. The locals made their livelihood on tourism and the lacquerware for which the area was famous.

Mamoru's father, Toshio Kusaka, had worked for city hall. He had been serving as assistant to the finance section chief when he disappeared, right after it was discovered that fifty million yen in public funds were missing.

Mamoru could vaguely remember a small family celebration when his father had been promoted. Who would have thought then that his father's position would one day be splashed across the headlines proclaiming the crime that had made Mamoru and his mother social outcasts?

Not only that, but there had been a woman involved.

After his father disappeared, Mamoru and his mother had stayed in Hirakawa. Twelve years later, last December, Keiko Kusaka had died suddenly of a stroke at the age of thirty-eight.

After she collapsed, Keiko had briefly regained consciousness and had told Mamoru about an aunt he had never known—her sister in Tokyo. She instructed him to contact his aunt if anything should happen to her.

Mamoru had quickly found his mother's address book and called. Both Yoriko and Taizo had come immediately, and they had been with Mamoru when his mother died. It was only then that Yoriko had filled him in on the family history.

"I married your uncle when I was eighteen," she told him. "Oh, your grandparents refused to give their permission, so we eloped." Yoriko spoke in the forthright tone typical of Tokyoites. "I knew why they were so mad. Now he's an honest taxi driver, but in those days he wasn't going anywhere. After we got married, I almost left him lots of times. But I had my pride. I wasn't about to run back to that country town with a baby in my arms. There wasn't anything for me there."

Yoriko had finally decided to reconnect with her parents and sister a few years before. "You can laugh if you like, but I was watching a soap opera on TV, and I just decided to do it. I guess it was time. Taizo was making a steady living, and I suppose I just didn't need to rebel anymore. Maki and your uncle both agreed I should do it, so I wrote to the old address."

The letter was sent back stamped "return to sender." Yoriko, however, was determined to make contact with her family, so she jumped on a train and headed for Hirakawa. She soon found someone she knew in her old neighborhood and learned where her sister was.

"I went straight to the factory where your mother was working, and I recognized her right away. She hadn't changed much. I hadn't seen her for more than fifteen years, but I knew her as soon as I saw her. Of course things weren't easy. I'd left and we'd never really been all that close, so we didn't have much to say to each other. She took me to our parents' grave, and I apologized to them for everything. After that she finally started telling me about herself. She wasn't very specific, and she didn't even let me meet you. It was my fault, so I couldn't complain. I was the big sister who hadn't even been there for our parents' funerals."

Yoriko made no further attempts to see her nephew. She didn't feel any pull from her old hometown, and it was clear that Keiko had little interest in resuming the relationship.

"I didn't blame her," said Yoriko. "It wasn't something she could ever forgive me for." The two sisters did begin a sort of correspondence, however, writing letters to each other every month or so. Finally, after about a year, Keiko told her sister what had happened to her family.

"What a shock! I felt so sorry for her. But she was exasperating, too. I don't know how many times I told her to forget that awful husband of hers and come here with you to live with us. But she refused. She said she knew Toshio would come back someday, and she wanted to be there when he did. She always was stubborn. She said she'd brought you up to believe your father would eventually come home."

There was something else Mamoru never knew until after his mother died: when his father had disappeared twelve years before, he had left divorce papers behind. His name was on them, and he had affixed his personal seal. All Keiko had had to do was sign her own name and submit them to the authorities, but she had never done so.

Mamoru told his aunt that it made him feel as if he had never really known his mother. Yoriko nodded sympathetically, and then added, "But it was just like her to do that. And you know, I don't even know what your father looked like. Keiko never showed me a photo, and I didn't want to see one anyway. I heard somewhere that he was tall, and not too bad looking."

Yoriko paused and took a long look at her nephew. "You look like your mother. Especially around the eyes. It makes me worry that you'll be like her. She was strong, but you just can't live all alone. She took everything on herself. And then . . . well, I lost her."

After Keiko's funeral, Yoriko asked Mamoru to come and live with her family in Tokyo. One of the reasons he decided to go may have been that he saw something in his aunt's eyes that he had never seen in his mother's.

Life in Tokyo had not been easy at first. He got used to the city soon enough, but it was hard learning to live with a new family. Maki was the one who had helped him out with that. From the very first she treated him like he'd always lived there. At first he thought it was out of pity, but he gradually realized that it was just the way she was.

The first time they met, she had laughed and said, "So now that I've suddenly got a sixteen-year-old brother, it makes me an old lady at twenty-one." Mamoru found out later that Taizo had summed up his first impression of his nephew as, "He's a gloomy kid, isn't he?" Maki's response had been, "Actually, that's my favorite type."

Once Maki had called Mamoru from the station after a night out drinking with her friends. "I can't find a taxi. Come get me." Mamoru had found Maki leaning against a utility pole singing as a male friend stood by looking on.

"Are you her brother?" The guy scratched his head and motioned at Maki. "I was going to walk her home . . ."

"Leave him alone," Maki called out drunkenly to her friend. "Mamoru, I don't want you to ever become a city boy like him!"

Mamoru was stuck dragging her home, and Maki never stopped singing. When Mamoru finally burst out laughing, she laughed right along.

"See?" she said. "Life in Tokyo isn't so bad!"

No, it wasn't bad at all, decided Mamoru. And that was why it was so hard tonight, looking out into the dark and listening to Maki weeping.

Mamoru finally jumped out of bed and went to the window. There was a canal right in front of the house. Between the house and the canal was a sloping concrete bank. Depending on the wind direction, you could smell the river from inside the house. It wasn't too bad, except on the hottest summer days.

Mamoru had never seen a canal before he came to Tokyo. They flowed in artificially straight concrete beds, going exactly where they were told. In Hirakawa, rivers were no danger to the population, and were left in their natural state. They were lively, and they all had their own forms of self-expression. The canals in Tokyo were all drowsy and tame, and they seemed to like it that way.

When Mamoru had mentioned this to his uncle, the response had been quick. "You say that now, but just you wait till a typhoon comes through."

In mid-September, a large storm hit the Kanto Plain. Mamoru put on a raincoat, and went out to stand on the concrete bank with Taizo, finally understanding what he meant.

The river was howling. *We rivers have awoken!* it seemed to say as it gathered up the swiftly falling rainwater and pulled its power inside, all the while continuing its relentless flow. *When you have this much power, you don't have to hurry. If you don't watch out, we'll break down these banks and, at a single stroke, flatten out the land that was ours to begin with. We'll take back the land, along with everything you humans think is yours, and wash it all out to sea.*

As he recalled that night, Mamoru felt the urge to go out for a look right now. The river was still; it looked like a smooth black board. On the opposite bank was a garage for a tour bus company that was lit up all night, its bright lights standing out in the quiet streets. Traffic signals interspersed along the road occasionally blinked red and green; beautiful in a melancholy sort of way.

Mamoru climbed up the bank and walked along the top just as he had the time the typhoon came through. He climbed down the rusty iron staircase that led down under the bridge, where a single thin column was marked with numbers to measure the height of the water. During the typhoon, he had stood there with Taizo, both of them blinking hard to keep the rain out of their eyes as they looked up at it. The stone column was marked at the levels the river had reached long ago during typhoons that had destroyed the entire area. There was one mark right about the height of Mamoru's head and another a foot or so higher. Next to each was the name of the typhoon and the date. To the side of these inscriptions was a red line labeled "Danger level."

Taizo had pointed at that mark. "The water will never get that high again," he said. "Those floods are a thing of the past. It's safe here now; you'll never have to worry about that."

After a childhood cursed by bad luck, Mamoru had started a new life in a new home with a new family. But now fate had intervened again. He was sure that it was he who had brought this calamity on the Asano family, and now he was having doubts about whether the neighborhood would be safe from flooding with him living there.

The river was sleeping. Mamoru found a rock at his feet, picked it up and threw it into the water. He heard it plop down surprisingly close to him. It must be high tide.

Something darker than night began to seep into Mamoru's heart.

---·---

College Co-ed Hit by Taxi

About midnight on November 14 Yoko Sugano (21), a junior at Toa Women's College, was struck by a taxi driven by Taizo Asano (50) at the Midori Itchome intersection in K—— Ward, Tokyo. Sugano died of her injuries at the scene. Asano was arrested for reckless driving and taken to Joto Police Station for questioning.

The man learned about the accident in the morning paper when the headline caught his eye. The report was in a small typeface near the bottom of an inside page. He scanned it and went on, and it was a few seconds before the meaning sank in. He went back and read it again, carefully checking the details, then folded up the paper, took off his glasses, and rubbed his eyes. There was no mistaking either the name or the address.

Next he reached for a business newspaper, and opened it up. The same accident had been reported with an additional couple of lines stating that the taxi driver had been charged with running a red light.

The man shook his head as he stared at the print. It wasn't fair.

He heard his late-rising wife on the stairs. He could tell from the sound of her footsteps that she was still not quite awake. What would she say when she saw his face? *Have the stocks dropped? Did you lose a customer? An accident? Someone you know die?* She'd come out with something like that, wanting to know why he looked so grim.

But he couldn't talk about it to her—or to anybody else.

He stood up and left the living room so she wouldn't see him, went into the bathroom, turned the water on in the sink, and let it run over his hands. The water was almost as cold as the memory of a certain cold, rainy morning many years before. He splashed water on his face over and over again. The water still dripping from his chin, he looked at his face in the clouded mirror. His complexion was gray.

He could hear the sound of the TV. His wife must have turned it on. He spoke to himself in a low voice that she wouldn't be able to hear.

"It's not fair."

He wiped his face with a towel, walked through the kitchen filled with the aroma of coffee, and climbed the stairs. Going into his study, he carefully closed the door, pulled out a key, and opened the bottom drawer of his desk. In the drawer was a blue-jacketed photo album. He pulled it out and opened it. There were three photos. One was of a boy, fifteen or sixteen years old. He was wearing a school uniform and shouldering a backpack. Another photo was of the same boy walking with a young woman who looked about twenty. The third was of a dark green taxi. A heavy-set middle-aged man was washing it. The boy was there, too, a hose in his hands. It looked like he might turn it on the man at any moment. Both of them were smiling. The man thumbed through the rest of the album.

On another page was a single photo of a woman wearing white work clothes with a matching scarf covering her head. She held a wooden serving tray in her left hand and a brush in her right. She looked to be in her late thirties. Possibly surprised by the photographer, she had turned suddenly to be faced with the camera and was squinting her eyes in a modest smile. She wasn't a beauty, but the line of her rounded cheeks was soft.

The man stared steadily at the photo of the woman. Then he turned back to the photos of the boy. He spoke again in a low voice.

"Mamoru, how could this have happened?"

The boy looked back at him, smiling.

That same morning, in another part of Tokyo, a young woman was looking at the same article. She never used to read the newspaper—not until all this had started. Now she read through the inside pages every morning; it had become part of her routine. She read the article three times. Then she lit up a cigarette and took several long, slow drags. Her hands were shaking.

After she had smoked two cigarettes, she got up and began to change her clothes. It was time to go to work. She chose a bright red suit, and carefully applied her makeup. Before she left, she made sure the windows and doors were all locked, poured the leftover coffee down the sink, then on an impulse grabbed the newspaper off the table as she left her apartment.

As she walked down the outside stairs, a woman with a broom in her hand called out to her. It was the wife of her landlord, who lived in the apartment beneath. They were fussy about rent payments, but not about much else. It was a comfortable place to live.

"Miss Takagi, you got a package from your mother yesterday, but you were so late last night I couldn't bring it up to you."

"I'll stop by for it when I get home tonight," she said brusquely as she hurried past.

"All right," the woman called after her retreating figure, and then muttered to herself, "It wouldn't kill you to say thank you!" By then Kazuko Takagi had already crossed the street in front of the building and was heading at a quick pace off toward the station. She tossed the newspaper onto a pile of trash waiting for the morning pickup.

"What a waste," muttered the landlord's wife, screwing up her face and getting back to her chores.

In yet another corner of the city, a different person altogether was reading the same article. The bony fingers of the bleached-white hands carefully cut it out with a pair of scissors. Then they pulled out the scrapbook and deliberately positioned the article on a new page. Fumie Kato, Atsuko Mita, and Yoko Sugano. Three reports about the deaths of three women.

———•———

The Asano family also started the morning with the newspaper article. Neither Mamoru nor Maki had got another wink of sleep. After the phone call, Yoriko had rushed down to the police station, and had returned at dawn looking pale and drawn.

"They wouldn't let me see him because it was the middle of the night! That's not a reason."

It took the three of them to spread out the paper with their unsteady hands.

"Here it is. There's no mistake." Maki was still trying to persuade herself it had really happened. Mamoru was having trouble believing it, too. There was nothing in the dry report to convince him that the tragedy had actually occurred. The midnight call was starting to seem like a dream.

It was like looking at a photo that you never knew had been taken. When you saw it, you were sure it was of someone you didn't know. That was how Mamoru felt when he saw the name "Taizo Asano" in print. This bad luck had befallen another Taizo Asano, and his uncle would walk through the door at any moment.

"It's cruel," said Yoriko, folding up the newspaper. The three of them ate their breakfast in silence. Maki was unable to eat much. She sat at the table with a cold, wet towel against her face, trying to bring down the swelling around her eyes caused by hours of crying.

"You've got to eat," urged Yoriko.

"It doesn't matter, I'm not going to work today."

"You can't do that! You told me how busy everyone was. And haven't you used up all your vacation days?"

Maki looked up and answered her mother angrily, "How can you say that? Who cares about vacation days and work? Dad's been arrested! What am I supposed to do?"

"There's nothing for you to do here."

"Mom!"

"You listen to me," Yoriko put down her chopsticks, placed her plump elbows on the table, and leaned toward her daughter. "Just because there was an accident doesn't mean your father was at fault. He's at the police station, but they might release him today. I trust him. Now calm down and go to work." She softened her expression as if trying to comfort Maki. "If you stay home, you're going to sit here and fret all day. It'll just make things worse."

Mamoru spoke up. "Aunt Yoriko, what are you planning to do today?"

"I'm going to visit your uncle's old boss and ask him to call Mr. Sayama for us. He's a lawyer, and I'll ask him to go to the police station with me. I want to take your father something to eat and a change of clothes. They told me I could bring him some change for the vending machines, too. I've got to buy him some new underwear, but they told me to cut off the tags and make sure there were no strings . . ."

Yoriko spoke distractedly, almost mumbling the details to herself until she realized Maki and Mamoru were still there. She quickly pulled herself together again.

"Then I'll go back to Mr. Sayama's office to hear what he has to say."

Taizo had had a long career with Tokai Taxi before he went independent. His boss had been Mr. Satomi, and Mr. Sayama was the company lawyer.

Maki pulled herself up from the table reluctantly and, glancing at the clock, headed off to her room. Yoriko called out, "And put on some extra makeup. You'll be breaking mirrors all day with that face."

As usual, Maki and Mamoru left the house together.

"Would you give me a ride to the station?" Maki asked, pointing at the back of Mamoru's bicycle. "I don't want to take a bus looking like this."

Mamoru waited for her to climb on the back and put an arm around his waist. After a few minutes, Maki wondered aloud, "I wonder if they gave Dad breakfast."

Mamoru tried to think of a response that wouldn't make her cry and spoil her makeup. "Sure they did. The police'll treat him right."

"Even though they arrested him?"

"It was an *accident*." Mamoru tried to sound optimistic. "Uncle Taizo's got all those safe driver awards. The police must know that. He'll be fine."

"I don't know . . ." Maki scratched her head, and the change in balance made Mamoru's bicycle wobble. "You know Dad doesn't like *donburi*—everything piled on top of a bowl of rice. Isn't that what the police feed people?"

"That's what they do on TV. But they've got to order it from somewhere, and shops aren't open that early."

"Rice and miso soup, then?" Maki was thoroughly engrossed in the images running through her mind. "I don't really care what they give him; I just hope it's hot."

Mamoru had been thinking the same thing. It was cold this morning; winter was stealthily taking over from autumn. He let Maki off at the station.

"No crying at work!" he warned her affectionately.

"I know, I know."

"But when you see your boyfriend, you can look as sad as you like. Let him take good care of you."

"Are you talking about Maekawa?" Maki never could keep a secret, and she had already told her family about the young man from work she had started seeing. Mamoru had spoken to him once on the phone when he'd called for her.

"Yeah, I think you can trust him. He sounded like a good guy to me."

He had finally coaxed a smile out of his cousin. Maki flipped her hair off her shoulders. Mamoru got back on his bike and took off. Before turning the corner, he looked back and waved. Maki was watching him go, and waved back.

Mamoru went to a public high school a twenty-minute bike ride from the Asano home. It had been built only two years before and was equipped with the latest in heating and air conditioning. The gardens out front were neat and tidy, and balanced well with the new white buildings.

The bicycle sheds were behind the cafeteria, and you could ride straight through to them without slowing down. When Mamoru arrived, there was nobody else around. Three mops set out to dry on a balcony were all that was there to greet him.

He took the stairs up to his class, 1-A, and opened the door, feeling somewhat better than when he left the house. The next instant, however, his improved mood vanished.

Not again, thought Mamoru.

Next to the door was a bulletin board to which the article about his uncle's accident, neatly clipped, had been fastened with thumbtacks. Written on the blackboard in large, crude lettering in red chalk was "MURDERER!" An arrow pointed toward the article.

Everywhere you went there were people who did things like this. Mamoru tried to keep his anger in check. Jerks who got their kicks from the misery of others were like cockroaches; no matter how many you got rid of, there were always hundreds more.

The article on Taizo was little more than a space filler, and the lines were spaced awkwardly to serve this purpose, with one line jutting out from all the rest and two words dangling at the end. Mamoru could feel the animosity of the person who had taken the time and energy to cut it out so neatly.

The same sort of thing had happened in Hirakawa after his father's crime had come to light. Compared with the big city, criminal incidents there were few and far between. In towns that were peaceful and saw few changes in the population, scandals took on a life of their own, putting down roots and settling in. Mamoru had been dogged by rumors and lies right up until his mother died and he himself left town. He had always been known as "the son of that Toshio Kusaka." The fact that it was starting all over again was more hurtful than the act itself, and Mamoru had a good idea who was behind it.

Public schools were not fussy about tardies; they seemed to expect a certain percentage of students to be late each day. Kunihiko Miura was one of the regulars, and he showed up near the end of the first period. He opened the door at the back of the room, entered at a leisurely pace, and took his time pulling up a chair.

Mamoru didn't turn around to look, but he knew Miura was watching him. Tall and athletic, Miura was the type who always stopped to check his hair in windows and drove a 400 cc motorcycle on which he sported a different girl every few months or so. Unable to bear the gaze he felt on his back, Mamoru turned around once. Miura stared back at him and broke out in an enormous grin. Other slack-offs in the back of the room snickered in refrain.

Miura was the one who had done it. There was no mistake.

Miura and his crowd had a mental age of ten, thought Mamoru, just like the boys in Hirakawa.

"Miura, hurry up and find a seat!" The teacher at the front of the room gestured with the English text in his hand. He was the homeroom teacher for the class, and Mamoru was chagrined that this was as far as he would ever go in terms of discipline. When he had walked into the room before class, he had done no more than glance at what was written on the blackboard, erase it, and open his book. His name was Mr. Nozaki, but the students called him Nonashi, or "Mr. Incompetent."

Maintaining an expressionless face, Mr. Incompetent added, "Kusaka, keep your eyes in front!" There was more snickering in the back.

"What *is* this? How stupid can you get?"

After the end of the first period, one of Mamoru's classmates, a cheerful girl known as Anego, or "Big Sis," pulled the offending article off the bulletin board. As she balled it up and tossed it in the wastebasket, she glared at Miura out of the corner of her eye. Miura paid no attention and continued chatting with his friends as they leaned against the windowsills.

Mamoru had got off to a bad start with Miura at the beginning of the school year. It hadn't been a big deal and he occasionally wished he had just stayed out of the matter to begin with. There was a girl in the class next door who was known throughout the school for being extraordinarily beautiful. Mamoru had seen her a few times and noted that her reputation was warranted.

It all started at the end of April, when the girl lost her wallet one day after classes and a search turned up nothing. The normal course of action would have been to report it to the office and go home, but the wallet held the key to the lock on her bike. She and her friends had just decided it would be best if she walked home and brought the spare key with her the next day, when Miura and his group passed by. Miura offered to take her home on his motorcycle.

This girl was not the type to hop on the motorcycle of a boy she didn't know. She was the quiet sort, and could be trusted to obey the rules, ride her bike instead of a motorcycle, and go to a movie—with her parent's permission, of course—and not a disco. Looking truly frightened, she turned Miura down, but Miura wouldn't take no for an answer. He told her to wait there while he went to get his motorcycle, and hurried off, smirking at his good fortune.

Mamoru overheard most of the conversation, and he saw that the girl was almost in tears, terrified of what would happen later if she just walked off. Mamoru suggested that he remove the lock from her bike and she could pretend that she'd found her wallet.

She looked hopeful. "Can you really do that?"

"Bike locks are easy," he'd responded, careful not to let on that he was capable of a lot more. By the time Miura got back, the girl was on her bike and ready to leave. Miura had been completely outwitted.

Mamoru didn't know who had told Miura what happened, and he didn't really care. Within a couple of days, though, the story had spread throughout the class, and Miura began to look at Mamoru with an evil gleam in his eye. A couple of weeks later, when the student roster was distributed, everyone learned that Mamoru's last name was different from that of his guardians, and it didn't take long for Miura to figure out how to get revenge. Within a week he had dug up the story of Toshio Kusaka. Mamoru's breath was taken away by the warped energy Miura had put into the project.

One morning he had come to school to find the old saying "A thief begets a thief" painted on his desk. Mamoru had known this was coming and had tried to prepare himself for it, but he involuntarily stiffened at the sight.

It was none other than the resourceful Anego who had tracked down the school janitor and got hold of a can of paint remover. This was when Mamoru had learned that her real name was Saori Tokida. "You can call me Anego, like everyone else. After all, my parents named me without asking me how I felt about it!" She'd laughed heartily at her own joke.

After Anego had torn the article off the bulletin board, she went straight over to Mamoru and plopped down into the chair next to him, a clouded expression on her shiny freckled face.

"I saw it in the morning paper. It must be awful for you." Her simple words of concern moved something in his heart that had been frozen since the accident had happened. The two were silent for a few moments.

"But it was an accident," she reassured him. "It was only an accident." Mamoru nodded in agreement and looked out the window.

East Cosmetics, Ltd., the company where Kazuko Takagi worked, was a five-minute walk from Shinjuku Station.

"I notice your sales are down. Aren't you feeling well?" asked her supervisor after the morning meeting. The implicit criticism was not lost on Kazuko and she ignored him, busily writing up her plan for the day. Her boss put a cigarette in his mouth and came to stand behind her seat, waiting for an answer.

"I've been a little under the weather," she eventually managed to spit out.

The man blew cigarette smoke through his nose and sniffed unsympathetically. "Well then, take it easy why don't you?"

She left the office at ten on the dot and decided to start out in front of the station. The weather was good and there was a comfortable breeze. The people she passed appeared to be in fine spirits. Kazuko, though, walked with her head down.

It was only after she had settled into this job that it had occurred to her that she was back in Shinjuku. *And that's not where I want to be.* She hated it here. She hated the way the buildings were all crowded together. She hated the trash and the stench in underground passageways and in the shrubs around high-rises. She hated the money spent here and the people who spent it.

So why did I come back to make myself the money that others spend? The thought made her angrier and more impatient than ever.

This morning she was unable to get any work done. All she could think of was that report in the morning paper. It just kept coming back no matter how hard she tried to push it aside in her mind. She stopped in a coffee shop, had a cup of coffee and smoked more than usual. She killed time staring at the skyscrapers. There was a pink public phone in the shop, and it was being used by a constant stream of people. A man in a business suit, another in a flashy checked suit who looked like he worked in a bar, a woman, probably a housewife who had come to shop in the department stores. They all took their turns putting coins in the slot and making calls.

At about noon, Kazuko finally stood up and walked over to the phone. She thumbed through her address book until she found S. On a page crammed with names and numbers, there was only one name of a personal friend: Yoko Sugano. The address and phone number had been erased and then rewritten. When Yoko had moved, she'd given Kazuko the details and begged her not to tell anyone else.

Kazuko dialed the number and listened to it ring. She couldn't remember what she had planned to say if anyone answered, so she pulled the receiver away from her ear to think about it.

"Hello? Hello?"

Hearing the distant voice calling out to her, Kazuko came to her senses. "Is this the home of Yoko Sugano?"

After a pause, the person on the other end responded. "That's right."

"I'm a friend of Yoko's. I, ah . . . I saw the, uh, newspaper this morning . . ."

"I see," the voice said. "I'm Yoko's mother."

"Did she really die? Is it true? I . . ."

"We're having a hard time believing it, too."

Kazuko gripped the receiver harder and squeezed her eyes shut. "Is it true that it was an accident?"

"Yes," Yoko's mother sounded angry. "And the driver claims it wasn't his fault!"

"I'm so sorry. Is she . . . is her body . . . at home . . . ?"

"We're taking her back home with us this afternoon. That's where we're going to have the funeral."

"I'd like to go. Could you please give me the time and place?"

Yoko's mother carefully told Kazuko how to get to their town, and Kazuko wrote it all down. When they were finished, Yoko's mother asked, "Are you a friend of hers from school?"

Kazuko was silent, not knowing what to say.

"Hello? Are you still there?"

"Ah . . . she and I worked together," Kazuko finally answered, and set the receiver back on the cradle.

The coffee shop had begun to serve lunch and was filling up with young women in their company uniforms. Kazuko suddenly felt unpleasantly out of place in her red suit. She walked to the train station and got in line at the travel center. When her turn came, she bought a ticket for a city that was a two-hour express ride from Tokyo. She remembered Yoko telling her that it was a dull place and there was nothing to do there.

Kazuko, I'm scared. That's what Yoko had said the last time she'd seen her. *Can it all be a coincidence? Things don't just happen like this!* Then she'd burst into tears.

I'm scared, too, thought Kazuko. *But Yoko, you died in an accident. You were killed by a taxi driver running a red light. It's all over now. It all died along with you.*

As she walked, Kazuko told herself that she did believe in coincidences. Anything at all could happen in Tokyo. The sunlight was so bright, she had to squint her eyes against it.

About three months before, she had got into a crowded elevator. During the few seconds before the doors closed, a young man walked past. He was poorly dressed and had a stoop to his walk that she thought she had seen before. Kazuko was startled, and the man suddenly noticed her, too. He had been one of her "clients." It was a suffocating moment. Kazuko tried to make herself smaller as he turned toward her and put his hand out to stop the elevator. "We're full here," said someone next to her, and as the doors closed the young man with the surprised expression had disappeared from view.

That had been a coincidence, too. In the midst of the millions of people in Tokyo, the chances of her running into a client that she was finished with were remote indeed.

Anything can happen here. You can't worry about every little thing.

That night, Yoriko took Maki and Mamoru to a neighborhood steak house to, as she put it, get something in their stomachs so they could keep their strength up. The restaurant, with its rugged wooden interior and bright lighting, was almost full, and the delicious smell of steak sauce permeated the entire place. After the three had been seated and placed their orders, Yoriko started telling Maki and Mamoru about her day.

"Your father was very upset for a while, but he's calmer now. You don't have to worry," Yoriko said firmly.

Maki was not reassured. "But why does he have to stay at the police station? They should let him come home."

Mamoru looked at his cousin and thought that the day's anxiety had already taken its toll on her. She had the beginnings of dark circles under her eyes.

Yoriko seemed the more optimistic of the two. "I've got more to tell you," she continued. She took a memo pad out of the large handbag she always had with her. It was printed with the Sayama Law Office letterhead. "You know I can never remember details. I had Mr. Sayama write it all down so I could tell you about what was going on."

The intersection where the accident took place was one that Taizo knew well. It was just behind the main thoroughfare, in a residential area. The southeast corner was occupied by a large playground, and there was an apartment building that was still under construction on the opposite corner. The northwest and southwest corners were occupied by private residences. The house on the former had a small family-operated cigarette shop on the first floor, and outside it were a public phone and a vending machine. The patrolman who had arrived on the scene of the accident had called an ambulance from that phone.

"So the police were there immediately after it happened?"

"That's right. He had been making his rounds in the area, and came running when he heard the commotion. That turned out to be bad luck for your father, too. Since he was the driver, the patrolman gave him a chewing out, and that made him even more upset."

"Did Dad hit him?" Maki's eyes opened wide in concern.

"It didn't come to that, but it wasn't much better. The patrolman was young, and he lost his temper, too. He arrested your father on the spot."

"How could he!" Maki managed to sputter out.

Mamoru finally spoke up in a hesitant voice. "It's hard to imagine Uncle Taizo being confused about the signal . . ."

"It looked bad," continued Yoriko, "and you know your uncle has never had an accident before. He's been hit from behind, but he has always been proud of his safety record."

Their meals arrived, but none of them could even pick up a fork.

"Let's eat before it gets cold," urged Yoriko, but Maki still had questions.

"What about how the accident happened? Are they saying it was Dad's fault? I can't believe it!"

Yoriko sighed. "Mr. Sayama says they don't know."

"Don't know what?"

"They don't have any witnesses. Of course there was quite a crowd after it happened, but nobody saw the car hit the girl." Yoriko began to sound tired. "And since the girl is dead . . ."

"What does Dad say?"

"He says that the girl, Yoko Sugano, just ran out into the street. He insists that he had the green light."

"Well, that must be the truth! Dad would never lie." Maki was adamant, but she knew that Taizo's word alone would not convince the police of anything.

After a few moments, Yoriko continued. "Miss Sugano died in the ambulance, but she said something about the accident."

"What did she say?"

Yoriko looked down at the table. Maki and Mamoru looked at each other.

"She was barely conscious, but she kept repeating 'It's awful, awful! How *could* he?' Both the patrolman and the ambulance medics distinctly heard her say it."

The words of the dead woman seemed to float in the air over the restaurant table. Mamoru shivered.

"Your father says Miss Sugano ran into the intersection, and he tried to avoid her, but couldn't. He had the green light. The police don't think that's what happened, and nobody else saw anything. They say that you can investigate the scene to figure out how fast the car was going, where the brakes were applied, and where the car stopped. But they'll never know whether the light was red or green, or whether or not Miss Sugano suddenly appeared out of nowhere."

"What's going to happen?" Maki was clearly upset. "What's going to happen to him if they don't know?"

"They can't say for sure," Yoriko began, "but if they can't find any evidence to support his story, he might go to prison. Your father is a professional driver, and the victim died."

Maki covered her face with her hands, and Mamoru spoke up again.

"But what happens if they do find evidence? Then what will happen?"

"They can't just let him off. Whether there's a trial or a summary order, the least he would get would be probation. Mr. Sayama said he would do what he could."

Yoriko tried to put on a brave smile. "If nothing else, they'll get him for not keeping his eyes on the road. It's just bad luck. He was a bit over the speed limit, which wouldn't be a problem normally. He was used to driving in the area, and knew there was never anyone out on that street after ten."

Yoriko looked up at Maki and Mamoru. "Come on, let's eat. Your father is eating, too. He told me it wasn't just *donburi*."

Maki didn't move. Finally, she picked up her water glass and took a drink. "Why can't he come home? They should let him come home when they're through questioning him. He won't try to run away."

"Well, I asked about that, too . . ." Yoriko looked back at the memo. "When there's a fatal accident, they usually keep the driver in custody for ten days. They do that no matter who it is."

"Can we go see him?" asked Mamoru.

Yoriko frowned and read the memo again. "Umm . . . no."

"But why?"

"They aren't allowing it this time."

"What do you mean, *this time*?" Maki was growing more and more agitated, and Yoriko found it difficult to go on.

"You know your father knows the Midori area like the back of his hand. The police are afraid he'll try to talk to the people in that all-night coffee shop where he often goes, and get them to testify that they saw the accident and that it wasn't his fault."

"How suspicious can they get?"

"I guess it's happened before."

"He would never do that!" Maki almost spit out the words.

"I know!" Yoriko was beginning to look and sound tired. "I'd never dream of suspecting him of doing anything like that."

Mamoru stepped in. "Is there anything we can do?"

Yoriko's expression softened. "Just try to take care of yourselves. Mr. Sayama and I will take care of the rest. Don't worry!" As if remembering a chore she had to do, Yoriko continued in a deceptively light tone. "Tomorrow, Mr. Sayama and I are going to Miss Sugano's parents' home. She lived in Tokyo because she was going to school, and her family home is rather far away. We might have to stay the night, so I hope you two will look after things here."

"The funeral?"

"That's right. We might not agree on how the accident happened, but these people have lost their daughter. Sooner or later, we'll have to settle things with them."

The three managed to eat their dinner, and walked back home. As they got to the door, they could hear the phone ringing. Yoriko hurriedly unlocked the door, and Maki flew inside.

"Hello? Hello? Yes, this is the Asanos."

Mamoru watched her expression go taut, and reached for the receiver a second before Maki threw it to the floor. "Troublemaker," he muttered as he picked up the phone and set it back on the cradle. The caller had already disconnected.

"What did they say?" Yoriko looked terrified.

"'Murderer. Anyone who kills a woman should get the death sentence.' I couldn't listen to any more. He sounded drunk."

"Just forget about it," Yoriko said, and headed toward the living room.

Maki stood staring at the phone and asked, "Mom, have there been other calls like that?" Yoriko was silent. "Why didn't you tell us?"

Mamoru stood watching the two of them. Maki began to cry. "Why did this have to happen? It's not fair!"

"You're not helping any of us by crying like that," scolded Yoriko.

"But when I went to work, the section chief called me over and showed me the paper. He knew it was Dad."

"So what?" Yoriko's face was tense. "Are you going to be punished in some way?"

"No, he didn't say anything like that. But everyone wanted to know about it. They asked what would happen to Dad and whether he really ran a red light." Maki bit her lip and tears glistened in her eyes. "I bet something happened today at school to you too, Mamoru. What did the other kids say? It's just awful the way people act!" she exploded, and ran to her room, slamming the door.

Mamoru turned to his aunt. "Let me answer the phone for a while."

Yoriko looked at Mamoru and gave him a crooked smile. "You've had enough trouble already . . . you don't need any more." Then, as if struck by something, she turned back to him. "Is this what happened when your father disappeared, too?"

You have no idea, thought Mamoru. But all he said was, "I don't know. I was too small to know what anything anyone said meant."

There were two more calls during the next hour. One was a hysterical woman ranting about the state of traffic safety. But the second caller was different from the others. "Thank you for taking care of Yoko Sugano." The voice sounded raspy and high with excitement. "I'm serious. Thanks for killing her. She had it coming." He hung up before Mamoru could reply.

At about eleven that night, there was another call. Mamoru picked it up and answered in what he hoped was a threatening voice.

"If you keep up that tone of voice, you'll never get a girlfriend!" It was Anego.

Mamoru laughed and apologized. "I appreciate what you did today."

"You mean throwing out that article? Forget it. I've got something to tell you. After school I went looking for Miura to teach him a thing or two, and he told me he didn't do it. He said he had an alibi."

"An alibi?"

"He was late as usual this morning, right? Just before he walked in, he got collared by a teacher; he said he wasn't there early enough to put anything up on the wall or scribble on the blackboard. He said the teacher could prove it. I don't know who that jackass thinks he can fool."

Mamoru listened to Anego. He appreciated her directness but winced at her language. "If it wasn't him it was one of the idiots he hangs out with. Who cares which one it was? Stay away from him, Anego. You don't need him any more riled up than he already is."

"Don't worry, Miura won't come after me. But it's strange, isn't it?" Anego was oddly pensive. "Miura isn't ugly. He's even kind of good looking. Girls like that type. He plays basketball, and he's the youngest starting player on the team. His grades are okay. So why does he always have to pick on kids when they're down?"

"He's sick; it's easier to think of it that way."

"Yeah, or he has some kind of complex." Anego had said what she had to say, so she said good night and hung up.

She was right, Mamoru thought. Miura had everything. His father worked in a big insurance company, and his family had money. He must be greedy, Mamoru decided. He had everything, but so did lots of other people. The only way to feel superior was to take something away from someone else. In order to be happy, Miura and countless others could no longer rely on addition, they had to do some subtracting to make it through life.

The fighting got worse some time after midnight. It was Maki and Yoriko. Mamoru was alone in his room, and the voices got louder and louder, coming right up the stairs.

"I can't believe it!" Maki yelled at her mother as she sobbed, the ends of her words shaking. "How can you say that about Dad? Do you really think he'd do something like that?"

"This is between your father and me. You've got no say in the matter." Yoriko was yelling, too, but she was still calmer than Maki. "I know your father is not irresponsible. But it doesn't matter what I believe. I've been the wife of a taxi driver since you were in diapers! I know much better than you about what accidents do and don't involve."

"Dad would never run a red light, hit and kill someone, and then lie about it."

"And who said he would?"

"You did! You're planning to apologize to that girl's parents and settle the matter with them. You're going to tell them Dad was wrong!"

"You don't know what you're talking about!" Mamoru heard the sound of Yoriko's fist hitting the table. "A girl died. There's nothing shameful about trying to compensate her parents for that. I've said the same thing over and over: this is for your father's sake, too!"

"I don't agree," Maki persisted. "I'll never forgive you for compromising like this."

"Do whatever you like, then," replied Yoriko, and she was silent for a moment before continuing. "Maki," her voice had begun to tremble, too. "You keep saying you're only thinking of your father, but aren't you really thinking about what it will mean for you if he has a criminal record? Aren't you worried about what people will think? If you ask me, that's pretty selfish."

Silence.

Then Mamoru heard Maki break down in angry sobs and run upstairs. She slammed the door of her room, and the house went quiet.

About ten minutes later, Mamoru went out into the hall and knocked on Maki's door. There was no reply. "Maki?" he called softly and opened the door a crack. His cousin was sitting on her bed with her face in her hands.

"I don't care if she is my mother," she sniffed. "There are some things you just shouldn't say."

Mamoru leaned against the door, watching her.

"Is there something wrong with what I said?" she asked.

"No, of course not."

"Then why does she—"

"She's not wrong, either."

Maki brushed her hair back and looked up. "How can you agree with us both?"

Mamoru smiled. "You're both right."

"What do *you* think, Mamoru?"

"I know Uncle Taizo would never break the law like that."

"That's not what I mean. I'm talking about your father." Maki looked up at him, her cheeks still wet.

"It was different. My father did something wrong. He really did embezzle that money."

"Was there evidence? Did they prove he did it?"

Mamoru nodded.

"It must have been awful for you."

Mamoru didn't answer. He didn't want to explain to her what had happened all those years ago. He wasn't sure he could tell her the truth.

The reason he wouldn't forgive his father had nothing to do with the money—it was because he had abandoned them. He'd avoided punishment for his crime the way you might take off a pair of slippers, and he was the only one of them that got to put on a new pair.

"Maki?"

"What?"

"You really are both right."

"What do you mean?"

"You believe Uncle Taizo and don't want your mother to settle without trying to make a case for him. And it's true that you *are* worried about him having a criminal record."

Maki didn't even blink. "So, you feel that way about me, too?"

Mamoru refused to back down. "They're both true, and you feel them both in equal amounts. You know how your mother feels. You know how angry she must feel because nobody believes Uncle Taizo. Her blood must be boiling to hear the police say there's nothing they can do unless someone comes up with evidence."

Sometimes Mamoru believed that the shape of the human heart was like two hands clasped together, the fingers of the right hand and those of the left hand lined up and pulling alternately in opposite directions. Having two different feelings inside your heart had to be the same way. They were diametrically opposed to each other, but both belonged to the same person. He was sure his mother had had similar feelings. She had never touched the divorce papers, and never said a word against her husband. She kept his family name. But Mamoru knew that she must have felt betrayed by him.

Maki stood up and pulled a small bag out of her closet. She began to fill it with her clothes.

"Are you leaving?"

"I'm going to stay with a friend," she said, and then smiled in a vaguely reassuring manner. "But I'll be back."

"Are you going to stay with Maekawa?"

"No, he lives with his parents. Things don't always work out the way they do in romance novels. And . . ." Maki closed her mouth. Mamoru was sure she had something more to say, and he waited, but she was silent.

Mamoru went outside with her and made sure she caught a taxi. Back in the house, he found his Aunt Yoriko in the living room, uncharacteristically smoking a cigarette.

"It's not the first time she's done this," she said, her eyes red. "Don't worry about it."

Mamoru decided to go out for a run. Every night he ran the same two-kilometer course. He changed into his running clothes, and when he came back downstairs he could see that his aunt had turned out the lights in her room, but he heard a loud sigh as he walked past her door.

She sounds a lot like Mom, he thought.

———•———

It was late. The man turned off the engine and lights, and sat alone in the car, gazing out the window.

He had stopped next to the bank of the canal, at the foot of the bridge. The street lamps shone the faintest of lights on the silver gray car.

He waited.

He knew that the boy went running at the same time every night, and he wanted to see him. He lit a cigarette, and then opened the car window a crack to let in some air. In came a faint breeze and the smell of the canal.

The town was asleep, and there were stars in the sky.

He looked up at them as if he had made a new discovery. He had forgotten for so long that there were stars.

The stagnant water. The low-lying houses. In between the plants and out-of-date mortar-coated homes were flashy Western-style apartment buildings. One of the houses on the side of the road had laundry hanging outside that someone had forgotten to take in. A white shirt and a pair of children's pants kept the man company in the dark.

The boy finally showed up about four cigarettes later. He came around the corner at a slow trot, appearing in the man's rearview mirror. The man quickly put out his cigarette and slid down in his seat.

The boy was smaller than he had thought. He probably hadn't got his growth spurt yet. In his light blue running outfit he looked clean, wholesome, and entirely too defenseless.

Left, right, left, right. He kept up a steady pace. He didn't seem winded. He had rolled up his sleeves to his elbows, and his arms moved in time with his legs.

He was going to be a good runner. For an instant, the man was almost proud of the fact. The boy drew closer. He continued to face straight ahead; he had not noticed the man in the car. He ran a few steps past the car and then stopped, his shoulders heaving up and down. His shape filled up the view through the windshield.

The man tried instinctively to pull himself even lower, but his body wouldn't move. He realized the boy wouldn't be able to see his face. The boy was standing under the light of the street lamp and wouldn't be able to see anyone lurking in the dark. He was probably just suspicious of the unfamiliar car stopped on the street.

The man couldn't move. He couldn't even take his gaze off the boy who was unwittingly staring straight at him.

The boy tilted his head as if trying to hear something. He had delicate features; he was good looking and would certainly remain that way into adulthood. He took after his mother, the man thought. The only difference was the firm set of his mouth that revealed his strength of character.

During those few moments, the man had to fight an overwhelming impulse to open the door, walk out into the street, and call out to the boy. It didn't matter what he said, he just wanted to hear what the boy's voice sounded like, find out how he would answer, see how his expression changed. But he knew he didn't yet have the courage to do that.

The boy straightened up, turned around, and started running again. The farther away he got, the whiter his blue running outfit appeared. He finally turned a corner and disappeared from sight.

The man unclenched his sweaty fist, and sat there for a while staring at the corner.

It's me. It's me! The words repeated themselves over and over inside his head; they were like a hammer. *It's me, it's me!*

The man was careful not to budge until he had recovered from the temptation to run after the boy, screaming these words at him. He finally took a deep breath and leaned forward, searching for something in the inside pocket of his jacket.

It was small and it sparkled in his hand.

It was a ring. The man had kept the ring stored with the album of the photos of the boy and his mother. It was Toshio Kusaka's wedding ring. The initials engraved inside it were still legible. Nowadays, he carried it with him and kept it as close to his heart as possible. He put the ring back in his pocket, then turned the key in the ignition and started the engine.

I'm going to make it up to you, he said to himself. *I've finally found my chance. Mamoru, I'll be back to see you.*

CHAPTER
2

Suspicion

The next day was Saturday, and Mamoru only had a half-day of classes. As soon as school was over he headed for Laurel, a large department store two stations away. On Saturday afternoons and Sundays he worked in the Books section on the fourth floor. Going in the employees' entrance, he stamped his blue time card and slipped into the locker room. Employees in Books and Audio wore orange jackets, and Mamoru's name tag had a blue line to indicate his part-time status.

On his way out, he checked himself in the mirror. Laurel was fussy about appearance. Long hair and sandals were not allowed. Women had to keep their hair tied back and nail polish was forbidden.

He climbed the service stairway to the fourth floor, coming out at the side of the storeroom. The afternoon delivery had just arrived and employees were busy opening and checking the boxes.

"Hey, Mamoru!" Sato, another part-timer, greeted him as he opened a box with a large cutter. He'd been working at Laurel for some years and had taught Mamoru the ropes. Most of Mamoru's work involved heavy lifting. There were receipts, shipments, stocking, delivery, and returns that needed processing. In terms of handling, books were as heavy as electric appliances. Of the twenty-five employees in this section, twenty were young men in their teens through their thirties. Four women operated the cash registers, and the only man over fifty was a plainclothes security officer.

"Takano said to go see him when you got here." Sato delivered this message while expertly dividing up the contents of the boxes. He had rolled up his sleeves in defiance of the rules to reveal darkly tanned arms. As soon as he had saved up enough, Sato would head off on a trip equipped with his sleeping bag and backpack, and he'd be back again only when he ran out of money.

He had returned from his most recent travels a month before. When Mamoru had inquired where he'd been this time, the brief reply had been, "The Gobi Desert." Whenever Sato was away, the rest of the employees would speculate about where he'd gone, and they liked to say the surface of the moon was the only place they'd rule out—for now anyway.

"So where is Takano?"

"Probably in the office. He was getting ready for the monthly meeting." Sato indicated the door at the back of the storage area with his chin.

Hajime Takano was the chief of the Books section; a low-ranking middle manager. He was just thirty. Laurel promoted its full-time employees strictly on the basis of ability, and there were cases of store managers who had only been out of college a few years.

Another interesting thing about Laurel was that, contrary to the norm in Japan, employees did not use ranks or honorific language when addressing each other. Job descriptions were detailed and the store frequently moved its employees around, which meant that ranks changed often. The company had decided it was inefficient to have employees spend time and energy figuring out how to address each other. They also realized that this would make it easier for their customers and suppliers when it came to doing business. They didn't even print titles on business cards. The Laurel organization was committed to surviving the cutthroat competition among large-scale retailers. Anything unrelated to this goal was eliminated as a waste of resources.

This system made life easier for employees, too. Mamoru knocked on the office door without having to switch into a formal mode. Takano's hands were full of sales records that he had just printed out, but his face took on a look of concern as soon as he saw Mamoru.

"Hi there. I heard about the accident. Are you all right? Have you heard from your uncle?" Mamoru almost panicked, afraid that he was going to be grilled the way Maki had been at work. Takano continued, "Let me know if there's anything I can do for you. Don't be afraid to ask for time off."

Relief set in quickly, along with a twinge of guilt. He had worked here for six months, long enough to know Takano cared about the people working under him.

"There's not much any of us can do right now. A lawyer is taking care of it, but thanks for asking." Mamoru pulled up a stool, and filled Takano in on what had happened.

"So everyone has a different story?" Takano leaned back in his chair, looked up at the ceiling and clasped his hands behind his head. "There's no evidence to prove what color the light was or what the woman actually did?"

"Well, we all believe my uncle. Not that it does him any good."

"And it doesn't help that the medics heard what Yoko Sugano said before she died."

"You mean, 'It's awful, awful. How *could* he?'"

Takano uncrossed his long legs and sat up. "Yeah, if I were a policeman on the scene, I guess I'd have to think about what that meant."

"You'd have to believe a dying person wouldn't lie."

"Hmm," Takano pulled at his chin the way he always did when he was thinking. "But the person who heard what she said might turn it into a lie."

"What do you mean?"

"I mean, the words are what she said, but she might not have been talking about your uncle."

"But she was alone when it happened."

"You don't know that. She might have had a fight with her boyfriend and been on her way home. Some dirty old man might have tried to molest her. A quiet, dark neighborhood like that, it could have been anything. Something happened, and she ran into the intersection and got hit by a car. And she cried out, 'It's awful, how *could* he?' Make sense?"

"And whoever was chasing her probably ran away when they saw her get hit."

"Right. I wonder if the police are checking into what she was doing at the time."

"I haven't heard anything about that." Mamoru felt a glimmer of hope at this new possibility. Then he remembered the phone call he got the night before. "You know, I got a strange phone call from some guy." He told Takano about how the man had thanked them for killing Yoko Sugano and that she had deserved to die.

Takano frowned, furrowing his thick eyebrows. "Did you mention that to your lawyer?"

"No, we didn't think much about it at the time."

"You ought to tell him. It's pretty odd even for a prank call."

"But I don't know if it's worth anything . . ."

"Why?"

"A lot of weird people get busy when something like this happens. It was the same when my father disappeared. Phone calls, letters, lies. We got anonymous letters with addresses and directions to the place where someone claimed my father was living. It all turned out to be lies. Then we'd hear from people who said my father wasn't the one who had stolen the money—somebody else had done it and framed him for it. Those were all lies, too."

Mamoru shrugged his shoulders as if trying to work a kink out of them. Talking about his father always made him tense. "Anyway, that's why I don't really want to follow up on that call."

"I see."

"But there might have been someone else there when the accident happened. I'll ask the lawyer about that."

Takano was one of the few people Mamoru had voluntarily told about his father. Minors had to have permission from a guardian to work. When Mamoru applied at Laurel, he had told Takano that both of his parents were dead and that he lived with his aunt. As he got to know Takano, he began to think of him as a friend, but he'd still had his doubts. Would his attitude toward Mamoru change if he knew about his family history? Prepared for disappointment, he'd decided to test Takano by telling him the story. Takano, however, had not even batted an eyelid.

"Look," he'd said. "I might get worried if you started talking about looking for your father so he could teach you how to embezzle on your own. But on the other hand," he'd started laughing, "I might want to tag along!"

---•---

As Mamoru got down to work he soon noticed a new addition to the décor. It was a video display about two meters high by two meters wide. The screen, currently featuring a video of a mountain forest in fall colors, was positioned to be the first thing customers saw as they stepped off the escalator.

"It really is something, isn't it? They're calling it their latest weapon." One of the girls at the cash register called over to Mamoru when she noticed him staring at the screen open-mouthed. "It's been here since Monday."

"Is that what they call an environmental video?"

"I guess so. It looks better than plastic leaves pinned up on the wall; the customers like it, anyway. But I hear it was pretty expensive."

"Have they got one on every floor?"

"Of course. It's all controlled centrally, and there's someone in charge of operating it. They had a terrible time finding the space. Thanks to the new security control room they have for this thing, the women's locker room is now quite a bit smaller."

"Watch out—it might be Big Brother!" Sato, scowling, appeared from an aisle where he was straightening the racks.

Mamoru and the girl exchanged a look. *Here we go again!* Sato liked science fiction almost as much as he enjoyed wandering around the world. Everyone knew that *Nineteen Eighty-Four* by George Orwell was his favorite novel.

"You can laugh all you like, but they're using that video to keep an eye on us. The pretty pictures are nothing but camouflage."

"And just last week you were telling us to be careful not to badmouth the bosses because you were sure the toilets were bugged!" the girl retorted.

"And I was right, wasn't I? The managers all knew which one of you ladies were planning to sneak Takano chocolates for Valentine's Day."

"Oh really! We all bought them together. You got some, too, I believe."

"I said 'sneak.'"

The girl leaned closer. "So who was it?"

"Go ask the managers."

Mamoru walked over to the screen and peered up at it. There was no switch or control panel. It was no more than a giant screen, now showing tourists gathering chestnuts. In the lower left-hand corner of the frame, Mamoru spotted the initials M and A linked together in a logo. He thought he'd seen it somewhere before, but he couldn't remember where.

"As long as they're showing videos, why don't they let us see *2001: A Space Odyssey,* or something interesting like that?" Sato was still griping.

"Are you kidding?" Mamoru laughed. "It would put the customers to sleep before they got around to buying anything."

"Kusaka, you've got a visitor!" Mamoru turned around to find Yoichi Miyashita, a classmate of his. Yoichi looked uncomfortable, clenching and unclenching his fists nervously, almost as though he was trying to work up the courage to say something. He was pale and slight, and had the sort of soft, light-skinned complexion so coveted by girls.

Mamoru rarely saw him talking to anyone outside of class. His grades were barely average and he was often absent. Everyone knew that Miura and his goons were the cause.

"Hey, come to do some shopping?" Yoichi looked so uncomfortable that Mamoru wished Anego was there to smooth things over. "*Modern Art* is over there . . ." Mamoru knew that Yoichi was in the art club, and he'd seen him reading *Modern Art* magazine. It was the sort of professional journal that Mamoru would never have noticed had he not worked in Books.

At the time, he had looked over Yoichi's shoulder. The picture he was looking at was of faceless figures of undetermined sex standing in something like a coliseum.

"What's that?" he had asked.

Yoichi's eyes had shone. "It's *The Disquieting Muses* by Giorgio de Chirico. It's my favorite."

Muses . . . now that he mentioned it, Mamoru saw that they were wearing long robes. The title on the page was for an exhibit of de Chirico's work in Osaka.

"There's going to be a major exhibit with works flown in from overseas."

"Women sure paint strange pictures," muttered Mamoru, mistaking the name "Chirico" for the Japanese "Kiriko."

"It's not a Japanese woman!" Yoichi had laughed, and Mamoru was sure it was the first time he had ever seen him doing so. "He's a wonderful Italian artist. One of the first surrealists."

Yoichi had talked about de Chirico as if he were talking about his favorite teenage rock star. After that exchange, Yoichi and Mamoru became friends, although Mamoru remained unable to comprehend the complexities of his love of art. Mamoru was sure that Miura hated Yoichi if only because he refused to hide his passion for works of art that others found difficult to appreciate.

"So, what's the matter? Do you need to talk?" Mamoru asked. "Is Miura up to something again?" He knew Miura took every opportunity to pick on Yoichi for his slight figure and confused attitude. And he also knew that Mr. Incompetent ignored it all.

"No, it's nothing like that," Yoichi denied quickly. "I was in the area and remembered you said you worked here, so I thought I'd stop by."

Mamoru was surprised and pleased. He'd always thought Yoichi was the type who'd take off whenever he saw anyone he knew on the street, no matter how friendly.

"I'll be off in about half an hour. If you don't mind waiting, we could leave together."

"Ummm . . ." Yoichi began rocking on the balls of his feet, looking down the whole time. "Actually I'm here because—"

"Excuse me!" a customer called out to Mamoru. "Do you have the second volume of this novel?"

"You're busy," concluded Yoichi hastily. "I'll talk to you later." Without waiting for a reply, he dashed off to the escalator.

"Excuse me!" The customer called out insistently. Still wondering what Yoichi had wanted to say, Mamoru ran off to look for the book in the romance section.

———————•———————

The wake had already begun when Kazuko Takagi arrived at Yoko Sugano's home. The town was as small as Yoko had told her it was. She had followed the black-framed signs indicating a funeral for the Sugano family up a narrow mountain road until she came to a flat piece of land with three houses built on it. Yoko's was on the far end.

The wind was strong. The top of the tent set up to the side of the house to register mourners flapped astonishingly loudly as a gust of wind passed through.

A young girl who looked quite a bit like Yoko sat bowing mechanically to each visitor. So this must be her younger sister, Kazuko thought. She had heard that she, too, had been anxious to come live in Tokyo, but Yoko had refused to allow it and had told her sister there was nothing worthwhile for her there.

Kazuko had brought along the customary envelope of condolence money, but hadn't signed it with her real name. There were so many people there she was sure that the entire town had turned out. The casket and an altar had been set up in a tatami room at the front of the house, and a Buddhist priest sat in front of it, chanting. The floor-to-ceiling windows of the room had been opened so the mourners could offer incense and prayers without having to come into the house. Kazuko waited in line for her turn, and then stepped to the side to listen to the priest. When she began to shiver from the cold wind, the neighbors who had turned up to help invited her to warm herself by a fire they had made.

"Are you from Tokyo?" a middle-aged woman asked her in the distinct intonation of the local dialect.

"Yes, I got here about two o'clock." When Kazuko had arrived at the station, she had been drawn to the broad riverbed that spread out before it. She had walked for a while along a gently sloping footpath, over a bridge, along the riverbed, and through the woods. She felt as if she had been relieved of a burden, and could feel the tension leave her shoulders. It had been five o'clock before she knew it, and the sky was turning dark.

"Are you from Yoko's college?" persisted the woman.

Kazuko nodded as she warmed her fingers. The woman stopped a girl walking by with a tray of cups, removed two, and gave one to Kazuko. The cup was full of weak but comfortingly hot tea.

"Yoko was the same age as my daughter," the woman offered. "But she did well in school and was pretty, too. The Suganos wanted to let her do whatever she wanted to, so they sent her to college."

"Yes . . . I know."

"And now she's dead. It didn't make any difference."

Kazuko, unable to respond, continued to sip her tea.

"Tokyo is a scary place."

"Traffic accidents happen everywhere," said Kazuko. "Yoko was just unlucky."

The woman gave Kazuko a questioning look, but Kazuko stared into the fire, blinking every time one of the logs crackled and popped as it burned.

That's right, she assured herself. *Yoko just had bad luck. There had been two suicides and one accident. There had been three dead bodies, but there was nothing to link their deaths.*

The girl in the reception tent got up and walked toward the entrance of the house. Kazuko gave the woman a polite parting bow, put her tea-cup back on the tray, and walked toward the girl.

"Are you Yoko's sister?"

"Yes, my name is Yukiko."

"I live in Tokyo; I was a friend of Yoko's."

"Thank you for making the long trip out here." The two stepped to the side to stay out of the path of the line of mourners. Kazuko brushed against the branches of a tree that had lost all of its leaves.

"Had you talked to your sister recently?" she inquired.

Yukiko shrugged. "The last phone call we had from her was a couple of weeks ago. Why do you ask?"

"No reason." Kazuko tried to act as if there really were no reason, giving the only hint of a smile an occasion like this would allow. "It was all so sudden, and it had been a while since I had spoken to her. I'm so sorry . . ."

"Yoko told us she wanted to come home," Yukiko said.

"Come home?"

"She said she was lonely. Mom talked to her and convinced her to stay. She only had a year of college left, and it wasn't long till winter vacation. Mom said she would go visit her and see how she was doing."

Kazuko remembered Yoko telling her how scared she was. "Yoko told me that you wanted to come to Tokyo, too."

"I did for a while, but I changed my mind."

"Why?"

"Nothing really. I got a good job here, and it wasn't as though I was going to school. Yoko wanted to study English; that's why she went to college." Yukiko looked resentful. "And my parents didn't have enough money to send both of us."

There was a constant hum of voices, and the scent of incense was everywhere.

"I can't believe she died like this. What a fool." Yukiko sounded like a petulant child, and her eyes filled with tears.

"So you didn't hear anything . . ." Kazuko said in a small voice.

"Hear what?"

Kazuko opened her purse, took out a handkerchief, and handed it to Yukiko. "Nothing, nothing at all."

Kazuko went to look at Yoko's picture one more time and decided to head back to the station. *I want to get back to Tokyo.*

Suddenly she heard a commotion at the front of the house. There was yelling, and the sound of something being hit. One of the large wreaths of funeral flowers had begun to tip over from the force of someone falling into it, and people rushed to right it.

"It's the wife of the driver," said Yukiko.

"You mean the one that hit Yuko?"

"Yes, she came with her lawyer. Uh-oh, there goes Dad."

Yukiko ran toward them and Kazuko followed her.

"Get out of here! Leave!" Angry voices were raised, and two people came flying out of the front door. One was a man in a suit. The other was a plump woman wearing black.

"We only want to apologize!"

"You can't bring our daughter back. So get out!" As if for emphasis, something black came flying out of the house and hit the woman full in the face.

"Mrs. Asano!" The man in the suit rushed to the woman's side to keep her from falling. Kazuko hurried forward to see what Yoko's father had thrown. It was a heavy, large-sized shoe.

The woman squatted down clutching the right side of her face. She was bleeding. The neighbors stood at a distance watching the exchange. No one stepped forward to help.

"Are you all right?" asked Kazuko.

"She's been hurt," said the man peering into the woman's face. He looked to be in as much pain as if he were the one who had been hit. Kazuko saw the shiny badge on his lapel; just as Yukiko had said, he was a lawyer. She and the lawyer helped the woman to a quieter spot and sat her down on the stone ledge of the next-door neighbor's house.

The woman used her free hand to gesture the two not to worry. "I'm all right."

"You don't look all right to me. Excuse me, Miss," the lawyer turned to Kazuko. "Would you mind staying with her until I get back? I'm going to call a taxi. I've got to get her to a doctor."

"Yes, of course."

The lawyer hastened off in the direction of the station. Kazuko felt anxious and hoped he'd be back soon.

"I'm sorry," the woman began speaking to her. "I don't even know you and here you are taking care of me. Please, I'm fine . . ."

"No, you're bleeding badly." Kazuko dabbed at the blood with the handkerchief the lawyer had left behind.

"Did you know Miss Sugano?" the woman asked.

"Yes, I came from Tokyo. You're from the family of the taxi driver, isn't that right?"

"Yes, I'm Yoriko, his wife."

"This must be difficult for you."

"That's the least of my worries. A girl has died," Yoriko Asano said bravely.

"But you know they're not going to forgive you just because you apologize."

"I suppose I shouldn't have shown up with Mr. Sayama. That man who was with me—he's a lawyer. But I wanted them to know that we are serious and that we intend to do the right thing. And I wanted them to hear what I had to say, too."

Kazuko lowered her eyes, embarrassed at how much Yoriko was sharing with her.

Yoriko looked up at her. "I'm sorry to bother you with this, especially since Miss Sugano was a friend of yours."

"It's all right. I wasn't so close to Yoko that I can't be open-minded about this." Kazuko was not being entirely truthful, but it did seem to calm Yoriko down.

"My husband claims that Miss Sugano ran out into the intersection."

Kazuko caught her breath.

"She was running so fast, it looked as though she was trying to escape from something. He couldn't avoid her. What she was doing was suicidal."

"Excuse me, but . . ."

"Yes?" Yoriko did her best to look up at Kazuko again.

"Was he telling the truth?"

"Yes, he was," Yoriko declared almost defiantly. "My husband doesn't lie." A pair of headlights began to shine in the distance. Mr. Sayama was back with a taxi. He helped Yoriko into the car, and they headed for the emergency room of the local hospital.

Kazuko said good-bye, and headed slowly down the mountain road toward the station. Yoko Sugano had run out into the road in front of the car. She had appeared so suddenly that the driver had been unable to swerve to avoid her. Kazuko heard Yoko's words in her head again. *I'm scared. Kazuko, you can see what happened, can't you? Those two didn't commit suicide. There was somebody else—*

No there wasn't! Kazuko cut off the memory. Who could have done it, and how? You could kill someone, but you couldn't make them commit suicide. You just couldn't! But . . .

Kazuko heard another pair of footsteps on the dark road. She turned around to look. A short distance a way she saw a small human shadow. The light of a single street lamp shone behind it, and she couldn't see the face.

"Did I frighten you?" the shadow spoke. "I'm so sorry, I didn't mean to."

Kazuko stood still, staring at it as it drew closer.

———•———

When Mamoru arrived home that night, he found a glass door in the back of the house shattered, the fragments scattered about. On the wall to the side of the door, someone had scrawled "Murderer" in brown paint.

A neighbor told him that she had heard the sound of glass breaking early in the evening. When she went to see what had happened, she saw a boy in a school uniform running away.

Mamoru swept up the glass and scrubbed the writing off the wall. It was then that he realized it hadn't been written in paint, but in blood.

When he was in the bathroom washing his hands, the phone rang. Thinking it might be his aunt, he went to pick it up, but it was the same raspy voice of the man who had called the night before.

"Is Mr. Asano, the one who did me the favor of killing Yoko Asano, still being held by the police?"

"Who are you?"

"They should let him go. The police are fools. They wouldn't have to search far to find out that she *had* to die."

"Just a minute! How can you say—"

The phone went dead. Frustrated, Mamoru continued to yell into it, but the caller was no longer on the line.

The police wouldn't have to search far? What would they find out? The house was so quiet that Mamoru could hear the clock ticking. He sat down to think, and wondered for a moment about the private life of Yoko Sugano. *But it was an accident!* Mamoru tried to put the questions out of his mind.

"Good evening!" a cheery voice called out. Anego stood at the front door, her arms full of shopping bags. Her brother Shinji was with her, and he was loaded down with bags, too.

"Good evening!" Shinji did his best to copy his big sister's tone of voice, and bowed in a grown-up way.

"When you said you'd be alone tonight, I thought I'd come over and make dinner for you." Anego was upbeat as always.

"I'm the chaperone!" Shinji giggled. "It would be dangerous for the two of you to be alone! I mean it would be dangerous for you, Mamoru!"

Anego's leg flew out to the side as she deftly kicked her brother. "Is your cousin still gone?"

"Sounds pretty strange to me." The three of them had finished their dinner of hamburgers, and Anego was adding milk and sugar to her second cup of coffee. High-pitched electronic beeps and blasting noises came from the living room where Shinji was playing with Maki's video game collection. From the soundtracks, Mamoru was sure he was going through all of them, one by one.

"Maybe you should talk to the police or to that lawyer. Takano might be right."

"Yeah, I will. The lawyer is with my aunt today. They went to the funeral for the girl who died." He looked up at the clock. It was eight-thirty. "She should have called home by now."

"If what that caller said was true, it might help your uncle out—but it's creepy the way someone you don't even know is bad-mouthing that girl. She was only twenty, right? Maybe it was some guy she blew off."

"That's exactly what I thought." Mamoru sighed. "We can't expect anything to come from it."

"What do you mean, *expect anything*?" Shinji poked his head in.

"Get out of here, you brat!" Anego balled up her fist at him. "Speaking of creeps, you haven't had Miura out here, have you?"

Mamoru was unable to deny this notion immediately, so he just tried to keep his face expressionless. He realized he had failed when he saw Anego's expression. He gave up and laughed.

"It's not funny," she said. "What's he done now?"

"Nothing really. Don't worry about it."

"But . . ."

"Come on, I've got my pride! I can't have a girl working as my bodyguard."

"That's not what I'm doing." Anego batted her eyes a few times at him, impressing Mamoru with her long lashes.

"I'm just joking," he did his best to laugh. "I appreciate it."

Anego smiled demurely. It was rare for her to do anything so overtly feminine—usually she just laughed out loud. Mamoru felt privileged.

"Promise you won't get mad?" she asked.

"What?"

"Promise!"

"All right, whatever. What is it?"

"I have this feeling that your father is upset about all this, too." Mamoru struggled to hide his surprise. "I feel like he's somewhere close by and that he's been keeping an eye on you and your mother. He knows you're here with the Asanos and he wants to come see you, but he just can't bring himself to."

"Now that you mention it, whenever I've gone to put flowers on my mother's grave on special days, someone has always been there before me—"

Anego's eyes opened wide, but Mamoru, unable to keep up the act, raised his hands in surrender and laughed. "No, that's a lie. It's never happened!"

Trying to cover up her embarrassment at having been so gullible, Anego quickly added, "Anyway, my mom says that's the way men are."

"Okay, I'll keep it in mind." The conversation had come to an uneasy halt, and Mamoru was anxious to cheer Anego up again. "But you know, sometimes I feel that way. Like my dad is somewhere close by. I wonder if we actually run into each other sometimes without knowing it."

"What do you mean? Don't you remember what he looked like?"

"No, I've forgotten, and I'm sure he doesn't remember me either."

"How old were you when he left?"

Mamoru held up four fingers.

"I guess you wouldn't remember. Don't you have any pictures?"

"It wasn't really the sort of situation where you'd hold on to family photos. If you looked through old newspapers from twelve years ago, you'd probably find one or two—out of focus."

"Didn't your mother leave anything for you?"

"She left me some pictures of the two of us and her wedding ring." Anego nodded, obviously moved. "Mom always wore her wedding ring . . ."

It had been raining the day Toshio Kusaka left his family. March rain was cold in the north. Mamoru had been small, but he recalled that it had begun raining the night before, and a downpour in the early hours had kept him awake. Toshio had left early, just after five—before the first express train passed through Hirakawa Station.

Mamoru's room was next to the front door of their home and he had heard his father leaving. Mamoru had pushed his door open just a crack. His father had been dressed in his suit, and he was tying his shoelaces. Mamoru thought that it must have been some kind of early morning meeting, and he remembered thinking that his mother must still be asleep. Looking back, he decided she must have been pretending to sleep. His father's lifestyle had become irregular, and there were days when he didn't even come home at night.

His mother must have realized that there was another woman involved, but Mamoru had never seen his parents arguing or his mother in tears. He wondered if it might have been easier on him if he had. The only impression he had had was that something in his home was being broken. It was almost as if he could hear the sound, not of destruction, but of collapse.

When his father had opened the front door, the sound of the rain became louder and it lasted for several long seconds as Toshio paused, looking back inside before turning to go. The door closed, and the sound was once again muffled. Toshio had left, and it was the last time Mamoru had ever seen him.

After his father left and the news of the embezzled funds got out, his mother spent more and more time in a daze. She would be cutting something in the kitchen or folding laundry, and just stop and stare into space. Mamoru's trials began when his friends all refused to play with him. He spent the rest of his childhood learning what it was to lose a father and exactly what it was his father had done.

My father abandoned me. Comprehension of this fact was similar to what a small child feels when first touching a hot stove and suddenly realizing that fire is dangerous. Mamoru did his best to forget the fact and distance himself from it.

Mamoru's mother had never blamed his father for anything nor tried to defend him. She only said that they had nothing to be ashamed of, and Mamoru should remember that.

Anego's voice brought Mamoru back to the present. "Didn't you ever think of leaving Hirakawa?"

"Yeah, but I never did."

"Why not?"

"I had a good friend that I didn't want to lose. He's dead now. And besides, my mother and I only had each other."

"I wonder why your mother wouldn't leave. Have you ever thought about that?"

Of course he had; sometimes it was all he thought about. He could never decide whether it was stubborn pride or some kind of hope, or simply a matter of having no other choices.

His father's girlfriend had worked in a bar in town. She was much younger than his mother, and her waist was tinier. And she didn't wait around for things to happen, either; she had left Hirakawa a week before Toshio.

The police had searched relentlessly for her, believing that she would lead them to Toshio Kusaka. They had finally located her in a condo in Sendai, but Toshio was nowhere to be found. He had already been replaced by her latest conquest, a salesman from a local loan company who was saved from her clutches by the arrival of the police.

She had passed all of the money Toshio had supplied her with to her pimp, a two-bit gangster type. The police suspected that the pimp might have been shaking Toshio down as well, but there was no evidence to prove it because they never found Toshio.

For his part, Mamoru suspected that his mother held on to hope when she found out who the woman was and what she had been up to. Her husband was sure to contact her; maybe he would even come home. That may have been why she refused to leave. She was afraid that if she left there'd be nobody there for Toshio when he did come home, and she'd miss her chance to be reunited with him.

"Your mother must really have loved your father," Anego concluded softly.

"That's not the way I saw it."

"Well, that's the way you *should* see it. It was good enough for her to live with. I'm sure that's how she felt—she never told you to be careful not to grow up like him, did she?"

"Not once."

"What a strong woman." Anego propped her chin in her hands and looked down at the table, speaking quietly. "But it must have been tough for you. She believed in your father. She wasn't the sort to compromise for her child's sake. I want to be like her . . ."

"Who likes who?" Shinji popped into the kitchen.

That evening, after Anego and Shinji had left, there was a call from the lawyer, Mr. Sayama.

"Why isn't my aunt calling?" Mamoru was immediately concerned. "Is something wrong?"

"She's been injured." Sayama's voice sounded agitated. "She's been to see a doctor and he wants to give her some tests. Someone from my office is on their way here to take care of things. You needn't worry."

"What happened?"

"I'm sure you can imagine the situation," the lawyer began and gave Mamoru the whole story.

Mamoru was speechless trying to imagine what his aunt had been through. He could feel his heart drop into his toes.

"Mr. Sayama?"

"What is it?"

"I've been thinking about the accident and wondering if Yoko Sugano was with someone when she got hit by the car."

"That would make everything a lot easier."

Mamoru explained to him what Takano and Anego had suggested.

"It's possible," concluded Sayama, "but we haven't had any reports of anyone leaving the scene."

"But it is possible?"

"Yes, but if everything happened just because it was possible, we'd all be sipping cocktails on Mars by now."

Mamoru continued to think for a long time after he hung up.

Why can't the police take a few minutes to look into it?

His Uncle Taizo was spending another night in jail, and his Aunt

Yoriko was in a hospital. Mr. Sayama had said that she had been hit in the face by a shoe.

A few minutes to look into it . . .

The clock struck ten.

I'll just have to be the one to do it.

———•———

It didn't take long for him to make the decision. And he was lucky, everything was set in his favor.

Lucky. He bit his lip at the irony of that particular word.

Just after ten, he made a call to someone who he knew would still be busy at work. When he heard the voice come onto the line, he got right to the point.

"Do you remember what we were talking about this morning? Right, that's what I mean. Look, I need to talk to you—there's more to the story. Can you make some time? Great, I'll be right over."

He hung up the phone and began to get ready to go out. The housekeeper his wife had recently hired gave him a concerned look.

"Are you going out so late?"

"Yes, I'll be gone for several hours, so don't wait up."

"What shall I tell your wife when she gets home?"

"You don't need to worry about her." He knew that within the week the housekeeper would come to understand the lack of interest he and his wife had in each other's activities.

He went to the garage and warmed up the car. The dull vibrations felt like they were shaking up his heart as well. Would this actually work? Would it clear up everything and leave him with no regrets? He closed his eyes and pictured the boy's face. He felt calmer by the time he eased the car out of the garage.

Standing in front of the building, he was afraid for the first time. Could he really pull this off? What if he lost control and began to spout the truth? Well, it was something he would just have to find out for himself.

———————•———————

Seated in an express train speeding toward Tokyo, Kazuko Takagi was having a dream. She felt a dull throbbing in her head, and she was terribly tired. She was even tired in her dream.

Kazuko, I'm dead! Yoko was standing next to her. Her expression was unbearably sad. *Poor Kazuko, now it's your turn. You'll be the last one.*

I'm not going to die! Kazuko screamed as hard as she could in her dream. She could see Yoko, Fumie Kato, and Atsuko Mita. Atsuko was headless. How come she was able to cry like that?

Kazuko, I've lost my head. Help me find it! Help me, look . . . look . . . Poor Kazuko. The last one will suffer the worst . . .

Kazuko woke up with a start. Her head ached and her heart was pounding. It was dark outside, and she could see her own face reflected in the window. She looked at her watch. She'd be in Tokyo in an hour. She wanted to go home and lie down in her own apartment. She wanted to be somewhere safe.

Why am I so afraid? Kazuko talked to herself as she tried to slow down her breathing. *I'm not going to commit suicide. There's no reason to be frightened.*

She looked at her watch again. She glanced at the timetable she had bought at the station when she left Tokyo, and suddenly realized why she ought to be afraid.

She had left Yoko's family home in plenty of time to catch an earlier train home. There was no reason for her to stay there any longer and nowhere for her to spend time even if she had wanted to.

So why was she on the last train to Tokyo?

Kazuko wrung her hands. *What was I doing all that time?*

CHAPTER 3

The Disquieting Muses

It was one in the morning, and Mamoru was standing at the intersection where the accident took place. He could see stars in the clear night sky. The air was cool, and everything looked as clean as a fishbowl that has just had its water changed. Everyone was asleep.

Mamoru stood for a while and watched the traffic signal change: red, yellow, green. It was a lonely electrical performance. During the day, it efficiently processed restless hordes of vehicles. Maybe its nighttime job was to keep order among the dreams of the sleeping masses.

Mamoru took a deep breath, drinking in the night. He had changed into a dark gray running suit and an old, thin-soled pair of jogging shoes before he left the house. The ones he usually wore to run had thick soles to protect his ankles from impact, but he was afraid they would squeak as he walked. On his hands were gloves with the fingertips cut out, and he had a white towel around his neck. If anyone asked him what he was doing, he'd have no trouble explaining. He'd heard that more and more joggers went out late at night when they could have the streets to themselves.

In the right-hand pocket of his pants were the tools he would need to complete his job tonight.

The signal turned green, and Mamoru crossed the silent intersection. Just as his aunt had said, there was a cigarette vending machine and a public phone in front of the shuttered store. Mamoru had checked a map, and he knew what direction to go. Turning his back on the intersection, he started off at a leisurely run.

The tiny apartment building where Yoko Sugano had lived was a mere fifty meters west facing a narrow side road. It was surfaced in red tile that, out of the light of the street lamps, looked like dried blood. Just beyond the narrow, paved driveway was a lighted concrete staircase. There was no inside corridor; all the apartments had outside entrances.

Mamoru stood running in place as he looked around. No one was on the road. He thought he heard the faint sound of singing; maybe there was a karaoke bar somewhere nearby. Mamoru ran across the driveway over to the staircase. A black cat with shining gold eyes ran out from behind the building and out into the street. Mamoru's heart stopped for an instant—that was one witness!

At the foot of the stairs were the aluminum mailboxes of the residents. They were divided into four rows, one for each floor, and each had a combination-lock padlock hanging from it. "Sugano 404" was written neatly on one of the boxes on the top row.

Mamoru took off his shoes, hid them in a bush, and climbed the stairs in his stocking feet—the sound of footsteps tended to carry late at night. The fourth floor seemed awfully far up. In weight training at school he wrapped sandbags around his ankles and climbed the stairs, but even that had never seemed this hard. The soles of his feet were cold, and he felt large and naked under the lights.

As he reached the third-floor landing, he heard voices. He couldn't tell where they were coming from, so he crouched down to listen. Someone was walking by on the street. His heart pounded as he waited for them to pass. Then he started climbing again.

He reached the fourth floor, and turned to look out for an overview of the area. Next door were two two-story houses and then another apartment building of about the same height as this one. Its windows all had the curtains pulled and none of the lights were on.

In the narrow hallway where he now stood, there were five white doors facing the road, each accompanied by a matching gas meter. Mamoru crouched down as low as he could and moved forward until he got to the one marked 404. There was no name on the door. Mamoru leaned against the railing and took a deep breath. He had come here to see what sort of place Yoko Sugano lived in, and he had the skills to do so.

Mamoru thought about Gramps, the good friend he'd told Anego he hadn't wanted to lose. Well, he had never imagined that he would be using everything Gramps had taught him for a situation like this.

After his father had disappeared, Mamoru's friends had refused to play with him anymore. To begin with he was merely perplexed, but as he grew older things got worse and he better understood what had happened. No baseball teams would take him and local mothers refused to look after him at the summer festivals. The discrimination began with the adults, but prejudice is a powerful disease, and it wasn't long before it spread to the children.

Soon after he started first grade, Mamoru found himself alone. No one invited him to play soccer after school. He had no one to do homework with, and no one to throw spitballs at during class. He supposed it was only natural: Toshio Kusaka had stolen from the taxpayers. If his wife and child were unable to put up with life in the town, they were free to leave.

About this time, his mother explained what had happened to him. She left nothing out. Mamoru would never forget her words as she finished her account. *Mamoru*, she had said, *you've done nothing to be ashamed of. Don't you ever forget that.* He was sure that she was telling herself the same thing in an attempt to make life somehow more tolerable.

Keiko was working at a paint plant at the time. She had found someone who had known her husband's family and was willing to help her out. Without that job, the only alternative to leaving Hirakawa would have been to murder her son and commit suicide. At least their ashes would have remained in the town.

Mamoru had nothing to be ashamed of, but he was always alone.

Then he met Gramps. It was a hot day in August. Mamoru had left his bike in the backyard and was sitting on the wall in front of his apartment building. He had nowhere to go and nothing to do, but he was bored of sitting at home alone.

"Awfully hot, isn't it?" Mamoru looked up when he heard someone talking to him. An older, thickset man was standing in the shade of the wall. He was wearing an open-necked gray shirt and held a small bag in his left hand. His almost-bald head was covered in perspiration. He pulled out a handkerchief to mop his head, and spoke again.

"You'll die of heat stroke sitting there in the sun. How about joining me for some shaved ice?"

Mamoru hesitated before standing up. He had a few coins in his pocket with which he had been instructed to buy his lunch.

And that was how it had all begun.

Gramps' real name was Goichi Takahashi, but Mamoru never called him anything but Gramps. He never knew his exact age, but he was probably over sixty when they first met.

Gramps was a retired locksmith who had specialized in safes. He had been born in Hirakawa but was apprenticed to a locksmith in Osaka after the war, and he had worked there his entire career. He had retired to Hirakawa, and that was about all he ever told Mamoru about himself.

All it took was a bowl of shaved ice. Afterward, Gramps had taken Mamoru home and shown him the workshop attached to his house. It was filled with shiny tools of all different shapes and sizes, and a safe big enough to hold Mamoru. There were some beautifully decorated boxes that were impossible to figure out how to open.

"This is my hobby," Gramps had announced with a smile. Mamoru couldn't help looking around at everything, and Gramps had had to laugh. "I get lonely if I don't have these things around me. And you know what? They get lonely, too, if no one's around to take care of them.

"You can look and touch and play with anything in this room that isn't dangerous." After that, Mamoru was allowed to do as he pleased whenever he came to visit. He loved to touch the cold "skin" of the safes and stare at the mazes that made up the devices inside the locks. He opened Gramps' old photo albums that were full of pictures of keys carved in wickerwork designs and safes that had to be more valuable than anything they held. Mamoru commented on how beautiful they were, and Gramps nodded in agreement.

Gramps was always engrossed in his work. After Mamoru had made the rounds and looked at everything, he would sit and watch him. Gramps' hands were quick and amazingly graceful, and he always had a contented look on his face as he worked on the safes and locks.

One day, when Mamoru had been coming around for a couple of weeks, Gramps turned to him and asked, "How about it, Mamoru? Would you like to try this?" He was using a fine file to get the rust off of an old safe.

"Do you think I can?"

"Of course you can!" Gramps smiled and handed him the file. "Be gentle with it, now."

Mamoru spent the next week gently filing the rust off the safe. Beneath the rust that had accumulated over the years, the safe had a shiny gray surface. On each corner of its door was an exquisitely engraved peony. When he was finished, Gramps smiled.

"She's a beauty, isn't she?" Mamoru had gone from being an observer to becoming a helper. From there it was only a matter of time until he became interested in the rest of Gramps' work.

Once Mamoru lost the key to his apartment. There were still two hours until his mother came home from work and could let him in. Outside the third-story window hung the laundry that he should have taken in hours earlier and, to make matters worse, it looked like it was going to rain. Mamoru ran to look for Gramps.

The lock took Gramps less than five minutes to pick. To Mamoru it looked like magic, but Gramps frowned and said, "You and your mother ought to have a better lock. This one is no better than a toy."

The next day he came over with a new lock for the door. When he was through, Mamoru asked, "Do you think I could do something like that?"

"Would you like to try?"

"Yes!"

"Well then," said Gramps, "you can do anything as long as you're interested."

That was how Mamoru began learning the locksmith's craft. He started out by learning about the different kinds of locks and how they worked. Different manufacturers made different types of locks, and each country had its own distinct models. When it came to actual techniques, there were so many to learn. He learned about padlocks that were opened by lining up numbers, bicycle keys, and car door locks. Next Gramps taught him about cylinder locks with pin tumblers, the most common type. Mamoru learned how to pick locks using two pieces of wire, and even made himself a picking gun. He learned how to make impressions of keys, and then practiced making duplicates of them using hundreds of uncut keys. He even learned how to open a lock using a key that was similar to the original but not exactly the same. It reminded him of trying to convince a stubborn person about something new. The final skill he learned was how to manipulate a combination lock to figure out what numbers would open it.

Looking back on it all, Mamoru realized that locks and keys did not constitute a hobby often pursued by young boys, but he had enjoyed it all. There was nothing else for him to do and he had come upon it all accidentally, but he had kept at it for pretty much ten years because it had been like play for him.

Last October, just as the final leaves were falling off the trees, Gramps had died suddenly of a heart attack. Mamoru felt as though his world had fallen apart.

Gramps had given him a set of tools just a few days before he died. Mamoru wondered later if Gramps had somehow known he didn't have long to live. He'd asked Mamoru a question.

"Do you know why I've taught you how to pick locks?"

Mamoru had been so delighted with the brand-new tools that he hadn't given it much thought. "It was because I asked you to, wasn't it?"

"No. Don't you remember what I told you when you first started? You can do anything as long as you're interested." He looked at Mamoru for a few moments before he continued. "You know, you've never talked to me about your dad."

Mamoru was confused. "I was sure you knew. Everybody does."

"Are there still people who bother you about that?"

"Sometimes. But not as many as before."

"People forget. They all forget eventually."

"I've forgotten about him, too."

"Did you enjoy learning about locks?"

"Yeah."

"Why?"

Mamoru thought a few moments. "Nobody else can do it!"

Gramps nodded and looked at Mamoru's hands. "Have you ever thought about using what you've learned to steal or to harm someone?"

"Never!" Mamoru was adamant. "Did you think I would?"

"No, of course not. A lot of the things I've taught you are outdated now. The times have changed, and there are new kinds of locks and keys. Before long you won't even see this sort anymore." Mamoru thought he sounded sad. "But that doesn't mean that everything you've learned will go to waste. You're a little bit different from other boys. You can see things that others want to hide away. You can get into places people don't want you to go. If you want to, that is."

Gramps looked into Mamoru's eyes. "You could have done all that already, but you didn't. It never even occurred to you. I believe in you, and that's why I taught you. Keys, Mamoru, are used to protect what is important to people. Your father," he continued sadly, "did not have the skills to pick locks, and he was not one to make spare keys. But he still did something he shouldn't have. He stole money. He used a key to a lock that people had given to him to protect what was important to them. It was their trust. And he opened that lock when he shouldn't have.

"Before you become an adult, you'll have to continue to suffer for what your father did. It won't be easy. But that's not what I'm worried about. Your father wasn't a bad man; he was weak. Everyone has that weakness inside themselves. Even you. And once you realize it's there, you'll understand your father. What I'm worried about is other people assuming that you'll take after him."

Mamoru looked at Gramps' face, but didn't say a word.

"As far as I can tell, there are two types of people. One type doesn't do what they don't want to even if they can. The other type doesn't give up until they achieve whatever it is they want. I can't tell you which type is better. What's bad is when you make up excuses to explain what you have or haven't done.

"Mamoru, never use your father as an excuse. Don't ever go looking for excuses. Someday you'll understand your father's weakness and what was so sad about that."

Gramps took Mamoru's hand—just the way he had when he first showed him how to hold the tools. His hand was dry and smooth, and surprisingly strong.

Which should I use? This was the first question Mamoru asked himself in front of Yoko Sugano's apartment. He didn't need any more light; the fluorescent lamp in the corridor was sufficient. You couldn't see inside locks anyway.

And this was a pitiful sort of lock. He looked at the doors of the apartments on either side. They were all the same. It was a common deadbolt that was even less effective than the type used in public housing. The deadbolt part was the only thing it had to say in its own defense, but Mamoru knew that as the lock and the door aged, it was only a matter of time until a credit card slipped into an expanding gap and a good push would open it up. It was not the sort of lock a young woman living alone would want to entrust her safety to. You could read the intentions of a building's owner just by looking at the locks on it. Mamoru saw that only two rivets had been used to attach the lock to the door, although there were holes for three.

Pin tumbler cylinder locks are made by combining several pins of varying lengths; when the right key is inserted into the cylindrical hole, the pins are manipulated to the exact height required to align them and turn the plug that opens the lock. Mamoru hadn't brought the ring of keys that he used to coax open locks, and his heart sank now as he realized it was all he had really needed.

Well then, he would just have to make one. It would be handy if he ever needed to come back here to return something. He wouldn't have to pick the lock a second time.

Mamoru dropped to one knee and took out his toolbox; it was about the same size as a pencil case. He opened it and took out a new key with a single groove in it. Gramps had taught him to sprinkle an uncut key with soot before inserting it into a lock, but Mamoru had decided to use baking soda he had borrowed from Maki's baking supplies. It would be easier to see where he needed to make notches.

He covered the key with the white powder and carefully inserted it in the lock. The biggest problem at a time like this was his own heartbeat. The more nervous he was, the more his heartbeat reverberated through his body and made his hand shake.

He removed the key and saw a fine line in the powder. Not everyone would be able to see it; you had to know what to look for. The line represented the silhouette of the lock. Mamoru took out a file and etched out the line, and then began to sculpt out the silhouette. The important thing was to take your time, trying it out now and then, to make sure you got it right. A lock was like a lady with principles; you had to do things right if you wanted to get close to her.

The fourth time Mamoru tried out the new key, he could feel the five notches fitting into the lock, and he slowly turned it. As he did so, he heard the deadbolt move. It had taken him twelve minutes.

He dropped the key into his pocket, and then blew gently into the lock. He was sure no one would go to the trouble to check, but he wanted to remove any traces of baking powder. Then he stood up and opened the door.

———————•———————

As Mamoru walked into the apartment, he found himself in a different sort of darkness. There was a smell of something sweet, but it was very faint. The dead woman had left behind the scent of her cologne. Mamoru stood still and pulled out a penlight. It was a strong, narrow-beamed light he had found in Akihabara. He switched it on and then adjusted it to the strongest setting so that he could get his bearings. The apartment had the tiniest of hallways, just large enough to remove one's shoes in. To his right was a cupboard for shoes, on top of which was an empty vase. On the wall behind it, there was a reproduction of a picture by Marie Laurencin.

Mamoru was unnerved to see the pale face of the girl in the painting looking down at him. His cousin liked the same artist and had all her books. The tones were romantic, but they were not the sort of pictures to look at in a dark place. Now Mamoru was sure that he would always hate them.

Next, shining the light on his feet, he was glad that he hadn't moved. Right by his right foot was a metal umbrella stand; if he'd kicked it over, it would surely have woken up the neighbors on either side. He stepped carefully around it and into the room.

He was now in the tiny kitchen. Two cups and saucers were set on the drainboard next to the sink. They were completely dry. There was a white table and two chairs. A ceiling lamp with a red shade was low enough to bump into. An oven toaster sat on top of a one-person refrigerator; both were white, as was the cupboard beside them. Next to this was another door with a sticker on it that said "Bathroom."

Mamoru opened the door and walked in. After using his penlight to confirm that there was no window, he flipped the light switch. The fluorescent light blinked on reluctantly.

Yoko Sugano was obviously very neat, and she liked the colors white and pink. Toiletries and slippers, all in pastel pink, were arranged neatly in the off-white single-unit bath and toilet. A single long hair was on the edge of the bathtub. It must have been Yoko's and she must have had long hair, realized Mamoru.

It occurred to him that he didn't know what she looked like, how she wore her hair, or even how tall she was. He hadn't gone to her funeral, and the newspapers had not printed her picture. He was almost certain that even his uncle hadn't clearly seen her face in the split-second before he hit her.

It was a realization that could destroy your courage at a single swipe. What did he think he was doing here? Mamoru slunk out of the bathroom, leaving the door ajar and the light on. The light wouldn't be visible from outside and it helped him see the entire apartment better. There was another room on the other side of the kitchen, and that was it. The room had a wooden floor and was about four meters square. In it was a simple bed and a low chest of drawers. Next to the window was the sort of desk and chair that a student might use. The rug in the center of the room matched the plastic-sided portable closet, the type you buy in a do-it-yourself shop and assemble at home. The zippered opening was half undone.

Mamoru imagined Yoko's mother must have gone through her things, looking for something to dress her in when she was laid in the casket. Mamoru drew closer and noticed a pleasant scent.

Where should he begin? He had considered this ahead of time and had planned to look for a diary, but now he decided what he needed was a photo album. He had to know what Yoko looked like before he could research her life any further. He found one on the bottom shelf of a tall bookcase. It was full of photos, mainly of women. Some looked like they were from a trip, showing a group dressed for hiking posing for the camera and making peace signs, a waterfall in the background. He decided that Yoko Sugano must be the tall, pale girl with straight hair down to the center of her back who showed up most frequently in the photos. There were pictures of her with another girl who resembled her, both of them wearing kimonos. This must be her younger sister. They had probably been photographed during the last New Year's holiday when she went back home.

As he moved to replace the album, a card fell out of a pocket on the inside of the back cover. It was an old student ID card for a cram school. This was Mamoru's proof that he had picked out the right girl as Yoko. She was very pretty, he thought. Not the type you might walk up to on the street and ask for directions. You'd expect to see her working in a fancy showroom for office equipment, or something like that.

Nice to meet you, and sorry to be here prying into your life.

Looking back at the bookcase, Mamoru saw that it was full. There were some mysteries and romance novels, but what stood out were the language books. Judging from the dictionaries, Yoko must have been studying English and French. There were books aimed at taking specific tests, guides for would-be interpreters, and others about studying abroad.

He couldn't find a diary. Maybe she wasn't in the habit of keeping one. Nor was there any appointment book or address book. Were they in her purse when she died?

How about letters?

Mamoru noticed a bulletin board at the head of her bed and a letter holder next to it. There were not many letters in it. *Everyone makes tele-*

phone calls these days, he thought, unable to remember the last time he himself had written a letter.

There was a postcard from a beauty salon and a picture postcard from a friend who had written from overseas. *How are you? I'm having a great time . . .* The only letter was from a Yukiko Sugano. The stationary had small flowers scattered over it and was written in the rounded hand-writing of a young woman. It was very short, saying that everyone was fine, that Yukiko had got a new job, and that if Yoko visited during the September holiday weekend she'd be able to see Ayako's baby. The final lines were taken up with asking after Yoko's health. She hadn't sounded well the last time they had spoken on the phone, was everything all right? Mamoru felt something heavy in the pit of his stomach.

He had been sure that he'd learn something by coming here. He never should have paid attention to that telephone call. Had he imagined he'd find a confession of some kind?

What would someone think if they found my lock-picking equipment in my room? he wondered. He might be suspected of being a career criminal. Then he'd be in trouble.

He sighed, sat down on the floor, and looked around the room again. He mentally compared it to his cousin Maki's room. It was painfully simple. The TV and radio were old, from a generation before. Yoko had probably got them secondhand. There was no video deck and even the lampshade was awkward and old-fashioned. The curtains were the cheapest sort available.

The entire building was old. Mamoru found two spots where water had leaked through the wall. The kitchen and bathroom faucets were old-fashioned, and the floor was covered with scratches. He wondered what the rent was here. Yoko probably got some money from her parents that she supplemented with a part-time job. Life couldn't have been easy. Not all female college students lived the rich life and wore designer clothes.

What *about* money?

Mamoru was not pleased with the extent of his own prying, but he went ahead and thought some more about it. What had Yoko's finances been like?

He might as well find out everything he could while he was here, he reasoned, as he began opening up drawers. In the second drawer of her desk he found a wad of receipts and a simple record of her housekeeping accounts along with two bankbooks. One had been stamped as out of use. He opened the newer one. She lived a frugal lifestyle, with the balance dropping to a few hundred yen each month. Once a month there was a deposit of 80,000 yen. This must have come from her parents. Within a day or so of this there was a bank transfer labeled "salary." The previous month she had earned 103,541 yen. Mamoru searched back over the preceding months. The figures were the same in September, August, July . . . but there was an enormous change the previous April.

She had been making much more.

There were deposits for 250,000 yen and even 600,000 yen, and they were cash deposits with no indication as to where they came from. There was little difference in the regular small payments she made, but every time the balance reached 500,000 yen, it had all been withdrawn. Mamoru kept flipping back the pages until he came to the one on which were listed long-term savings. She had made seven long-term deposits of 500,000 yen each. One had been withdrawn in April, but three million yen were left.

Mamoru looked around once again. Had Yoko really saved up three million yen while living such a modest lifestyle? He opened up the old savings book and discovered that the large deposits had begun in February of the preceding year. During the fifteen months between then and April of this year, Yoko Sugano had been extremely well off, and she had saved it all.

Why had she saved so much, and what had she done to earn it?

He opened up her housekeeping accounts. All of her expenses for each month had been duly recorded. On April 12, there was an entry for "cost of moving" and "deposit and key money." This is what she had used the one long-term savings deposit on. It had only been about six months since she had moved here.

For fifteen months she had been earning large amounts of money, and she had moved here at the same time as she stopped doing so. That point ran through Mamoru's brain over and over, just like a needle on a broken record.

Thanks for killing her. She had it coming.

But what was it she had done?

Mamoru put the bankbooks back, folded his arms across his chest, and thought a little longer. He considered whether he should look for anything else. Then he noticed a small red light shining in the dimly lit room.

It was the telephone answering machine. The red light meant it was set to take messages. Mamoru fumbled around with the phone until he located the tiny cassette tape in the machine.

There might be something on it.

Using his penlight to see, he rewound the tape and began playing it from the beginning.

"This is Morimoto. I'm going on a trip and I won't be in class tomorrow. Let me see your notes when I get back—I'll be sure to bring something back for you."

There was a high-pitched tone, and then the next voice began speaking.

"Hi, this is Yukiko. I'll call back again. Why are you out all the time?"

The next voice was a man.

"This is Sakamoto from the Hashida Prep School. Thank you for coming in for an interview the other day. We've decided to hire you and would like you to start work next week. Please call when you get this."

The next voice was another man, and his voice was animated.

"Did you change your phone number?" It was the raspy voice of the man who had called Mamoru's house. The one who had said *Thanks for killing her. She had it coming.* Mamoru listened more closely as the voice continued.

"It took some time. But it wasn't too hard to get your new number and address. Oh well. I wanted to tell you I found another copy of *Information Channel* at a used bookstore. I feel for you, I really do, but you can't escape. Talk to you later!"

It was the last call on the tape.

It was him, all right. The voice Mamoru kept hearing in his head. The same man who had called his house had also called Yoko Sugano.

When had he called her? How long before she died?

You can't escape.

She had moved and changed her phone number, too. What was *Information Channel*? Did it have anything to do with all that money she had made?

The questions kept running around and around his head in circles.

He decided that he was done for the night. He finally had some clues to work with. There *had* to be some kind of meaning in what that man had said.

Mamoru left the apartment and headed back toward the intersection where the accident had taken place. He stopped for a few moments there, and knelt down to tie his shoelace. Looking up again, he saw a silver gray car pass slowly through the intersection. It stopped by the playground on the other side. The car door opened and someone stepped out. Mamoru decided he'd better play it safe, so he withdrew to the side of the road and watched.

It was a man in a suit. He was tall, with broad shoulders. His back was to Mamoru, but Mamoru could tell he wasn't young. Purple smoke spread out over his head from the cigarette he was smoking. What was he doing here so late at night?

Just as Mamoru had done, he stood in the middle of the quiet intersection, looking up at the traffic light. Then he turned around in Mamoru's direction. Mamoru hurriedly stepped back further into the shadows. The man had a square jaw and neatly combed hair that was silver at the temples.

After about five minutes the man went back to his car and drove away. Mamoru set off at a run, headed for home. The scent of cigarette smoke still hung in the air as he passed through the intersection.

———•———

"Information Channel?"

Mamoru began work on Sunday by sorting the magazines that had passed their three-week shelf life and were to be returned to the publishers. The Books section was full of customers, and the atmosphere was noisy and bustling. Mamoru and Sato were bent over in uncomfortable positions, busy with their monotonous task.

Sato wrinkled his brow as he mulled over the unfamiliar name. "I've never heard of it. Are you sure it's the name of a magazine?"

"Yes, it was listed as a 'copy of,' so it's got to be either a magazine or a book. I was sure you'd know."

The voice on the answering machine had said he'd found *another copy* of Information Channel *at a used bookstore.*

"A suspicious-sounding name like that wouldn't be a book." Sato seemed to be enjoying the puzzle.

"And it probably wouldn't sell well either," Mamoru added.

"It probably went out of publication after a few months. I've heard of just about every magazine that's lasted at least a year. Do you have a copy yourself?"

"No, I just know the name. It's probably been in print during the last year or so."

"I guess we could look it up, but I wonder if it would be listed. It might be some kind of underground publication and probably has a weird subtitle attached to it."

Underground publication? Why hadn't he thought of that? Yoko Sugano was a beautiful girl; she might have been a model. And all that money in her bankbook . . . she'd never have earned that much in a typical part-time job!

As he and Sato removed the covers from the outdated magazines, Sato sighed, "All the beautiful girls on these are off to the pulp factory. You've got to feel sorry for them. But just think of how many magazines there are around! You're looking for a needle in a haystack!"

"Yeah, I guess you're right."

"Hail, young men! Working hard?" Makino, the plainclothes security man for the Books section, ambled over from the service stairway. Today he was wearing a suit and tie. Mamoru always admired the way he dressed—it wasn't what he wore so much as how he wore it. No matter what the outfit, he looked comfortable in it. When he had on an English suit, he looked like an executive who had a room with an enormous wardrobe full of beautiful clothes. When he wore a thin jacket with a pair of worn-out jeans and stuffed a racing form in his back pocket, no one would ever doubt he was a two-bit gambler on his way home from the track.

"Stay on your toes today, young men. Your youthful clientele are face-to-face with final exams, and they are fidgety."

"Hey, that's me you're talking about," Mamoru spoke up.

"And I'm glad it's you and not me." Sato kept up the patter, but Makino wasn't about to let him get away with it.

"And this from someone who took eight years to get through college, and still doesn't have a decent job?"

"This is a job."

"Right. How long are you going to continue your career as an occasional worker in a bookstore? You'll never earn enough to get a pension in your old age and lie around all day bothering your wife." Makino sniffed. "You know what they say about reading too much, don't you? Women miss their chance to marry, and men lose their balls."

"Come on, nobody believes that anymore," Mamoru laughed.

Just then Sato broke in. "Mamoru! I think I figured out how to find that *Information Channel* you were talking about."

"How?"

"Our Madame Anzai. She'll be able to tell us—if she hasn't broke up with that boyfriend of hers, that is."

"Hasn't broke up? That's a fine way of putting it," clucked Makino.

Masako Anzai's career in Books had been even longer than Sato's. She had an imposing presence that resulted in everyone calling her Madame, and she would not be pleased to learn that Sato had thought of her when someone mentioned women missing their chance to marry.

"I wouldn't do anything for that Sato, but I can't ignore Kusaka," was her response when asked about the mysterious publication.

"Have you ever heard of it?"

"Give me a little time, and I'm sure I'll come up with something. He's not someone who's easy to get a hold of." One of her boyfriends was a freelance writer who collected magazines as a hobby. "Someday he wants to open a library for magazines. He's got a database that will tell you more than a newspaper could."

As he continued to sort the magazines, Mamoru wondered what would come up. What did *Information Channel* possess that could have caused such misery for Yoko Sugano? If it was an underground publication, could someone have been using it to blackmail her?

She had been a college student. She might have unwittingly slipped into an unfortunate situation, led on by a glib tongue and the promise of a lot of money. It was just the sort of thing TV programs and magazines reported about modern young women.

She might have met her blackmailer at that intersection that night. She might have tried to escape when he refused to let her go.

Or—and a new thought occurred to Mamoru—she might have committed suicide, leaping into the path of a car because she was unable to deal with the situation any longer. She might have been describing what had happened to her when she groaned, *It's awful, awful! How* could *he?* before she died.

While they waited for word from Madame's boyfriend, Mamoru was able to get a look at Makino at work as he deftly caught several shoplifters.

One case involved two high school girls who tried to hide a book of photos of a popular rock band under a loose-fitting sweatshirt. Makino had tapped them on the shoulder the instant they put a foot on the stairway leading to the next floor. The girls had frozen in front of the giant screen, just then displaying a scene of a cool Canadian lake.

"What idiots!" noted Madame as she stood at the cash register and watched the girls being hauled off to the office. "Their school will expel them for sure."

Neither of the culprits looked too concerned.

"Do you think they'll be that hard on them? Those girls don't act like they think they've committed a crime."

"No, they don't. And the police don't always take it seriously when we call them, but schools are different." The girls were wearing the uniform of one of the top private girls' schools in Tokyo. "Makino told me strict schools like that call in the parents as soon as they find out anything, and make them stand in the hall with their daughters while the teachers decide how to punish them. Sometimes it takes hours; you'd almost think that was punishment enough."

"So they get expelled?"

"That's what I hear."

"Just for something they did on a whim?" Now Mamoru had begun to feel sorry for them.

"Hmm, on a whim . . ." Madame fixed the glasses that had begun sliding down her nose, and cocked her head. "I might be old-fashioned, and you might be speaking for the next generation, but I believe the term 'on a whim' is obsolete. Kids these days set out to steal; there's nothing impulsive about it. They think they can apologize for giving into momentary temptation. But that doesn't make up for losses of 4.5 million yen a year."

"Is that how much gets stolen?" Mamoru knew there was a lot of shoplifting, but he'd had no idea just how much it amounted to.

Madame Anzai nodded. "We make 20 million yen a month for a space of 300 square meters, and that's not good to start out with."

"Twenty million yen isn't good?" Mamoru was dumbfounded.

"Well, it's a little more than that now that Takano is in charge. The store has to pay the employees and other costs, right? So the actual profit only amounts to 4.4 million a month. That means that if shoplifting amounts to 4.5 million a year, we work for nothing for a whole month just to cover it.

"And it's the same in all the sales areas. It's even worse with CDs and videos. Stores that are any smaller than this get run out of business."

All those tiny thefts added up to a lot.

"I hear some of the kids get together to trade things they've lifted. They're all fencing stolen goods!"

Makino returned just as Madame finished her lecture.

"So what happened?" she asked.

"They begged Takano not to call the school. Their parents are on their way here, so I guess they get a lecture and go home." Makino looked unhappy about it. "I'm sure that wasn't the first time they've done it. They were just slow today, and that's why I caught them. I've probably missed them before."

Madame spoke in a purposely loud voice. "That Takano's a soft touch when it comes to girls!"

The other case of shoplifting was in direct contrast to the high school girls. A young man who claimed to be a member of a theater group that no one had ever heard of was discovered to have a large book of plays and a special issue of a magazine featuring photographs of onstage art. The total for the two was 12,000 yen.

The case, however, was not clear-cut. Makino caught the culprit before he had left the sales area, although he had clearly been heading for the elevator. He made no attempt to escape, instead claiming that he intended to pay, opening his wallet to show that he had 30,000 yen. He threatened Makino with suing the store for defamation of character.

Mamoru watched the scene anxiously from behind the shelf of recent publications. He knew that Laurel had had similar threats before, and that they had even made the papers. He also knew that a number of employees had been disciplined in connection with the incidents.

This time, however, luck was on Makino's side, as the guy also had two pieces of videogame software from the second floor. The police were called in, and it turned out that they had caught a shoplifter with eight previous convictions.

"I've had my eye on him for a long time; I knew I'd get him eventually," said Makino. "But you know, he was sloppy today. It's not the way he usually operates."

"It was your powers of perception!" Mamoru smiled.

Later when he was discussing the arrest with Sato, Sato told him, "Makino is hot this week, he's already caught four shoplifters. Maybe he's got some sixth sense going."

Mamoru finally got word from Madame Anzai during his lunch break. She walked into the storage room where Mamoru was drinking coffee, a memo in her hand. "My boyfriend says there definitely was a magazine called *Information Channel*."

"Really?" Mamoru stood up in his excitement and spilled his coffee. Madame moved quickly aside to avoid it.

"Come on, can it really be that important?"

"It really is."

"It has suspicious origins, you know. The first issue came out at the end of last year, and there were only four issues all told. It was sold through the usual channels, but it was put out by a publisher that no one's ever heard of."

"What kind of magazine was it? Who's the publisher?"

"My boyfriend only has a record of having seen it. There aren't any copies, so I really don't know, but he said it's not the sort of girlie magazine you'd put out for the kids to thumb through. Here you go." She handed Mamoru the memo.

"This is the publisher's name and address, and here's the information on the person in charge. I doubt you'll be able to get hold of them, though."

Mamoru handled the memo as though it was a ticket he'd won for a trip around the world.

"I'm sure you'd like to be on your way," frowned Madame, "but you know how busy we are today."

Mamoru knew that they were shorthanded; it was a busy weekend afternoon and one of the other girls had already gone home with a headache.

"But—"

Madame had kept her left hand behind her back. Now she whipped it out and flashed something in Mamoru's face. "Here's your permission to leave early. Takano told me to let you do whatever you needed to."

Mamoru headed off to the locker room, his heart full of thanks for Madame Anzai, her boyfriend, and Takano.

———————•———————

The phone was answered by a cheerful-sounding woman.

"Hello! This is Love Love."

Mamoru looked down at the memo Madame had handed him. There was no mistaking Madame's neat handwriting: "company president, Yoshiyuki Mizuno."

"Excuse me, I was given this number for the Mizunos."

"Yes, this is Mizuno."

"I'm looking for a Yoshiyuki Mizuno."

"That's my husband."

Mamoru breathed a sigh of relief. "I'd like to talk to him about a magazine he used to publish. *Information Channel*."

There was a brief pause before the woman spoke again, this time with a laugh in her voice. "What do you want to know about it?"

"I'm afraid I can't discuss it over the phone. My name is Mamoru Kusaka. I'm a student . . . I'm not out to cause any trouble."

"Well then, you might as well come by. We run a coffee shop called Love Love. Do you have the address? I'll give you directions."

There hadn't been any need for directions. Love Love was in a prime location in front of a train station. It was painted white, and had Western-style windows and awnings. Inside, a large ceiling fan turned slowly.

The shop was full of the Sunday afternoon crowd; most of the customers looked young. Music was playing in the background. Mamoru noticed a laser disc jukebox.

"My, what a sweet-looking boy!" A tall, thin woman in her mid-thirties greeted him. She wore a loose-fitting sweater, tight jeans, and leather sandals. She didn't appear to be wearing any makeup, but Mamoru noticed a scent of cologne. Her black hair came down to her shoulders, and one side had a single streak of light brown.

"I'm Akemi Mizuno, Yoshiyuki's wife. You're Mamoru, right? If you want to know about *Information Channel*, I'm sure I can help you out. I was the one who financed it, and I got stuck with cleaning up after it failed."

"Is Mr. Mizuno here?"

Akemi laughed. "I've got no idea where he is. Once he goes out, he's gone for a while."

Akemi stood behind the counter, and Mamoru took a seat in front of her. She fixed him a cup of coffee. "What business does a nice young man like you have with a filthy magazine like that? I know you boys have to have your fun, but there are lots of other magazines and videos you could get your hands on much more easily."

"So *Information Channel* was a porn magazine?"

"That was the category it was in, but it apparently wasn't dirty enough to sell. Good intentions, but nothing to back them up. That's Yoshiyuki for you."

"Do you have any copies left?"

Akemi's smile disappeared. "You're serious, aren't you? Why do I have a feeling that if I don't know what you're up to, it's going to cause me trouble later?"

Mamoru explained everything to her. That is, he gave her the story he had thought up on his way over. He told her that a friend of his had found a copy in a used book store, and told him that there was a picture in it of a girl who looked a lot like his long-lost sister.

"So why didn't your friend buy it to show you?"

"He never thought it was really her. So much for friends helping you out, huh?"

Akemi picked up her own coffee cup in a neatly manicured hand and thought hard. Mamoru pressed on.

"Are you sure you don't have any copies left over? If I could just get my hands on one . . . "

Akemi looked at Mamoru. "There was someone else in here a few months ago looking for copies of that magazine. He was a lot older than you, but he was doing the same thing. I didn't think anything of it at the time, but he was just as serious about it as you. We had some copies left, and he bought them all.

"I'm pretty sure that someone he was close to, a daughter or a grand-daughter, was a model in one of the issues. He wanted to buy them all and keep them out of circulation. Yoshiyuki and I had a fight over it. I told him I didn't care how much he paid those girls, what was wrong was wrong."

"So you don't have any copies left?" Mamoru felt his heart sink into his stomach.

"We've got one copy of each issue. Yoshiyuki insisted. Are you sure you want to see them? Aren't there any other ways of finding your sister? You're going to get a terrible shock if your friend was right."

"I don't mind. Please show them to me."

Akemi took Mamoru around the back and through an office of sorts.

The desk was lined with files, and there was a monthly calendar on the wall.

Akemi Mizuno was a businesswoman. Her husband seemed to be the type who, financed by his wife, was free to dabble in any new venture he put his mind to.

"Here they are. We closed up shop after the fourth one." Akemi put the magazines on the desk and left Mamoru alone to look through them.

Information Channel was the sort of magazine you'd go to a convenience store late at night to look through, keeping your back to the cash register. Mamoru looked at each page carefully, before turning it over to the next. He was glad there was no one else there to see him.

Then he found it.

When Mamoru went back into the shop, Akemi was chatting with a customer. Someone had put money in the jukebox; it was playing a song he knew. *Well we all have a face that we hide away forever, and we take them out and show ourselves when everyone has gone . . .*

"Did you find what you were looking for?" Akemi turned to look at him.

Mamoru nodded. "Do you know who wrote this article?"

He spread out a copy of the second issue of *Information Channel*. There was a photo of the upper bodies of four women. All of them beautiful. Their skin and hair shone even through the grainy photos. They were laughing and chatting together.

The second woman from the left was Yoko Sugano; Mamoru recognized her from the photos he had found in her apartment. Below the picture was a large headline: "These high-earners use every sexy trick in the book to get what they want. Lovers-for-hire talk about their real feelings."

Below that were quotes from the women. The first one read, "We're modern prostitutes: you pay us to fall in love with you."

———•———

The address Akemi gave Mamoru was another half-hour away, outside the city. The station only had one exit, and it led to a small town that was utterly unlike the district where the Asanos lived. Instead of an old, established neighborhood, there was a brand-new housing development with newly paved streets lined with trees.

Mamoru stopped in at a real estate office to ask for directions. A middle-aged man in a knitted vest sat at a desk, reading the paper. He kindly drew a map on the back of an old listing.

"Ten minutes at a slow stroll," he stated.

Mamoru arrived at a green house. Despite the modern design, the edges of the roof and the window frames were showing signs of wear, and the gate had come off its hinges and was leaning against the wall. Instead of curtains in the windows, battered Venetian blinds had been pulled down. The windows looked as if it had been at least a year since they were last cleaned.

Mamoru walked up three steps and found himself at the front door on which a nameplate announced "Nobuhiko and Masami Hashimoto." Nobuhiko Hashimoto was the name Akemi had given him.

Mamoru pushed the dusty doorbell just as someone said, "It's broken." He wheeled around to see a man with unshaved stubble around his jaw leaning out of a small window. "The electrician won't come to fix it. Can you believe that?"

It was already evening, but the man squinting in the light looked as if he had just woken up. "The door's not locked. Come on in. You need me to sign for something, don't you?" As soon as the man finished speaking, he pulled his head back inside.

Mamoru opened the door and stood in the tiny hallway. The shoe cupboard, with its mahogany veneer, had been badly damaged. It looked as though someone in a bad mood had hurled something at it, maybe one of the liquor bottles which were strewn in the hallway. It looked as though a number of people had just had a party there.

"Where is it?" the man asked.

"Are you Nobuhiko Hashimoto?" countered Mamoru, trying to maintain his composure.

"That's right. Where do I sign?"

"I'm not a deliveryman. I came to ask you about this article." Mamoru pulled out a copy of *Information Journal*, and one of the man's eyelids began to twitch. "I'm sorry to show up here all of a sudden, but there's something I need to know."

"Who gave you my name?"

When Mamoru told him that Akemi Mizuno had sent him, the man grimaced and gave Mamoru a hard look. "Aren't you a little too young for this sort of thing?" He laughed mirthlessly.

"She told me that you're the one who wrote this interview."

Hashimoto closed his eyes and put his hand to his temple. "Look, I've got a hangover. You'll understand one day. My head is pounding. I don't think I feel good enough to talk to anyone about work."

Mamoru implored, "Just listen to what I've got to say. I'm not here out of curiosity."

The man looked at Mamoru through narrowed eyes. Then he looked back at the magazine, and back at Mamoru. "All right. You'd better come in."

The kitchen was to the right of the narrow hallway. It was more like the ruins of a kitchen buried in piles of dirty dishes and rotten leftover food. Here, too, empty liquor bottles were scattered about. A number of flies patrolled overhead. Mamoru wondered how long it would take to excavate the kitchen from the mess.

The man led Mamoru into what had certainly been intended to be the living room. Now it was a home office in shambles. The room was divided in half by a large desk, on top of which were more bottles and a computer with a gray cover. Next to it was a smaller desk holding a printer. A bookcase reached up to the ceiling, equipped with shelves that could be slid to the side to reveal more shelves in the back. It was stuffed full of books. There were so many that it reminded Mamoru of the book stacks at Laurel. The only title he recognized was *Honor Thy Father*, by Gay Talese. It had been popular the year before, and Mamoru had picked it up, curious to see what it recommended for people without fathers to respect.

Everything in the room looked neglected and was covered with dust. The only things without a layer of dust were the bottles that still had something in them.

Mamoru sat down on the sofa opposite the desk. Stuffing poked through numerous holes, and indecipherable stains were scattered over it like so many islands. Mamoru decided that under no condition would he ask to use the toilet.

"So, what are you here for?" Hashimoto sat across from Mamoru and lit up a cigarette. He looked to be in his mid-thirties, but his expression gave the impression that he had lost all purpose in life. He didn't even run a hand through his disheveled hair in an attempt to be presentable.

Mamoru decided to tell him the truth. He started at the beginning, and told Hashimoto about the anonymous caller, the words spoken by Yoko Sugano before she died—everything.

Hashimoto chain-smoked as he listened. When a cigarette was so short it was about to burn his fingers, he used it to quickly light the next one before dropping the butt into an empty can.

"I see," he finally said. "So Yoko Sugano is dead."

"It was in the paper." Mamoru didn't mean to be rude, but his tone implied that someone who made their living writing articles ought to be reading newspapers.

Hashimoto flashed him a greasy grin. "Yeah, well, I haven't been reading the papers lately. Nothing exciting ever happens and the writing is so bad, I hate reading them."

"But you know who Yoko Sugano is. This is her in the photo, right?" The names of the women in the article were not given; the article referred to them as Miss A, Miss B, and so on.

Hashimoto was looking out the window, almost as if he had forgotten Mamoru was there. "Yeah, that's her." He turned back to his guest and spoke quietly. "Yoko Sugano was part of the interview. I was there talking to her. I remember her because, even though she made less money than the others, she was the prettiest."

Mamoru was so relieved that he felt dizzy. "So are these other women people you know, too?"

"No, I had to go looking for women who would agree to talk to me. I paid them well, of course. They each got 100,000 yen for the two-hour interview, plus dinner and taxi fare."

"Why so much?"

"So I could use their photos." Hashimoto laughed at Mamoru's confusion. "I didn't tell them that. They were supposed to be anonymous in the article. I told them I'd take pictures but not use them. They were used to making money for doing almost nothing, but they should have known that I wouldn't make an outlay like that without expecting something in return." Now Hashimoto was enjoying himself. "They all complained when the article was published. Yoko Sugano called, too."

"What did she say?"

"'How *could* you? You've ruined my life!' Things like that. So I said, 'Don't worry, your friends who aren't involved in this sort of thing wouldn't come within a mile of a magazine like this. No one will ever know.' She started crying—she obviously didn't have what it took to be in that line of work."

Mamoru knew that Yoko had been frightened. She had moved and changed her phone number. He recalled the message on her answering machine: *You can't escape.*

"So did the four women know each other before this interview?"

"I don't think so. I don't know if they became friends afterward. If it was me, I wouldn't want to have any friends from that side of my life."

Hashimoto stood up with an air of purpose. He grabbed one of the bottles lying nearby, and dug around in the piles on the desk until he found a dirty glass under a pile of books on economics. "You're a minor, right? So I won't offer you a drink."

Mamoru didn't think he would want a drink out of that bottle no matter how old he was.

Hashimoto simultaneously filled the glass from the bottle and plumped back down in his seat, spilling some of the amber liquid in the process. He indicated the bottle. "The king of whiskeys!"

Mamoru pondered the notion that Hashimoto had forsaken most of his life to serve this king, although there was no hint of regret in the way he sniffed at his glass. Mamoru's heart was getting heavier by the moment.

"Do you know what those girls did? What 'lovers for hire' means?"

Mamoru nodded. He had surreptitiously read the article on the train and was pretty sure he understood the basic idea.

"I wrote those 'quotes' under the photos. They never said those things. But I was wrong—it wasn't fair to women who do make their living as prostitutes. Real prostitutes give their customers something in return for their money."

A single fly buzzed through the room. Hashimoto tried to brush it away. He pointed at Mamoru with his glass. "OK, how about this? Imagine you work shifts at a computer company, or you're a truck driver, or a high school teacher. Anyway, you're always busy and you work long, irregular hours. You go days without even seeing a woman. Then, one day, you get a call from one."

Hashimoto put an imaginary receiver to his ear, and made a sound like a phone ringing. "Is this Mamoru Kusaka? A mutual friend of ours gave me your number. Do you think we could meet? I know girls shouldn't be calling boys, but your friend said you were so nice. If you don't already have a girlfriend, why don't we get together?"

Hashimoto spoke in an absurdly high-pitched voice and batted his eyelids. In any other situation, it would have made Mamoru laugh out loud.

"You'd be careful at first, and you'd ask who had given her your number. She'd laugh and say she'd been sworn to secrecy. Then she'd call you over and over; when you were tired and lonely and fed up eating cold dinners alone. One day you'd give in and agree to meet her. Where was the harm? You had a little bit of time to spare and you'd have a girl to spend it with."

Mamoru nodded, his eyes fixed on Hashimoto's face. He'd had a similar call from a girl with a cheery voice who'd started out by asking him to answer a few questions for some kind of survey.

"The girl who shows up," continued Hashimoto, "is beautiful. Before long, you're chatting together like old friends. She's full of smiles and knows how to talk. She's *delighted* to meet someone like you, and that makes you happy, too. You start seeing each other. You start out by going to the movies and taking walks. Or you might pick up something for lunch and go for a drive together. You, of course, are paying for everything because she is a lady. You start liking her. How could you not? She's beautiful, she's smart, and she acts like she's head over heels in love with you.

"One day she shows up for a date with two tickets, and asks if you want to go with her. It's a special show of leather coats or kimonos. Or maybe a special discount ticket for a jewelry fair. She puts her arm through yours, and off you go. The show is full of couples who look just like you. They're all looking at the showcases and chatting with the sales staff. Your girlfriend finds all kinds of things she wants, but oh, it's all so *expensive*! The salesman suggests that she use her credit card. She thinks it over and then asks you if you wouldn't mind signing for her because she doesn't have quite enough credit to cover it all. Or maybe you just decide to go ahead and buy it all for her. She's worth it, after all."

Hashimoto was still not finished. "And then one day she tells you that she works for a consumer finance company. She talks about how she's not making as many loans as she ought to be. Not only that, but the company is holding a campaign and she's far behind the others in the office. She asks you if she could borrow your name to make it look like she's drumming up more business than she really is. She swears she won't do anything to bother you. Or how about making an investment? She's got a friend in a securities company and there's a once-in-a-lifetime chance to make some money. There's no way it can fail—and we can use the money to go on a trip somewhere. She might tell you she can get you a membership to a luxury resort for a bargain price. You can sell it to someone else and make lots of money right away.

"You are seeing romantic dreams, and you hand over your savings to her. She's grateful, *so* grateful. She might even kiss you, she says."

Hashimoto finished his whiskey in a single gulp.

"And that's the end." He tossed out the line. "She stops calling you. You try calling her, and get her answering machine every time. If she answers, she acts bored and turns down your invitations. Some other guy might even answer for her. It'll be a guy with the kind of voice that'd make you piss your pants. You'll worry. You'll feel even lonelier than you did before you met her. That's about when you'll find the first late-payment warning in your mailbox."

We're modern prostitutes: you pay us to fall in love with you.

"The jewelry you bought for her. The fur coat. The payment on the resort membership you bought to help her out. Altogether, it comes to at least half your salary. That's when it hits home: she was just using you to make money."

Hashimoto lifted his arms in a show of resignation. "But it's too late. And you'll pay the money. Or you'll run to some consumer center, and they'll tell you how to file a complaint so you might not have to pay so much. But what about all that time you spent with her? What happened to all your dreams?"

Hashimoto's voice grew louder, and his punchy drunkard's façade was replaced by something much harder and unforgiving. "You were a fool. You were a defenseless, innocent fool. And you paid for it. But you weren't the only one. She was seeing more than one fool at the same time. Guys just like you. But no matter how stupid and ignorant a man is, he still has the right to dream. Dreams aren't things you buy with money. You don't sell them, either. Do you understand what I'm saying? The girl who snuggled up to you broke the one rule that should never be broken. She was after you *because* you were a lonely, soft-hearted idiot. And she knew she could make good money off of you."

Hashimoto's breathing was ragged. He opened the bottle, poured himself another shot of whiskey, and drank it down. "I really hadn't wanted to sell that interview to *Information Channel*. I didn't give it that sensational title. The idiot editor knew less about how to run a magazine than a baby in diapers." He looked at Mamoru. "But I didn't add anything to what those bitches said in it. I didn't have to add any dirty words or any slutty turns of phrase. They said it all themselves. All of it—every single bit of it.

"Those beautiful girls in their expensive clothes. You'd think they couldn't even swat a fly. They were raised by good parents in good homes. They went to decent schools and they all had boyfriends. You know, they even contributed to the end-of-the-year charities! They were *proud* of how they made their livings. Do you hear me? Proud! They bragged about the way they aimed for lonely men. Men who came home to empty apartments, had nowhere to go on Sundays, and shopped late at night for ready-made meals for one. They enjoyed taking those guys for everything they had. They laughed about the awful over-priced scarves the men bought for them, and how they threw them away in the station trash cans."

Hashimoto was angry now. Reeking of alcohol, he leaned forward and pointed a finger in Mamoru's face. "Young man, those women were scum. I don't have an ounce of sympathy for any of them. If one of them died, she got what she deserved."

Before he left, Mamoru gave Hashimoto his aunt and uncle's address and telephone number. "Would you be willing to tell that story to our lawyer or to the police?" he asked.

Hashimoto shrugged. "I suppose I'll have to. Someone might have been after Yoko Sugano, or she could have killed herself out of shame. And you need me to prove it?"

"That's right."

Hashimoto rooted around in the cabinet and pulled out a fat file that he tossed over to Mamoru. "Here are the transcripts from that interview, and all of the photos." The pictures were clear. The names of the girls were written on the back. Yoko Sugano, Fumie Kato, Atsuko Mita, and Kazuko Takagi. "You can use it all if it'll help."

"That would be great."

"There was someone here before. He said he wanted to sue the girl who had swindled him, and he needed some more details. He rewarded me for letting him copy this file." Hashimoto lifted his bottle triumphantly. "I don't know how the lawsuit is going, but he calls me up every once in a while, and he never forgets to send more whiskey."

"Well, we'll do what we can for you."

Hashimoto laughed and slurred, "Do whatever you think is right."

Looking at the file on the table, Mamoru remembered what Akemi Mizuno had told him about someone else who had come snooping around. "Was this man older?"

"Yeah, that's right. He was an old guy. How'd you know?"

"He came looking for you the same way I did. He bought all of the leftover copies of *Information Channel* from the publisher. Did he tell you which one he wanted to sue?"

Hashimoto tapped the picture of Kazuko Takagi. "This one."

Still holding his copy of the magazine in his hand, Mamoru stood up. "You hold onto this file for now," he said. "I'll let you know when we need it. Call this number if you're leaving town on a job." Mamoru indicated the memo he had written.

Hashimoto remained seated and waved his arms at the mess surrounding him. "You sure talk big for a kid. Do I look to you like I'm heading out of town?"

"Well, what are you writing about now?"

Hashimoto tilted the whiskey bottle at an angle. "What do you *think* I'm writing about?"

"Hard to say."

"Same here. My wife left me, you know."

Hashimoto's drunken laugh followed Mamoru out of the house.

———•———

"Just sign here . . . and here. Do you have your name seals with you?" The two young girls sitting before her shook their heads in unison. One had a sickly pale complexion and straight, greasy hair that she kept brushing off of her face. The other had a terrible case of acne.

Wondering how to show off her own blemish-free skin to its best effect, Kazuko continued, "Well then, I'll have to ask you both to give me your thumbprints. Sorry about the ink." The two did as they were asked. Kazuko waited until they were finished and then handed them tissues to wipe their fingers with. "All right then, the contract is now complete. It may look expensive, but it covers an entire year. If you work it out, it costs no more than the cosmetics you usually buy. The automatic bank transfer is only ten thousand yen a month—you won't even notice it!

"I've got something special for you, too." Kazuko pulled two light green tickets from her purse and gave one to each girl. "It's a special invitation to our Esthetique beauty salon. There's no expiration date, so go whenever you like. You can get a facial and a full-body massage using a special beauty cream. But don't tell anyone I gave this to you just for signing the contract. I'm not supposed to give them out for free," she said, giving the girls a just-between-us smile. They giggled in response.

Kazuko knew full well that if these girls showed up at the Esthetique salon, they would stop giggling in short order. The tickets she had given them covered only the rental bathrobes they would be given to wear and the soda they would be served in the waiting room. Kazuko had very carefully avoided saying that the facial and massage would be free.

She had come across the girls in the cosmetics section of a fancy department store filled with individual counters manned by beauty consultants for each of the many brands. Kazuko had stood just outside the section watching the young girls browsing through on their way to another sales area.

She settled on them as her targets and struck up a conversation in a soft, professional voice, letting them think that she too was a consultant. After that it was a matter of taking them gently by the arm out of the sales area and into an elegant coffee shop where the deal was closed.

"You're lucky, you both have lovely faces," Kazuko began as soon as they had settled themselves at a table, making out that she was studying their faces carefully. "Bone structure is the only thing I can't do a thing about; even plastic surgery has its limits. I've got other customers with such heavy jaws . . . the balance is just not there." At this point Kazuko looked up at the ceiling, holding up her hands in a gesture of utter defeat. The two girls couldn't help laughing.

"I'm always at a loss when women like that ask me for help. The only thing I can suggest is trying to hide the problem with makeup. The woman with the jaw? She's quite nice looking now. And you two? Well, you will be amazed at how good you can look."

Once Kazuko had put the completed application forms, pamphlets, ink, and credit payment papers back in her bag, she reached for the check, but then stopped to add, "I've got to be going now. I still have some customers to see. Do you know a company called HeartLux?"

The girls shook their heads, their eyes full of curiosity.

"It's a company based in Hollywood. Their makeup artists contract with actresses and models. Brooke Shields' and Phoebe Cates' careers began to take off when they started using HeartLux artists. They're about to open an office in Japan, and I'm . . ."

"You're going to work for them?" the girls were breathless.

Kazuko shrugged modestly, always careful to avoid any libelous claims. "I'm waiting to hear what they have to offer. My company puts more emphasis on skin care than makeup; I think our products are better. I'm not sure what I'll do."

"You must love your work!"

"I have to admit that it's more fun than sitting at a desk all day." Once more she reached out for the check.

One of the girls hesitated a second and then spoke quickly. "Why don't you leave it? We're going to have some dessert before we go." The showcase next to the cash register had a display of colorful French-style cakes.

"I can't let you do that," Kazuko protested, "at least let me pay for my own."

"Oh no, you gave us those tickets."

Kazuko favored the girls with a dazzling smile. "Are you sure? Well, then, thank you very much! You won't have to give up sweets when you use our products, so go ahead and enjoy yourselves!"

Kazuko pushed open the glass door and walked out. Before crossing the street, she turned around to wave at the girls through the window. One gave her a quick bow and the other waved back.

HeartLux was a name on a sign she had seen from the train this morning. Who knew what it was? Nor was she on her way to see other customers.

The cosmetics the two girls had contracted to pay for over the next twelve months were no different from the contents of jars and bottles lining any supermarket shelf. Of the 240,000 yen the girls would pay between them over the year, half went to Kazuko. The company she worked for, East Cosmetics Inc., had the ability to suck up money like a high-powered vacuum cleaner. While female employees posed as beauty consultants, men sold a sideline of "premium" feather beds and fire extinguishers.

Kazuko was working for East Cosmetics because she had got tired of her previous job. She just didn't have the determination it required. It had taken a lot of energy to seduce men who were overwhelmed with their jobs and had few opportunities to meet women, and to keep the relationship going until they came through with the goods. After every date, she would think of nothing but how long it was taking and whether the money she'd be able to wring out of her "clients" would be worth it. While she was with them, though, she had to act like she was having fun. She'd had to force herself to believe she was having fun.

It was a lot easier to swindle women. Women were like gamblers with decks of transparent cards. No matter how well a woman maintained a poker face, she would be yours for the having as long as you were able to tell her what cards she was holding. And it never took long.

Kazuko was very good at what she did, and she had also had the dramatic talent required of a "lover for hire." To whit, she had been able to delude herself. She'd made a lot of money and had spent it as she liked. For a while, she had traveled all over, going overseas twice a month. Her passport was full of visas, but no place she visited had made a lasting impression on her.

And after every trip, she'd returned to Tokyo to make even more money.

At first she had wanted to save up so she could start her own business. What she hadn't realized was that if there had been something she really wanted to do, she wouldn't have needed so much money to do it. She wouldn't have needed any more than she could have earned with honest labor, but she couldn't bear the thought of a regular job. She had long ago decided that the tedious jobs women were assigned were all pretty much the same no matter who you worked for.

The women she had met at the interview for *Information Channel* had had the same motivation. Money and escape from boring jobs. All four of them had been beautiful, but they didn't have quite what it took to live by their beauty alone.

Yoko Sugano had wanted to study overseas without having to rely on money from her parents. Fumie Kato had quit a job in a boutique that had kept her on her feet all day and required her to make a certain number of sales. Atsuko Mita had been looking for something to replace the constant competition she faced from the other female sales staff at her insurance company. They had all claimed they would quit this con game the second they had the money they needed.

The four of them had talked and laughed over drinks, and told each other everything. They'd never admit as much, but they weren't proud of what they did, and they wouldn't have been able to talk about it so openly if they hadn't let themselves laugh about it.

Those two girls could afford 240,000 yen, thought Kazuko. At least they'd had the illusion that they could pay it during the hour she was with them. And it was the illusion that enabled Kazuko to get what she wanted out of them.

It had been the same for the male clients for whom she had been a temporary lover who'd left them with a pile of debts. They'd been under the illusion that they'd found someone they got along well with, and who could make them happy. That was why Kazuko had been able to cheat them out of their money. Kazuko was always ready to stop the act the moment any of them had an inkling of doubt that something so wonderful could come to them so easily. That had happened more than once.

But most of Kazuko's clients had been irritatingly naive. They were like children who still believed that the Tooth Fairy would exchange their baby teeth for money. And that was why she didn't mind using them; she was sure they wouldn't be too badly hurt. She hated them all.

It was nearly evening, and Kazuko decided to call it a day. The two girls had been a jackpot, and she didn't want to push her luck any further. She stopped by a row of public phones in front of the station. She'd been thinking about calling her parents, and had been putting it off. She had felt shaken ever since she noticed there had been a couple of blank hours between the time she left Yoko Sugano's funeral and found herself on the train back to Tokyo. She was almost ready to leave the city and go home.

Kazuko had been born and raised in a town less than an hour away by train. Her brother and his wife lived with her mother in the family home. Her mother never came to see her, sending her packages rather than making the trip. It was all part of her sister-in-law's strategy to keep mother and daughter apart, Kazuko thought bitterly.

Whenever she called, her sister-in-law never failed to invite her to come visit. *You ought to come see your mother more. Her legs have been hurting, and she can't make the trip to go see you. I know how she misses you. Come stay for a while,* she'd say, and then she would hang up. But in that instant before the receiver hit the cradle, Kazuko would hear a deep sigh. That sigh communicated more to her than any complaints about sick children or endless household duties.

She decided not to make the call. She was deep in thought as she walked through the crowds, heading back to her apartment. She made a wish that was even more earnest than the eyes of the girls who had looked at her with awe, hanging on her every word. It was almost a prayer: *I wish HeartLux were real. Wouldn't it be wonderful if it really did exist?*

———————•———————

It was dark by the time Mamoru got home. His head felt heavy and his temples ached. He had come home with valuable information that would certainly help his Uncle Taizo, but he wasn't pleased with himself at all. Yoko Sugano had been running away from someone the night she had been hit by a car. She might even have been trying to escape from herself. Mamoru had discovered that she had reasons to be running outside late at night, plenty of them.

But she had died. Nothing could save her other than rewinding the clock back to that time. If what he had learned today came to light, it might have the effect of killing her twice. Mamoru wanted to be able to help his uncle without doing that. The whole way home he thought about how he could manage things.

"I'm home!" As soon as Mamoru stepped inside, someone came running down the hall. It was Maki, back from her brief stint as a runaway, and she flung herself at him. "W-w-wait a second! What happened?" he asked, startled.

Maki had grabbed his collar and couldn't stop crying. Eventually Yoriko appeared, with half her face covered in a bandage and the other half smiling.

"We got a call from Mr. Sayama not long after I got home this morning. A witness has come forward."

Maki wiped her face on Mamoru's shirt, and finally spoke. "Somebody witnessed the accident. He said the signal was green for Dad, and that Miss Sugano ran out in front of his taxi." Maki grabbed Mamoru's arm and shook it as she repeated herself. "Are you listening? Someone was there. Someone who saw the whole thing. We have a witness!"

CHAPTER

4

On a Chain

Over and over and over again.

The police interrogation just went on and on. He felt like a second-rate actor forced to repeat a scene until somebody gave him the okay to stop.

"I'm going to ask you again," said a detective. It must have been the fifth or sixth time. But he was compliant. It was a different detective from before, but this one, too, began with the now-familiar "Let's go over this again."

Humans were not equal: some were poor and others were rich; some had talent and others did not; some people were sick, others healthy. The court of law was the only place where everyone was treated the same. The man remembered hearing something like that when he was a student.

And he added to it now: humans were equal at the police station, too. Nothing he was familiar with was of any value here. His friends, who had helped him out in the past, were useless. All the detectives were impeccably polite, and they let him smoke whenever he wanted to. But the questions continued mercilessly. Any variation in response and they brought him up short. *Wait a minute, didn't you say it differently a while ago?*

He thought of himself as a piece of stale cheese, and the detectives were all mice running around taking tiny bites out of him. This time over here, the next time over on the other side. If they could only take him by surprise and bite in some unexpected spot, they would find out what they had suspected all along—that he wasn't cheese all the way through to the core.

I'd never be able to keep this up if the truth weren't such a simple thing, he thought. The part of him that was always able to maintain an objective eye on his own actions had to admire the persistence of the detectives.

"Where were you when you saw the accident?"

"Maybe ten meters away. She just kept running, heading toward the intersection. Farther and farther away from me."

"What were you doing there?"

"Just walking."

"What time was it?"

"Just after midnight."

"And where exactly were you heading at that time of night?"

"A friend of mine lives in an apartment near there. I was going to see her."

"How close is 'near'?"

"That same neighborhood. It was about a ten-minute walk."

"Would it take that long? So why were you walking? You said that you got out of the taxi on the same road as Yoko Sugano and walked from there. Why? Why didn't you just stay in the cab until you reached your friend's place?"

"It's the way I always do it when I go there. I take a taxi partway, and then I get out and walk."

"That's an unusual habit. Why do you do it?"

"I'm a successful businessman."

"Very successful."

"Right. Thank you. So, when I go places people recognize me. In other words . . ."

"Let me finish that up for you. In other words, when you, the vice-president of Shin Nippon Enterprises, decide to visit a lady friend in the middle of the night, you don't want anyone to see you. It would create a scandal, and things wouldn't be very pleasant if your wife found out. Is that what you mean?"

"Um, yes."

"This 'friend' you've been talking about. It's Hiromi Ida, age twenty-five."

"Yes."

"You pay the rent on her apartment, and visit her there. You go late at night, so you won't be seen."

The man looked down.

"So you admit that Hiromi Ida is your mistress?"

"I suppose that's what you would call her."

"Well, then, let's call her that. Hiromi Ida is your mistress. You were on your way to her apartment when you saw the accident. Am I right?"

"Yes."

"Does your wife know about her?"

"She might. I don't know. She'll certainly know about her before long."

"What color was the taxi that you saw?"

"It looked dark green, but I can't say for sure. It was a dark color."

"Were there any passengers in the car?"

"It looked empty to me."

"Were you able to see the traffic signal from where you were standing?"

"Yes, clearly. There is just the one road."

"Did you see the signal?"

"Yes."

"Why?"

"Do you really need a reason? I was walking down the road toward it, and I was planning to cross the road myself. I just looked up at it instinctively."

"Do you remember the license number of the taxi?"

"Which taxi?"

"The one that you say was in the accident."

"No, sorry."

"Did you notice the sign on the roof that said whether it was it a private taxi or from a taxi company?"

"I don't remember. It all happened so quickly."

"I see. What did you do after it happened?"

"I kept going—to Hiromi Ida's place."

"But why? You didn't think about stopping to help?"

"I didn't want to get involved. People began coming out to see what had happened. I figured there were plenty of people who would help."

"What do you mean 'get involved'? It didn't have anything to do with you."

"I didn't want anyone to know that I had been there."

"So you're saying that you ran away from it?"

"Well . . . yes."

"What time did you arrive at Hiromi Ida's apartment?"

"I took a sort of detour and got there just after twelve-thirty."

"That means you must have got home very late that night. Didn't your wife ask you where you'd been?"

"No, she's used to it."

"I see. But I imagine the reason you ran away from the accident was that you were terrified that someone would find out you were somewhere you had no business being at a very late hour."

"I'm not sure terrified is the right word. It just didn't seem advisable."

"Pardon me, then. I was just trying to be considerate of your social standing. Your wife, after all, is the president of Shin Nippon Enterprises, and the only daughter of its founder."

"Yes, but she is not involved in running the company. I am."

"If you say so. Did you tell Hiromi Ida about the accident?"

"No."

"Why was that?"

"I didn't want to worry her."

"It would have put you in a tight spot if she were to get involved in any way and your relationship became public. Is that what you didn't want her to worry about?"

"Exactly."

"I see. Now, you were standing in a spot where you could see the intersection. The victim ran that far. The traffic signal for the taxi . . ."

"Was green. There was no mistaking it."

"Are you saying that the signal for Yoko Sugano was red?"

"Yes, but she didn't even stop to check for cars."

"Why do you think that was? What did you think when you saw her?"

"It was late. I thought she was trying to get home in a hurry. She was a young woman. They're building an apartment building on the side of the street the taxi was on, and it was hard to see. Even I didn't see the taxi until it was too late. I imagined it had been the same for her. It happens all the time."

"What was the victim wearing?"

"I couldn't really see. Maybe a dark-colored suit. She had long hair and was rather pretty."

"You saw her face even though you were walking behind her?"

"I spoke to her beforehand."

"You *spoke* to her? What's this about?"

"When I got out of the taxi, I saw her on the road before it turns onto the street where the intersection was. I asked her the time. My watch is a little fast."

"Why did you ask her the time?"

"I figured I ought to know the time before I went to see Hiromi Ida. She might have been asleep."

"Do you always show up at her apartment without calling ahead first?"

"That's right."

"What did the victim do when you asked the time?"

"She looked surprised to have a strange man speak to her. But I asked nicely, and she answered."

"What time was it?"

"Five after twelve. That's what she said."

"And then she started running?"

"No she kept walking on a little ways. I don't think I looked suspicious, but it must have frightened her to have a man come up to her like that. She began to walk faster and faster, and then she started running."

"Didn't that seem unnatural to you?"

"No, I thought it was probably very natural for a young woman. I felt bad about it."

"And then the taxi hit her?"

"Yes, and I feel partly responsible for what happened."

"We'll be here all night if we start talking about responsibility. We're more interested in the fact that you left the scene."

"I understand that."

"By the way, nobody we talked to at the scene remembered seeing you leave."

"That's understandable. I didn't leave right away. I was there when it happened, but I was standing in the shadows."

"Pardon?"

"I thought it would attract attention if I left right away. I waited until some of the locals turned up, and then I joined them at the intersection. Then I left after a few minutes when everyone's attention was elsewhere."

"So, after going to all that trouble to make sure nobody noticed you, why did you decide to come forward?"

"As you know, I have friends on the police force. Very close friends."

"Yes, we know that."

"They told me about the incident, and it began to bother me. I heard there were no other witnesses and that the driver might be convicted for negligence. I was surprised to hear that because it wasn't what happened."

"So you're saying the taxi driver was telling the truth?"

"Yes. He had the green light. Miss Sugano ignored the red light and ran out in front of the taxi. I saw it clearly, and I deeply regret leaving the scene. If I had stayed and spoken up for him, the driver would not have been taken into custody."

The man lifted his face and looked directly into the eyes of the detectives. "I have a mistress, and my wife and I do not get along. I'm a man with my own problems, but I could never let an innocent man suffer. That's why I'm here."

"You've done the right thing."

———•———

After another sleepless night, the three members of the Asano household looked at each other over the breakfast table.

"I'm going to be at home today waiting for a call from Mr. Sayama," said Yoriko calmly as she made coffee. She sounded as if she was trying to stay in control for the sake of the younger two. "Just because a witness has come forward doesn't mean everything is over and done with."

"I think I'll stay home too," said Maki.

"Me too," added Mamoru.

"There's no reason why you two should—" Yoriko began to protest, but the two youngsters burst out in unison, "Nobody asked your opinion!"

Yoriko sent the two of them upstairs so she could clean, and gave Maki a basket of laundry to hang out on the rooftop. "Make sure it dries without wrinkles!"

Maki grumbled obligingly, but smiled as she opened the door on the second floor that led to the stairway up to the roof. "A beautiful fall day! Something good is bound to happen!"

Mamoru was just as anxious as Maki for things to go well, but for more complex reasons. What sort of person was the witness? Would the police be able to trust him? How would the testimony affect his uncle? Mamoru wanted it to solve the entire case. He wanted to avoid having Yoko Sugano's sordid past brought into the picture. Mamoru had not told his aunt or his cousin anything about what he had learned yesterday. His issue of *Information Channel* was hidden, crammed behind the other books on his bookshelf.

More than anything, he was concerned about Yukiko, Yoko's younger sister. He recalled her smile in the picture of her and Yoko in kimonos. What would happen to her if it became known that her sister had been involved in a scam that had made her lots of money, and that she had spent her last days on the run, terrified of some kind of threat?

Yukiko was about to start a new job and become a working member of society. Would she be able to survive the tidal wave that such a revelation would cause? The very idea depressed Mamoru. He would be glad if Yoko's hidden past could remain hidden—and he felt almost as strongly about that as he did about getting his uncle out of jail.

"Mamoru, have you got a sec?" Maki peeked into his room. "Were there any calls while I was away?"

"Nope, nothing."

Maki looked down in disappointment.

"You mean from your boyfriend?"

Maki nodded. Mamoru decided to offer a ray of hope. "I was out all day yesterday, too. He might have called when there was nobody here. I'm sure he's worried about you. Why don't you call him at the office?"

"That's a good idea." Her smile was back. "I'll call a little later."

Downstairs, the phone rang. Maki and Mamoru looked at each other and ran down the stairs. Yoriko was heading for the phone with a dust rag in one hand, but Mamoru got there first.

"Hello! This is the Asanos!"

"Kusaka, is that you?" It was Mr. Nozaki from Mamoru's school. Mamoru stuck out his tongue in disappointment and motioned to Yoriko and Maki that this was not the call they'd been waiting for.

"Yes, I forgot to call. Today, we're . . ."

"Get to school immediately!"

"What?"

"Get down here as fast as you can. Come see me in the staff room. I'll talk to you when you get here." The line went dead.

"Was that your school?"

"Yeah." Mamoru looked at the receiver a few seconds longer and finally replaced it. Mr. Incompetent was upset about something. "Mr. Nozaki told me to go see him right away."

"Did you forget to call?" Yoriko gave him a playful rap on the head. "I guess you better go then. I'll call the school if we hear anything."

Mamoru shrugged. Maki smiled as she picked up the phone to call in to work.

Unfortunately, there was nothing to laugh about. Nozaki was waiting for Mamoru and laid into him right away.

"There was a robbery on Saturday night."

Mamoru knew instantly what was coming. "What was stolen?"

"The monthly dues for the basketball club and the money for their New Year's camp was taken from the clubroom."

"How much was it?"

"About 500,000 yen. There was enough for twenty-two boys to spend a week at camp."

Mamoru closed his eyes. *Why was this happening?* "Why would they leave so much money there?"

Most boys' sports teams in Japanese schools have girls with the title of "manager," but who are more like volunteer maids. Five years ago, the head of the PE department and coach for the basketball team, Iwamoto, had decreed that this school would discontinue such a tradition. "You're not pros, so why should you have someone to do your laundry for you? Doing it yourself is part of being on the team. If you don't like it, then get out!"

The boys therefore had to clean up after themselves and collect their own dues. Sasaki, a freshman on the basketball team, had been given this job. And Sasaki was one of Miura's pals.

Nozaki continued, "Sasaki put the money in a locker and locked it. The clubroom was locked, too. When the team showed up to practice on Sunday morning, both of the locks had been cut with bolt cutters. Kusaka, the robbery took place sometime between six-thirty Saturday night after practice was over and seven-thirty Sunday morning. Where were you during that time?"

"At home."

"Was there someone with you?"

"There was nobody home. A friend was with me until nine Saturday night, but after that I was alone." Mamoru was becoming more and more irritated with the whole situation. "Am I a suspect?"

"Saturday afternoon in the classroom," Nozaki went on, ignoring Mamoru's question, "Miura, Sasaki, and Tsunamoto were discussing the accommodations for their New Year's camp, and they say you were there. They say they talked about how much money there was, too. They were trying to decide whether to leave it in the clubroom."

"They told you I heard them, and that makes me the thief?" Leave it to Miura and his no-good friends.

"They said no one else knew about the money."

"I don't know about any money. I didn't hear anything. You'll believe Miura and Sasaki, but not me?" Mamoru knew they had set him up. Miura had heard him tell Anego that no one would be at home that night. That was why she and her brother had come to visit. They knew he wouldn't have an alibi for Saturday night. "What about other members of the basketball team? They must have all known about the money."

"No, it wasn't any of them."

"How do you know that?"

Nozaki was silent. Mamoru could see the veins in his temples popping out.

"How can you blame me for it? Why?" Mamoru kept repeating the same question, but he knew the answer just looking at his teacher's face. *A thief begets a thief. The apple never falls far from the tree.*

Of course, Nozaki knew about Mamoru's father. All the teachers and all the students knew. Once Miura had found out his secret, word must have spread quickly. If rumors were infectious diseases, the school would have closed long ago. Mamoru felt a dull sword of despair cutting through his heart. Nothing had changed.

"Does Mr. Iwamoto think I did it, too?"

"He's suspending practice until this gets sorted out. He has cancelled the camp, whether they get the money back or not, and he's punishing the whole team for mishandling the money. He's heard what Miura has to say, but he's looking into it himself."

Mamoru felt a trace of relief. The students called him "Demon Iwamoto" because he was strict and stubborn, but he wasn't one to leave a matter half done. Mamoru was sure he would turn the entire school upside down looking for the stolen money.

Mamoru looked at Nozaki's pale face and asked, "What do you think? Do you think I did it?"

Nozaki refused to speak for a few seconds. He couldn't even bring himself to look Mamoru in the face. Finally he mumbled, "I—I just want you to tell me the truth."

"Then it's simple. I didn't do it. That's all."

"That's all?" Nozaki sputtered. "Are you sure that's all?"

Mamoru thought of his uncle in jail. He finally understood how he must be feeling right now. *Won't someone believe me? I'm telling the truth!* Now he was angry, and knew he couldn't stay there another second. *You're afraid of me!* He wanted to scream at the man standing before him, with his pursed lips and eyes that refused to meet his. Just the thought of one of his students having done something improper was enough to send this teacher into a hysterical tizzy.

"I won't be coming to school for a while," Mamoru spoke as he headed for the door. "I'm sure that will make it easier to investigate."

"Are you suspending yourself?"

"No, I'm just staying home." Mamoru couldn't hold it back anymore.

"Don't worry. I won't be suing you for infringing on my human rights. I won't be reporting you to the Department of Education."

"What the hell do you mean by that?" Nozaki's pale face had taken on a tinge of green.

"Just tell me one thing," Mamoru asked. "What kind of lock did the clubroom locker have?"

"A padlock. Mr. Iwamoto has the key to it."

Even if I was some kind of pathological sleepwalker, I would never cut a padlock with bolt cutters. Only an amateur would do something like that, Mamoru thought to himself.

Mamoru's feet were heavy as he left school. He felt like he was falling feet first down the stairs. He didn't want to go home—his Aunt Yoriko was an expert at reading the minds of young people. Mamoru always had to wonder where she had honed such a talent. If he went home looking as glum as he felt, it would just add to her problems.

He came to a pay phone in the hall, and dropped in a coin. Maybe Mr. Sayama had called and his aunt was trying to get hold of him.

"We haven't heard anything new," was the only news he got. Yoriko had picked up the phone on the first ring, and the pitch of her voice had fallen as soon as she heard Mamoru's voice. Mr. Sayama had let them know that the police were still investigating the matter and that it would take a couple of more days.

As he hung up, Mamoru heard someone calling him.

"Kusaka!" It was Yoichi Miyashita catching up with him, out of breath. "Finally! Anego and I have been looking all over for you."

"Thanks," Mamoru turned around and breathed in sharply. "What happened to you?"

Yoichi was covered in bandages, one all the way down his right arm, another around his left foot. He couldn't even get his shoe on, so he was dragging it along hooked on his toes. His lips were cut and scabbed, and his right eyelid was swollen.

"I fell off my bike," he said quickly. "Can you believe it?"

"All that from a fall? Did you break your arm?"

"No, it's just some cuts."

"How did it happen?"

"It's no big deal. The doctor overdid it with these bandages." Yoichi was trying hard to smile, but that made him look all the worse.

"How are you going to get your picture finished for that exhibition?"

"I'll be fine in no time. Forget about me. What are *you* going to do?"

"What should I do?" Mamoru tried to laugh, too. "I don't know."

"They're lying, all of them!" Yoichi was furious. "They've got no proof. Miura set you up."

"Yeah, that's the way it looks."

"How can Mr. Nozaki believe them and not you?"

"I'm the one with a criminal for a father," Mamoru muttered. Yoichi's sympathetic face made Mamoru let down his guard. "Don't you think so, too? It's Mendel's law of heredity."

Yoichi blinked back tears as he looked at Mamoru, but pulled himself together and said, "My Dad used to draw a funny picture when I was small. It was more like graffiti than art, something he called *tsurusan*. I used to copy him, and he finally told me to draw something else, too. Trains or flowers or something. Then he sent me to a drawing class with one of my neighbors. My Dad was really bad at drawing; he could never do anything besides that stupid *tsurusan*." Yoichi finally grinned. "When I become a real artist, I'm going to use that *tsurusan* as my signature. The only thing is, every time I do it, it looks like my Dad's face!"

●

Taizo didn't come home the next day, or the next. The three other members of the Asano household waited as patiently as they could, aware that the doubts and irritation they felt were reflected in their faces.

Mamoru got up each morning, put on his school uniform and set off as usual, but headed to Laurel instead of school. He had gone to see Takano and explained the situation to him, and Takano had promised to let him spend his days at work for the time being.

"Do you plan to quit school and work?" he had asked.

"No," Mamoru had replied. "Not unless I get expelled, that is."

"Don't worry. They'll get the culprit."

Takano had also rejoiced with Mamoru about finding a witness to his uncle's accident. "Everything will work out fine," he had assured him. "It may take a while, but don't give up."

The other employees in Books had been surprised to see Mamoru there on a weekday.

"Shouldn't you be in school?" Madame Anzai registered her obvious disapproval.

"Uh . . ."

"I hear your school closed because of an outbreak of something bad. Isn't that right?" Sato came over and clapped Mamoru on the shoulder.

"It's too early in the flu season for that." Madame was not convinced.

"Mumps, isn't it, Mamoru?" Sato refused to give up.

"Mumps?"

"That's right, Miss Anzai. Did you have it as a child?"

"No, I don't think so."

"Then you'd better watch out. It's going around. And you better tell your boyfriend, too. You know what happens when men get mumps!"

"Is that true?" Now she looked worried.

"Sure is—he'll be firing blanks. You don't want that to happen!" Sato pulled Mamoru off to the side, out of Madame's sight.

"Thanks," said Mamoru.

"Forget it, I'm glad to have you around. I know something's going on with you, but you don't have to worry about it. Missing school won't kill you."

There was a lot of work to do. It was almost December, and the new calendars and schedule books were arriving and had to be sorted out and displayed. As long as he was busy, Mamoru was able to forget both his uncle and the half million yen.

Thursday afternoon, while he was taking a break in the storage room, Makino, the security officer, paid him a visit.

"Young man! Are you skipping classes to pursue honest labor?"

Sato climbed on top of a pile of cardboard boxes and began singing some old labor union anthem, swinging his arms to the rhythm.

"That'll do," Makino intoned. "Have a seat."

"Thank you, sir!" Sato was having fun.

"Is it true that you're twenty-six? I pity your poor parents."

Mamoru laughed out loud. "And how are you, Mr. Makino?"

"Full of energy, and operating at one-hundred-twenty percent. I can't deal with the free time."

"Free time? With a store full of customers?"

Makino himself looked mystified. "Go ahead and ask the other officers in the store."

"The economy is in good shape, I guess," said Sato nonchalantly.

"Don't be a fool. Shoplifting increases as the economy grows. It's robberies that go up during rough times. And besides, the economy has been like this for years now."

"A better class of customer?" guessed Mamoru.

"I don't think so. I haven't heard about any new courses on morals and manners."

Just then, Takano stuck his head in and called for Makino, who rushed out. Just as Sato and Mamoru exchanged a glance, Makino ran back in.

"Call the police! Someone's threatening to jump off the roof! Call the fire department, too! But tell them not to run their sirens or I'll shoot them!" Then he disappeared again.

Sato grabbed the phone and Mamoru followed Makino. He ran down the hallway and saw Takano and Makino climbing the stairs two at a time. The music being played on the speakers changed from classical to pops. This was how employees were notified of an emergency.

When they got up to the roof, the miniature garden and amusement park area was full of onlookers. Mamoru grabbed the arm of another employee.

"Where?"

"Over by the water tank. I think it's a girl."

Mamoru spun around and ran down to the floor below and headed for the opposite side of the roof. He had memorized the floor plan of the store so he could give directions when needed, and made for a hall-way guarded with a No Entry sign. Turning at the first corner, there was a fireproof steel door. Mamoru pulled it open and rushed up a nar-row flight of stairs that generally provided repairmen and cleaners with access to the roof.

At the top of the stairs was a door with a wired-glass window that let the sunlight through. It was kept shut with a simple padlock. For all the shine and glamour of the store's interior, the building was quite old. Secu-rity alarms and electronic locks had been added in recent years, but doors like this that could only be reached from outside by climbing up the outer wall and then down from the roof still had their original hardware.

Feeling like the cat who'd got the cream, Mamoru began searching his pockets. He must have something he could use. Then he remembered his name tag: on the back was a safety pin about three centimeters long. If the cylinder of a pin tumbler lock was a labyrinth, a padlock was like the road on a stretch of farmland that had just been cleared for develop-ment. Mamoru dropped to his knees, and within a minute he heard the satisfying click of the lock opening. He carefully opened the door and looked out onto the roof. The sun was so bright it made him blink. But he was right on target.

The concrete wall partially surrounding the water tank was in front of him, and the tank itself was just beyond.

The girl in question sat on top of the tank with her back to Mamoru. She was wearing a red sweater. Mamoru could only see a part of the red sweater and the back of her head. As he watched, she inched toward the fence at the edge of the roof. He wondered how she'd managed to climb on top of the tank. It was over two meters high. There were footholds, but it would still have been hard work for a young girl.

The girl was now at the edge of the tank, up against the fence. All she had to do was lean over and she'd plunge down six stories. She had her back to Mamoru and showed no sign of having noticed him. Her eyes appeared to be locked on the crowd of onlookers who were trying to persuade her to come down off the tank.

Mamoru moved around until he could see through the legs of the tank. The crowd was five or six meters away, and to his right. In front was a female security guard. Next to her was a middle-aged woman with both arms outstretched—probably the girl's mother. Takano stood almost directly across from Mamoru, and Makino stood behind him. Mamoru could hear the buzz of the crowd.

Mamoru thought for a few moments, and decided he had to climb the tank and try to overpower the girl and pull her down.

"Nobody is going to hurt you. What you're doing is very dangerous; why don't you just come on down now?" It was the gentle voice of a female guard.

The girl howled, "Don't come any closer!"

Mamoru poked his head out and tried to get Takano's attention. When Takano finally saw him, his eyes opened wide and his jaw dropped open. Mamoru motioned him to silence. Takano nodded almost imperceptibly, glancing at the girl out of the corner of his eye.

He gestured as if to ask Mamoru what he was going to do. Just then the girl shrieked again. "Don't come near me! I'll jump!"

Mamoru motioned that he would climb up and move around behind the girl. He also indicated that he wanted Takano to talk to her and try to keep her occupied. Takano blinked rapidly to indicate he understood.

He looked as if he wanted to leap to Mamoru's aid, but was doing his best to stay put. Mamoru went back behind the tank so the girl wouldn't see him. He would climb the wall and move toward her from behind. He jumped and managed to touch the top of the wall, but couldn't get hold of it.

"Young lady," Takano called out. "There's no need to worry. We'll let you stay up there if you like. Why don't we chat a bit? My name is Takano and I work here. Hajime Takano. I write my name with the character for 'one.' What's your name? Won't you tell me?"

"Her name is Misuzu!" the girl's mother cried out in anguish. "Come down! Misuzu, please come down!" she pleaded with her daughter.

Mamoru jumped again. This time he grabbed hold of the wall, and got a purchase on a foothold. Now he just needed to pull himself up. He heard Takano continue in a soothing tone of voice, "You came shopping with your mother today, didn't you? What did you buy?"

Mamoru pulled himself up and suddenly had a view of both the girl's back and the store employees on the other side. Takano had moved to the front.

"Keep away!" the girl screamed out to Takano. Mamoru moved forward slowly, trying to stay as low as he could. He could see the red sweater buffeted by the wind. He was careful not to look toward the fence at the edge of the roof, but he felt queasy just the same.

Takano continued to talk. "Did you come to the Book section? That's where I work. Do you like books?"

Mamoru was almost at the tank, just two meters from the girl.

"I hate them," the girl whispered.

"You hate them?" repeated Takano. "Why's that?"

Mamoru was ready to pounce.

"I'm scared," she said in a small voice that began to sound more like a moan. "I hate them. I'm scared . . . scared . . . I'm so scared."

By now some of the other onlookers had noticed Mamoru. A look of surprise passed over the female security officer's face. The girl noticed this and turned around. Seeing Mamoru, she screamed so loudly and shrilly that he almost shrank back. Instead, he leaped blindly toward the red sweater, grabbing the girl and pulling her away from the fence. He fell over backward and had to use his feet to keep himself from falling off the tank.

The girl continued to scream. As the onlookers rushed toward the tank, Takano climbed up and threw his arms around the girl and Mamoru, keeping them from the edge.

"It's okay, it's okay. You're all right. Just calm down, calm down," Takano chanted the words over and over like a magical charm as he held onto her, and finally it began to work. The girl stopped struggling and dissolved into tears. They needed a ladder to get her off the tank, and it was left to the firemen to bring her down and load her onto a stretcher.

"That was close!" Mamoru and Takano sat on the top of the water tank a little longer mopping the sweat off their foreheads.

Takano heaved a sigh, shaking his head. "One false move and you would have gone over the side with her."

"But it didn't happen, did it?"

"Hey, young man! You've been watching too many police shows!" Makino bellowed up at Mamoru from where he stood below the tank with his hands on his hips. Mamoru gave a quick nod of mock remorse. "I'll have to talk to the manager about getting a higher fence around this tank."

"How did she get up here?"

"Just like you did," Takano replied. "Apparently, she was looking at musical instruments and went into some kind of trance. She was like an animal fleeing a mountain fire; she just kept going higher and higher, and ended up here."

"What happened to her?"

"They said she looked like she was being chased." Takano shrugged and then looked back at Mamoru. "How did *you* get out here?"

"I came up the service stairs."

"Isn't that door locked?"

"Not today it wasn't." Mamoru finally stopped shaking enough to climb down. A fireman looked up at him and frowned.

"Sorry for the fuss," Takano spoke first, bowing.

"We can't have people doing things like this!"

Mamoru had to answer questions from both the police and the fire department. Not to mention the work he still had left to do. He ended up working an hour of overtime before he headed home, exhausted.

He rode his bike along the riverbank almost all the way home, and as he descended onto the road, someone called his name. Looking back, he saw Maki running to catch up with him, her open jacket flapping behind her.

They arrived home together, pulled the old-style sliding door open, and called out in unison, "I'm home!"

"Welcome back!" It was a familiar voice, but one that they hadn't heard in a while. As they looked at each other in surprise, Taizo opened the living room door.

"I'm home, too!" he said with a smile.

———————•———————

That night Yoriko prepared so much food that they couldn't fit it all on the table.

"Dad said he dreamed of drinking beer!" Maki scowled. "Imagine— wanting beer more than your own daughter!"

Taizo looked thinner and tired. But his smile after a large glass of beer was just the same as it had always been.

"I don't care what he dreamed about as long as he's home," said Yoriko as she picked up the bottle to pour him some more.

Taizo sat up straight in a formal position. "I don't know how to apologize to all of you for what happened. All the worry I caused you. You even got hurt, Yoriko. Well anyway, I'm thankful for you all." Having said this, Taizo bowed down low on the tatami mats.

"Aw, come off it Dad, you're embarrassing us!" Maki protested. "Come on, let's eat!"

After they had eaten, Maki and Mamoru got the full story about what had led to Taizo's release.

"What sort of person was the witness? Was that what convinced the police you were innocent?"

"Maki, have you ever heard of Shin Nippon Enterprises?" asked Taizo.

"Of course! Our salesmen are always out trying to get their account." Maki worked for an air cargo company. "Shin Nippon used to deal exclusively in expensive imported furniture and antiques, but about five years ago they expanded into condominiums and resort hotels. All their buildings are built with the best materials and furnished with the finest interiors. They've had a lot of success with them, and the company is doing well. They were behind that retro fad a few years ago."

"What about Shin Nippon?" asked Mamoru.

"The witness was the vice-president, Koichi Yoshitake."

"I've heard of him," Maki said excitedly. "He had a magazine column called 'Fly on the Wall.' A collection of them were published as a book."

"Hey! I've seen that," broke in Mamoru. "It's a big book full of pictures."

"That's right. Photos and comments on the workplaces of journalists, authors, architects, and other famous people."

"It sold pretty well."

"So he's famous," murmured Yoriko. "That's why it took so long for him to come forward."

"Why's that?" asked Mamoru.

Yoriko looked over at Taizo, who coughed and said, "Mr. Yoshitake was on his way to see his mistress when he saw the accident."

Maki and Mamoru were speechless.

Yoriko took over the explanation. "The police were suspicious because he didn't turn up until several days later. They had to check out his story carefully. He had spoken to Miss Sugano right before the accident, when he asked her for the time . . . He says she was probably trying to get home as fast as she could."

"It makes sense," said Maki nodding in agreement. "That's the way I feel when I'm on my way home. Why do they always have to doubt everyone? I'd never marry a policeman."

"Not that any would have you!" countered Yoriko.

"Anyway, someone like Mr. Yoshitake wouldn't have any reason to go out of his way and lie about what he saw. It's thanks to him that I'm back home," said Taizo with feeling. "He married into his wife's family. His wife is the company president. One of the detectives told me she might seek a divorce after this."

"It must have been hard," Yoriko added. "He went to the police in spite of all that. He must have needed to think about it first."

"Wait a minute!" Now Maki was indignant. "Dad would never have been arrested if that man had stayed at the scene. Don't forget that we had to go through all of this because he ran away!"

"Maki, you're a hard one to please!" said Taizo with a wry grin. "It must have been rough for you. And you, too, Mamoru. I heard about school."

"It was no big deal," Mamoru responded. Maki was silent. "So what's going to happen now?" Mamoru continued, changing the subject.

"Your uncle is still charged with negligence," picked up Yoriko. "Mr. Sayama is doing his best to see that all he gets is a fine. He says that he's close to an out-of-court settlement."

Mamoru knew that his uncle still might lose his driver's license, and that would lead to more problems. But for now, they were all relieved just to have him back home. He was also glad that he wouldn't have to bring up Yoko Sugano's secret. Mamoru decided to focus on the positive. It looked like they were going to be able to take care of the whole incident with the minimal amount of damage.

"Some things you just can't take back . . . ," muttered Maki. It was as if she could read Mamoru's mind and was arguing back.

At nine that evening Mamoru called Nobuhiko Hashimoto to let him know that he wouldn't have to testify, and got his answering machine. Mamoru quickly summed up the situation, thanked Hashimoto for his cooperation, and hung up. He was just as glad not to speak to him directly.

Later he got a call from Anego. She let him know she had taken notes for him in class, and updated him on what was happening with Mr. Incompetent, Mr. Iwamoto, and Miura. She was delighted to hear that Mamoru's Uncle Taizo was home and things were looking up.

Mamoru went out running at ten o'clock on the dot. He decided to skip his usual route, and went back to the intersection where the accident had taken place. The same stars were in the sky as on the night he had broken into Yoko Sugano's apartment, and the half moon looked close enough to cut your hand on. The intersection was quiet. There were no other people around; the only movement was from the traffic signal as it changed colors.

Forgive me for poking around. I won't tell anyone what I found out. Rest in peace. Mamoru's heart was light as he ran back home. As he neared his house, he saw a white figure sitting on the riverbank. It was his Uncle Taizo.

"Can't sleep?" Mamoru sat down next to him. The cold concrete felt good after his run. Over his pajamas Taizo was wearing a sweater Maki had knitted for his birthday. He flicked his cigarette butt into the water. It made a brief red arc and then disappeared.

"You'll catch cold in that outfit," Taizo gently scolded his nephew.

"I'm fine."

Taizo asked Mamoru to wait a minute, and went over to a nearby vending machine. He came back with two cans of coffee and handed one to him.

"Be careful, it's hot."

The two drank the coffee in silence.

"I'm sorry for all the trouble," murmured Taizo.

"I'm just sorry there was nothing I could do for you," replied Mamoru.

They were silent again. Taizo finished his drink, and put the can at his feet. "I hear you've been skipping school."

Mamoru spat out a mouthful of coffee in surprise and began choking. Taizo clapped him on the back.

"How did you know?" Mamoru finally got out.

"After I got home and your aunt went out shopping, there was a call from your school. It was about three."

Mamoru broke out in a cold sweat. "I'm glad *you* took it! Who was it from?"

"A Mr. Iwamoto. He asked me to make sure you went tomorrow. He wants to see you as soon as you get there."

Mamoru was perplexed. Did it mean they had found the culprit, or was he going to be punished?

"Uncle Taizo, I want you to know I'm not skipping school because of your accident." Taizo just looked at the river. "It's the truth. It's completely unrelated." He went on to explain the entire situation.

Taizo listened quietly. "So, what's going to happen?" he asked when Mamoru was through.

"I don't know. I think I can trust Mr. Iwamoto to do things right. I'll go to school tomorrow and find out what he has to say."

The two sank into silence once more, gazing at the huge sign for the bus company on the other side of the river. They watched as a large bus pulled into the garage. Mamoru wondered what sort of tour bus was on the road at this time of night.

"Things have been rough on you, Mamoru." Taizo said after a while. "Kids have experiences that are tough too, don't they?"

Mamoru looked at his uncle and finally figured out what was on his mind. "Maki's growing up," he offered.

"That's right," Taizo chuckled to himself.

Mamoru remembered how nervous Maki had looked when asking if there had been any calls for her. And the way she had said, *Some things you just can't take back.*

"I won't be able to drive anymore," Taizo mumbled as if to himself.

"They might suspend your license, but it won't be for long."

"That's not what I mean." Taizo lit another cigarette with a faraway look in his eyes. "I drove for all those years without a single accident. I was proud of my record."

"Not many people can say that."

"I was responsible for someone's death. A young woman who had her whole life ahead of her."

Well, maybe not, thought Mamoru to himself.

"I was lucky until now, but I didn't realize it. I became proud, and now I'm being punished for it. That's what it feels like. I was feeling good that night." Taizo told Mamoru how he had felt a cold coming on, and had decided to stop work early. Just as he had put up his Out of Service sign, he was flagged down. It was a woman in her forties headed for the Narita airport, a long, expensive taxi ride from Tokyo. Her husband, who was stationed overseas by his company, had fallen ill, and she was on her way to be with him. She had called for a taxi, but had been told there'd be a long wait, so she'd gone outside to look for one.

"That was lucky for you."

"It was that new housing development out in Mitomo. You'll never find taxis in that area! The woman said it was a miracle that I'd come along just then."

Taizo had removed the Out of Service sign and taken the woman to Narita. At the taxi stand at the airport, he'd picked up a young man.

His wife had just had their first baby, and he had flown home from an overseas business trip. Taizo had dropped the man off a few blocks away from the intersection where the accident occurred.

"I felt good. I was pleased with the work I did and what it meant to people. And then I hit that girl. She looked as if she was being chased, the way she dashed out in front of me." Taizo spoke evenly. "I tried to swerve away from her, but I couldn't. The bumper hit her, and she flew up in the air and bounced off the hood of the car, hitting the windshield." Taizo rubbed his face with his hands, and sighed before continuing. "It made a sound . . . a sound I'd never heard before. I never want to hear it again. But I hear it in my dreams. Sometimes I hear it inside my head—like while the police were interrogating me, and when I was locked up in a cell by myself."

Mamoru tried to imagine what it had sounded like. What about the girl in the red sweater? What if she had fallen?

"I jumped out of the car, and she was lying on the ground on her back. She was still breathing. I remember telling her to stay with me. But I don't think she heard. That astonished look was still on her face, and she kept repeating something in a small voice. *It's awful, awful!* My head was pounding and I didn't know what was happening. There wasn't anybody around until a police officer came running."

It's awful, awful! How could *he?* Mamoru could almost hear her gasping out the words.

"I was agitated, and the police officer was probably worked up, too. I don't remember what happened. I think I yelled at him to call an ambulance and said something about her being chased. I probably yelled at him to find out who it was."

"When did you find out she had died?"

"At the police station. I was sure they'd never let me go home again."

Neither of them spoke for a while. They listened to the sound of the water. The tide was going out.

"I can't drive anymore," Taizo repeated. "As long as I live, I'll never sit behind a steering wheel again." He sat with his head in his hands, looking out over the river.

Mamoru caught sight of a raft gently bobbing up and down, and watched it for a while. He thought about the water receding after a flood.

"There's no way Miyashita did it!"

In a corner of a room off the gym, Iwamoto sat on one chair with his feet braced against another.

Mamoru took a step forward. "After all this time, this is all you've come up with?"

Iwamoto was not one to take such disrespect from a student, but the gravity of the matter must have somehow led him to overlook Mamoru's outburst. "That's what I thought when he showed up to confess to me."

"When was that?"

"Yesterday during the noon break. I asked him about it, but he couldn't give me any straightforward answers. I sent him home to calm down." Iwamoto frowned and went on. "He went home and hung himself in his room."

Mamoru went white as a sheet, and Iwamoto hurriedly continued. "He tried to kill himself, but the rope came undone and he fell on the floor. His parents were home, and they took care of him. He's fine. Wipe that look off your face! If anybody came in here, they'd think I was trying to kill you!"

"So . . ." Mamoru swallowed a few times and finally got a few words out. "Where is he now?"

"He's at home today. He's asking to see you. He refuses to tell me why he made such a ridiculous confession. He wants to talk to you."

"I'll go see him right away."

"No, you go to your classes and visit him after school. That'll be soon enough. I told him you'd be there this evening. I can't have you missing any more school." Iwamoto gave Mamoru a rap on the head, and Mamoru's vision swam for a few moments. "That one is my 'seal of approval' for the four days you've missed so far. If it hurt, think a little harder next time. You're much too stubborn for your own good."

"Just like you!"

"Touché." Iwamoto kept an exasperated expression on his face, but his eyes were laughing.

"So, what happened to the stolen money? Does this mean I'm going to be accused of taking it?"

Iwamoto stared at him. "Don't be an idiot. I never believed that was possible."

"But—"

"Miura and his cohorts planned the whole thing. Give me credit for understanding that. But I don't have any proof. I've been wandering around town every night since it happened, and I finally caught Miura and Sasaki coming out of an adult movie theater. And they were drunk." Iwamoto was obviously disgusted. "I got the police to lend a hand, but it took a long time to just get this far."

"Even if they were out spending money, it doesn't mean they stole it."

"That's right. All you kids have jobs these days. I think there are still rules against that." Iwamoto glared at Mamoru again, and Mamoru hung his head. "But they broke the rules of the school and of the basket-ball club. I got all the club members together and raked them over the coals. When you have freshmen breaking the rules like that it leads to things like lost money. The older boys should have been paying atten-tion. The basketball club is on toilet-cleaning duty until winter vacation. They can work to make back the money they lost."

Iwamoto pulled a handkerchief out of his pocket, and blew his nose explosively. "And that is how I'm handling the theft. It's my fault for not having supervised them more closely to begin with. And you had to take the brunt of it, Kusaka. I apologize." Iwamoto stood up and bowed formally to Mamoru. "The punishment might seem lenient, but I'm going to keep Miura and the others on the basketball team. I don't care if they beg to be let go. It's thugs like that who need the training. Do you understand what I'm saying?"

Mamoru nodded.

"Now get to class. But before you go, I want you to see Mr. Nozaki and apologize for your absences. He's serious about his job."

"Okay." Mamoru turned to leave.

Iwamoto suddenly spoke as if remembering something. "Kusaka, I don't believe we inherit our characters."

Mamoru stopped in his tracks.

"If frogs only produced frogs, we'd have nothing but frogs everywhere making a racket. I'm not too bright myself, but the reason I manage to stick with this job is that it's so interesting to watch the polliwogs turn into dogs and horses and other types of animals."

Mamoru felt some of the tension leave his face, and he laughed. It felt good to feel it rumble through his body on its way out.

"But there are lots of idiots out there with bad eyes. They see the tail of an elephant and start screaming that it's a snake. They grab the horns of a cow and are sure they've got a rhinoceros. They can't see past the tips of their own noses. They'll drive you nuts every time. You've got to do your best to avoid them. They're not going to go out of their way to make things easier for you."

Yoichi Miyashita lived in a three-story building. His parents were both notary publics and used the first floor as their office. Yoichi had painted the sign announcing "All Registration Procedures. Real Estate Appraisals" over a landscape of the local scenery.

Yoichi took after his mother, who was short and fine-featured. Mrs. Miyashita led Mamoru up to her son's room on the third floor. One of Yoichi's works was in a frame on the wall next to the door.

Mamoru knocked and a small voice answered, "Who is it?"

"A friend of *tsurusan*."

The door opened and Yoichi's face poked out.

"I'm hopeless. I can't even tie a knot." Yoichi couldn't bring himself to look Mamoru in the eye.

Mamoru looked up at the ceiling at the grating from which Yoichi had tried to hang himself: it was strong enough to hold his weight. He was glad about the clumsy knot. Still bandaged up from his previous injuries, Yoichi looked smaller than ever.

"Why'd you do it?"

Yoichi was silent.

"I heard about it from Mr. Iwamoto. Were you afraid I'd get into trouble for it and be expelled? Were you trying to help me out by lying about stealing the money?" It was awfully quiet. Mamoru got the feeling that Yoichi's parents were trying to avoid making any noise while their son recuperated. "Well, you were wrong. What if you really had died? Did you ever think about how we would have felt about it? Think of the responsibility that would have left me with!"

Finally, in a voice no louder than that of a mosquito, Yoichi answered. "I did it."

"Of course you didn't."

But Yoichi continued. "I did it. I did it all. If you knew what I'd done, you'd never talk to me again."

"What do you mean?" Now he had Mamoru worried. "What exactly did you do?"

Tears had begun to fall on Yoichi's cheeks. "I did it all," he repeated. "I put that article about your uncle on the bulletin board, I wrote that stuff on the blackboard, and I wrote 'Murderer' in blood on the wall of your house. I did it all."

Mamoru was speechless. He stared at Yoichi's head as he turned away, trying to hide his tears, and then at his bandaged hand. "Did you cut your hand when you broke our window?"

Yoichi nodded.

Suddenly it was all clear. "Miura and the others threatened you into doing it," said Mamoru in a low voice.

Yoichi nodded again.

"They used you so that they wouldn't be caught." Mamoru remembered the time Yoichi had showed up at Laurel. He had started to say something, but then stopped. This must have been what it was about. "You didn't get injured falling off your bike, did you? One of them found out you showed up where I work and tried to tell me what they were doing. They beat you up."

Yoichi wiped his face with his left hand.

"They must have threatened to hurt you so badly that you'd never be able to paint again." Mamoru could feel the blood rushing in his ears.

"I can't do anything," Yoichi was saying. "I'm no good at sports, I'm not a great student, and the girls won't give me the time of day. But I can draw and paint. It's the only thing I can do better than other people. If I lost that, I wouldn't have anything. Those bastards scared me. It would have been different if they had threatened to kill me, but they threatened to cut off my hands and put my eyes out. Then I might as well be dead. It would have been like pulling out all my insides and leaving just the shell of me behind. I couldn't go against them."

Yoichi finally looked at Mamoru. "But I felt like dirt, Kusaka. You tried to understand me. You were the only person who ever took me seriously. I wanted to make up for it somehow."

"Make up for it?"

"If I came out and took responsibility for the theft, that would get you off the hook. But I couldn't even pull that off. I thought about it all night before I went in, but I couldn't manage to convince Mr. Iwamoto. He told me to stick to my painting and not worry about you. I went home feeling worse than ever. Life just wasn't worth living. But I couldn't even hang myself!"

Mamoru took a deep breath. "Thank heaven for that!"

Mamoru left the Miyashita home and headed back to school. It was six thirty when he arrived. He climbed over the closed gate and slipped through the night entrance. The sun had set long ago, and the grounds were empty. Mamoru went up to the second floor, took out a penlight, and started looking for Miura's locker. It was at the end of the fifth row on the right, equipped with a brand new bright-red combination padlock.

It was the work of a few seconds to pop it open. Mamoru opened up Miura's locker, and set about putting the entire crumpled contents into perfect order. There were dirty towels, books, papers, notebooks with bent covers, smelly T-shirts, and a half-finished box of cigarettes. Mamoru tore a page out of one of the notebooks and wrote on it, "Kunihiko Miura believes in heredity."

Mamoru placed it on top of the entire pile, closed the door, and replaced the lock.

As soon as he had left the school grounds, he found a pay phone and called Miura's house.

"Hello?" Miura sounded unnaturally pleasant; he must have been waiting for a call from his girlfriend.

"Is this Miura?"

"Yeah, but . . . wait a minute! Is that you, Kusaka?"

Mamoru could feel his blood pressure rising, and his temples throbbed. He tried to speak as clearly and deliberately as possible. "I'm only going to say this once, Miura. I know about everything you've done. And why you did it. It's because I'm new in town, I'm from the boondocks, and I'm a parasite orphan with a father who was a thief. Isn't that right? And that's the type you like to pick on. But I pity you, and you know why? You've opened up a door you should've left shut."

There was a moment of silence before Miura began to yell, but Mamoru was prepared for this, and shouted right over him. "Are you listening? This is your only chance. I won't be there to have another chat the next time you feel like one! All right? I'm an ungrateful sponge with a thief for a father. But there's more you don't know. My father swindled money, that's for sure, but he was also a murderer. He killed my mother. Nobody ever found out about that." Mamoru wasn't lying—he held his father responsible for his mother's early death. "That graffiti you put on my house? It's true! I'm the son of a murderer!"

Miura was silent again.

"You were right, Miura! I'm the son of a murderer. And you believe things like that are inherited, don't you? A thief begets a thief. That's the way it is. That's the way things are. So you'd better be careful. I've got the blood of a killer flowing through my veins."

"Now . . . now, just wait . . . wait a minute," Miura sputtered.

"Shut up! Think back now. Remember that girl you liked? Her bike? She said she found her key and that's why she went home without you? Well, you were right. I was behind all that. I took the lock off her bike, it wasn't the key. I was born doing things like that. I can do it because I'm the son of a killer. A bike lock is no big deal. And there are lots more things I can break than bike locks."

The more he spoke, the more his anger flowed. Finally, Mamoru blasted out with the last thing he had to say.

"If you ever, EVER, do anything to me, any of my friends, or my family, I won't hold anything back. You can close yourself in with as many locks as you like or you can try to run away—but it won't do you any good. I'll be on your trail. How about that motorcycle of yours? Is it locked up nice and tight in a safe place? You'd better check it over before you ride it next time. You could be driving full throttle when the brakes go out."

Mamoru could almost hear the sound of Miura's knees knocking together. "Got it? Don't forget, it's all in the genes. Now you watch out for yourself."

Mamoru slammed down the receiver for good measure. The heavy weight in the pit of his stomach dissolved. He realized his own knees were shaking. Mamoru leaned against the glass of the phone booth and heaved a deep sigh.

————•————

From the weekly tabloid *Spider*, November 30:

A Good Heart or a Sweetheart?
The witness who followed his conscience

Do any of our readers have an annual income of ten billion yen? Are any married to a beautiful heiress and have a mistress who is even more gorgeous? The photo to the left is Koichi Yoshitake, vice-president of Shin Nippon Enterprises and the possessor of just such rare good fortune. Not only that, but he also has a rare sense of justice and fairness.

It all began late at night on November 13. A twenty-one-year-old college student was hit by a taxi. Without any witnesses, there was a direct conflict between the driver, who swore that the victim came running into the street despite the fact that she had a red light, and the dying words of the victim, which appeared to contradict him. Enter Mr. Yoshitake. Thanks to his testimony, the taxi driver, who had been detained during the investigation, is once again a free man.

The location of the accident was far from Yoshitake's home, and he had no respectable motive for being there at that time of night. The reason he did in fact have was that he had been on his way to the home of his mistress, Miss I——, who lives in an apartment near the site.

Yoshitake is forty-five years old and a native of Hirakawa. He is a shrewd businessman who raised himself from the position of lowly salesman to his current status. Shin Nippon Enterprises, where he is vice-president, was founded and is owned by the father of Yoshitake's wife. Naturally, he is required to exercise a certain discretion with regard to paramours.

Yoshitake showed up at the Joto Police Station when he learned that the taxi driver was being held because no one was available to testify on his behalf. His testimony matched that of the driver. He remembered that just before the accident he had stopped the victim and asked her the time. Her response was "Five past twelve." This convinced the police of the credibility of his testimony, and led them to conclude that the accident had been caused by the victim. It also proved that Yoshitake had the courage to put justice over his family, although some say it is only a matter of time before his wife has him served with divorce papers.

And one must pity the unfortunate Miss I——. Once her relationship with Yoshitake became public, she quit the nightclub where she was working, and has reportedly gone to stay with a friend until matters between Yoshitake and his wife are settled. And to any other such fortunate men among our readership, in order to avoid the wrath of your wife and keep your lover from tears, please take care to avoid any traffic accidents on the way to your secret rendezvous.

At first glance, everything seemed back to normal in the Asano household. Maki wasn't as cheerful as usual, but she went to work each morning. Yoriko roused Mamoru out of bed, made his lunch and packed him off to school, and then started her housework.

Only Taizo had a new routine. Previously he'd worked late at night, and had been sound asleep when Maki and Mamoru left the house. Nowadays, he sat next to the window and saw them off. He spent more time than he used to reading the newspaper. When they noticed him studying it especially closely, they knew he was reading the Help Wanted ads. His dark green taxi was returned to him the day after he was released, but he had washed it once and then left it untouched.

Mr. Satomi from the Tokai Taxi Company had visited the house and invited Taizo to come back and work for him until he got his license back. There was lots of work he could do besides driving, such as cleaning, paperwork, and personnel management. Taizo turned the offer down without a second thought. His determination to avoid the taxi business was holding fast.

"He's a stubborn one!" Mr. Satomi had said in exasperation as he left.

"We'll get by somehow," Yoriko had forced a smile as she saw him off.

Things had also settled down for Mamoru at school. His strategy seemed to have worked on Miura and his gang; they had completely stopped bothering him. Yoichi Miyashita's injuries had healed and he, too, was back in class.

One evening as the Asano household sat down to dinner with the six o'clock news on in the background, Mamoru looked over at the TV screen and saw footage of a familiar building.

"At three o'clock this afternoon at the Laurel department store in K——— ward," said the announcer, "a middle-aged man suddenly became violent."

Mamoru put down his rice bowl and listened intently.

"The man took a knife from Housewares and stabbed two employees. The culprit was later identified as Kazunobu Kakiyama, a local resident."

"Mamoru, isn't that where you work?" Maki asked excitedly as she reached down to pick up the chopsticks Mamoru had dropped on the floor.

"The two injured employees were Goro Makino, a security guard aged fifty-seven, and Hajime Takano, aged thirty. Takano was stabbed in the shoulder and seriously wounded. Although there were approximately fifteen hundred customers in the store at the time, none of them were hurt. Police apprehended Kakiyama and took him to the Joto precinct for questioning. Due to Kakiyama's state of agitation immediately following the attack and his history of substance abuse, police believe he was under the influence of drugs at the time."

By the time Mamoru arrived at the hospital, visiting hours were almost over. Takano was lying on the hospital bed with bandages around his neck and shoulder and an IV attached to his uninjured right arm, but he did his best to lift his head when Mamoru peeked into the room.

"Well, come in!" he greeted Mamoru with a smile. "It must have been a shock to hear about this."

"I saw it on the news while I was eating dinner. You should have seen me choking."

Takano told him that the police had been there to talk to him, and that they would be back for a formal interview the next day.

"It's awful what happened. Does it hurt much?" asked Mamoru.

"It's not as bad as it looks. They wrapped me up like this to keep it from getting any worse." Takano used his chin to indicate where he had been cut. Any higher and he would have had his throat slit. Any lower and the knife would have gone through his heart. Mamoru felt shivers down his back. "I'm not as fast as I thought. I was sure I could duck and avoid it. Well, at least no customers were injured."

"How about Mr. Makino?"

"He hurt his back when he was holding the attacker down, but his tests were clear. He's probably at home with his feet up."

"Who would have thought something like this could happen at our Laurel?"

Books and Housewares were on opposite ends of the fourth floor. When Kakiyama broke the glass showcase with his bare hand and took out the knife, a female employee had pressed the emergency bell and Takano and Makino had come running. Otherwise, customers would certainly have been involved.

"They ought to give you a medal. What with that girl on the roof and now this attack, what would the store do without you?"

"Didn't you know? They keep a few of us incompetents on the payroll for emergencies like this when they need a little brute force." Takano laughed, but Mamoru could tell that it hurt. "And besides, you were the one that pulled it off last time!"

As they talked, the IV solution dripped steadily into Takano's arm. It appeared to be taking effect, as Takano started to look drowsy. Mamoru was just drawing quietly away from his bed when Takano began talking again.

". . . But it's a good opportunity, you know."

"What is?"

"Do you remember that girl? The one in the red sweater?"

"Of course I do."

"She's a top student at her school. She wasn't the type to do something like that. Apparently she can't even remember why . . ." Takano began slurring his words and, seeing his eyes were drooping, Mamoru tiptoed out of the room.

On his way down the hall, he passed a young nurse with a clipboard in her hands. Mamoru turned around to admire her, and watched her walk into Takano's room.

When Sato from work had had his appendix out, he had told Mamoru that single men always went crazy over the nurses. Mamoru wondered if Takano's time had come and, if so, maybe that meant there would be a silver lining to this whole incident.

But what had Takano meant by a good opportunity? That wasn't something you'd expect to hear from someone who had just escaped death. As he went out the emergency exit, an ambulance with flashing lights pulled up and medics hurriedly carried out someone wrapped in yellow blankets on a stretcher.

How come that girl who had almost jumped off the roof couldn't even remember why she had done it?

———•———

The end of the year was a time when customers would come to shop even if the store's blinds were drawn. Sales targets were set high, and employees were harried.

On the first Sunday of the month, Sato and Mamoru spent the morning away from the Books section running the lottery set up in the large foyer on the first floor. Customers got a number of chances according to the amount of purchases they had made. This was another special feature of the year-end season.

The lottery machine was computer-run and resembled a slot machine.

An employee pulled a lever, and numbers rotated rapidly across the screen. The customer pushed a button to stop it, and the number it stopped at showed what prize they'd won. It looked good and wasn't too noisy—and the kids loved it. There were two such machines, and a single employee operated each. Pulling the lever and pushing it back into place for one customer after another in a line that never got any shorter quickly wore the two out.

"Hey, Mamoru, have you ever heard of Shurado?" asked Sato, struggling to keep a smile on his face.

"Shurado? What's that? Some kind of martial art?"

"No, no, it's one of the six levels of Buddhist hell. The place where those who are killed in battle go."

"And what has that got to do with this lottery?" Mamoru asked, handing a customer a packet of tissues as a consolation prize. The customer gave a lingering last look at the grand prize, a seven-day cruise on the Aegean Sea, and walked off.

Sato continued. "They fall into Shurado, full of the hatred of battle, their hearts brimming with bitterness and spite. And what should await them there but yet another battlefield! The morning sun comes up and the enemy arrives with their swords drawn, and they have to fight again. They are wounded and fall, but they stand up again and wave their swords. By evening their arms fall off and then their legs. They moan and groan and cry in pain."

"You've been reading too much again."

"I'm not done yet. Even then they don't die; they become immortal. Which is natural, of course, because they've already died once. No matter how mortal their wounds, as soon as the sun comes up, they're healed. And then off they go again to fight their enemy. All they can do is fight. And so it goes on, over and over again. Sounds terrible, huh?"

"It sounds like the Japanese national rugby team having to play the All Blacks."

"We stand here hour after hour, pulling this lever," continued Sato.

"But all we're doing here is fooling the customers."

"Why do you say that? They enjoy it."

"That's what I mean. They really believe that grand prize is in there. I've never seen anything higher than third prize, that stereo video deck."

"Is that true?" The woman who had moved to the front of the line broke into their conversation, her eyebrows wrinkled in consternation.

"Of course not!" said Sato with a fake smile on his face. "Of course there's a grand prize!" He took the woman's ticket and pulled the lever. She got a fourth prize.

"You talk way too much," Mamoru warned him, and then turned back to the woman. "Fourth prize. Would you like a roll of plastic wrap or some cough drops?"

Sato refused to stop talking, but at least he lowered his voice.

"Customers show up with their tickets in their fist and a dream in their heart. They end up buying things they don't need just to get an extra ticket. When we die, we're going to Shurado for our sins, Mamoru. The lottery hell. We'll be pulling this lever from morning until night till our arms drop off. Every morning we'll wake up and there'll be another line of customers waiting for us. They'll all have handfuls of tickets, and we'll do it over and over and over."

"What nonsense are you filling this boy's mind with?" It was Madame Anzai, who was covering for Takano while he was out. "I'll take over now, so go have lunch. Then I want you to spend the afternoon checking stock in the storage room."

"Merciful Lord Buddha, I thank you!" exclaimed Sato.

During lunch in the employee cafeteria with Sato, Mamoru excused himself and went to phone Hashimoto. Yoriko had left a message for him with Madame Anzai while he'd been working at the lottery.

"She said that right after you left this morning, you got a call from someone named Hashimoto. He wants you to call him back."

What could Nobuhiko Hashimoto have to say to him? When he

called, the line was busy. He tried three more times at intervals of two minutes, but the line remained engaged, so he hung up. Sato was grinning at him when he returned.

"Was it your girlfriend calling to break up?"

"Yeah, but I'm not worried. We've broken up lots of times and we always kiss and make up."

Sato bowed in mock defeat. "You win! And here I am traveling from one place to the next. Don't try to stop me, love!"

"So where are you going at New Year's?" Mamoru neatly changed the subject.

"I'm going to see the Paris–Dakar Rally."

"Wow! It'll cost you though."

"Yeah, I suppose, but that's what I'm working and saving for. I'll be counting on you to look after things while I'm gone. And if I don't come back, stand looking toward the Eurasian continent and pray that I rest in peace."

This reminded Mamoru of their previous conversation about Shurado, and he decided to run by Sato something that had been weighing on his mind about Yoko Sugano. "Sato, have you ever thought about getting a better job to make money so you could travel?"

"Better job?"

"You know, something easier that would bring in lots of money."

Sato looked confused. "What's all this about all of a sudden?"

"Nothing, I just wondered."

Sato scratched his nose and thought. "Lots of money . . . That would be nice, but that sort of thing is usually trouble. You have to scam someone, or they're trying to scam you. Nope, I'm not interested. I enjoy the bookshop and it suits me. I work for what I earn."

Back at the storage room, they found goods to be inspected and a mountain of books and magazines to return. On top of that, the video display was airing a fashion show of next year's bathing suits. Sato was in and out watching it.

"You should see the high legs on those suits! It's more naked than naked! Go take a look!"

Within an hour, the T-shirt Mamoru wore under his uniform was soaking wet with sweat, and the mountain of work hadn't shrunk a bit. Mamoru decided this was more of a Shurado than the lottery. He looked at the piles of magazines they had tied in bundles to be returned, and thought about *Information Channel*.

How many copies had it sold? How many people had read that article? He was pretty sure that most of the copies had gone this route, getting sent back to the publisher with their covers cut off.

We had some copies left, and he bought them all.

That man had apparently talked of suing, but could you really take someone to court for pretending to be your girlfriend and swindling you out of money? Lost in thought, Mamoru let his eyes roam over the cover of another sort of publication, the type known as a "cutout magazine." The editors cut out articles from newspapers, magazines, and tabloids, re-edited them, and printed them by genre. Mamoru knew of a couple of such magazines, one of book reviews and another on new computer technology. There was a demand for both of them, and they sold well.

The magazine he was looking at now was a little different. It was full of "page three" news, such as crimes, accidents, and scandals. It wasn't the sort of thing many people would be interested in or have work-related needs for. Anyone that curious would probably make their own scrapbook. Very few people would go the route of buying this magazine, especially since it was expensive—cutout magazines are put together by hand. This one had come directly from the publisher rather than through the normal distribution channels. Takano had carefully explained to the man who delivered them that he would have to come pick up any unsold copies after three weeks.

Mamoru noticed the title, "Accidents and Suicides, etc., in September and October," and he picked up a copy. He wondered if he would find an article about his uncle's accident.

There was one short mention. There were clippings from the three largest papers, the business paper, and the *Tokyo Daily News*, which the Asanos took. It took up only half as much space as a kidnapping case. Mamoru thought about how there were probably many other things, too, that hadn't made the papers. Any incident was equally earthshaking for the people involved in it.

As he flipped through the magazine, he noticed another heading: "Woman Jumps to Death from Tozai Line Platform." Maki took that line to work, and he remembered her mentioning it.

I heard at the station that the head of the woman who jumped was found on the coupling between two cars. I'm not kidding!

His attention caught, Mamoru sat down on the floor to read it. "The woman who died was Atsuko Mita (20), a company employee . . ." *Atsuko Mita!* Wasn't she one of the women interviewed for *Information Channel?* Mamoru looked up, blinked a few times, and then read the article again. Atsuko Mita. Suicide. No suicide note, no will.

October: Atsuko Mita committed suicide by jumping in front of a train. November: Yoko Sugano died in an accident—but it was similar to a suicide since she'd run out in front of a car. Still holding the magazine, Mamoru ran to the pay phone on the same floor. He tried calling Hashimoto again, but the line was still busy.

He thought for a while longer and decided to call the publisher of the cutout magazine to ask about something that might have appeared in a previous issue. Mamoru called, explained what he wanted, and was put on hold. He tapped his foot in impatience as he listened to the music box melody. Finally someone came on the line.

"Hello? Sorry to keep you waiting. Yes, there is something on Fumie Kato. It was in an article on September 2. She jumped off the roof of her apartment building."

"Does it say whether she left a will?"

"They didn't find a will. It says they were searching for a motive."

So Fumie Kato had also committed suicide without leaving a will.

"Are there any articles about Kazuko Takagi?"

There was silence for a few moments. Mamoru heard the sound of pages being turned.

"No, I don't see that name here."

That made three. It was still only three. There were already three. Of the four women in the *Information Channel* article, three had died.

Mamoru suddenly realized that Sato had come up and was standing beside him.

"Hey, what's the matter? You look like you just donated a couple liters of blood."

"Ah, look . . . something just came up." Mamoru sprinted for the stairs. He had to go see Hashimoto. This had to be what he wanted to talk about. Three of the four women . . . it couldn't be a coincidence.

———•———

Nobuhiko Hashimoto was gone. And it wasn't just him. Everything he owned was gone. All that was left was the burned-out shell of that green house. The walls left standing were cracked and covered in soot. In other places only the steel frame remained poking up toward the sky. The whole place resembled a blackened skeleton.

Mamoru walked up to the rope labeled with a sign that said "Danger! No Entry!" He felt something crunching under his feet. Pieces of sharp window and rounded bottle glass floated in puddles of water along with the ash.

Everything had burned. The filing cabinet was partially melted, and nothing was left of the desk but the steel rim. There were a few springs from the couch that Mamoru had sat on.

What had happened? What had happened to Hashimoto?

"Did you know Hashimoto?"

Mamoru spun around to see who was speaking. It was a woman

wearing a red apron and holding a broom in one hand. "Uh . . . yes."

"Are you a relative?"

"No, I barely know him. What happened here?"

"Hashimoto's dead."

"Dead?" Mamoru stood there with his mouth open.

"It was a propane gas explosion," the woman answered. "It was awful. All the houses on the street had their windows blown out. What a mess." The woman took a closer look at Mamoru. "Are you all right? You don't look too good."

"Did Mr. Hashimoto die in the explosion?"

"That's right. Burned to a crisp, or so I hear." The women motioned to Mamoru with the hand that wasn't holding the broom. "Now, you get out of there. It's dangerous. The police said to stay away."

Mamoru moved away from the house, giving it one more long backward look. On the mountain of black rubble he noticed the clock he'd seen before on the wall. The glass was broken and the hands had stopped at ten past two.

Everything was gone; blown to smithereens. That was why he hadn't got through on the phone. He'd heard that phone lines temporarily retained the appearance of being connected after lines were cut in an accident or a disaster.

"Do you know what caused the explosion?"

"Who knows whether it was the alcohol or the fact that his wife had left him. He was a strange one. Nobody knew what he was thinking."

Mamoru wasn't sure what she was talking about. "What do you mean?"

"It was suicide." The woman dangled the broom from her fingers. "The gas lines were open, and he had poured a tank of gasoline over everything. I guess he lit a match and that took care of the rest. The fire department is doing an investigation. Are you sure you're all right? Can you get in touch with his family? Someone's got to take responsibility for my broken windows and the water all over everything."

Mamoru didn't hear the rest of what she said. He couldn't hear anything.

Nobuhiko Hashimoto was dead. Mamoru leaned against the fence of the house across the street. Another suicide. It wasn't three out of four. It was now four out of the five people who were involved in the *Information Channel* interview. It just wasn't possible. It *couldn't* be a coincidence.

It *had* to be murder. Someone had plotted to kill these four. It was as cold and calculated as slitting their throats with a knife. Hashimoto was the only connection to the four women. He was the link that could connect the three corpses to each other. The filing cabinet had contained records of the interview and photographs which must have been in the way of whoever had planned the murders.

If Hashimoto had put the three deaths together—no, he *must* have put them together. That was why he had had to die.

The only question was—Mamoru looked up into the sky—how had the murders been carried out? Yoko Sugano's death had an explanation of sorts, but what about the others? From all appearances they were suicides. Each of them was witnessed. It was possible to push someone off a roof or in front of a train, but how could you make someone kill himself?

A burned smell mixed with the stench of gasoline floated on the wind. Gasoline! That was it. The propane gas alone would have been enough to finish off Hashimoto. Gasoline and a flame had been added to make sure the contents of the filing cabinet were destroyed, too.

But how? If the murderer had been there, he or she would have been hurt. That was why the police had judged it to be suicide.

So how had it been done?

What had Hashimoto wanted to tell me? Mamoru remembered the phone call that morning. Did he want me to know the three women had died? Or had he figured out how they'd been killed?

The ruins of the house were cold. When had the explosion taken place? The clock had stopped at ten past two. It was just past four thirty now. It must have happened at ten past two in the morning.

That meant Hashimoto couldn't have called him—somebody else had called using his name. All of a sudden it became clear. Mamoru had the only remaining copy of the *Information Channel* article. That made him a link. He had the only remaining proof of the connection between the four women. Mamoru broke out in a cold sweat.

The magazine is at home! He remembered that he had given Hashimoto a memo with his phone number and address. Whoever it was had found it and called him—to warn him that he was next!

Mamoru had to find a phone and call his aunt. He ran for several blocks until he came across one. In a panic, he struggled to remember his own phone number. He gripped the receiver and heard the metallic dial tone. He might be too late already. What if all he got was a busy signal?

"Hello, Asano speaking," answered his Aunt Yoriko.

"Auntie, you've got to get out of the house!"

"What? Who is this?"

"It's Mamoru. I don't have time to explain. Just do what I say. Just get out of the house. Don't take anything with you. Make sure Uncle Taizo and Maki are with you, too. Now!"

"Mamoru, what on earth's the matter with you?"

"Just do what I say! I'm begging you!"

"I don't know what your problem is, but someone called again while you were out. This Hashimoto wants you to call him—"

"I know, that's why—"

"He gave me his number. Shall I give it to you?"

Mamoru went silent. He gave a number?

"He said he had something important to talk to you about. I'm going to read it out."

It wasn't Hashimoto's home phone number. It had a midtown prefix. Mamoru's head began to pound. He felt like he was playing dodgeball with the Invisible Man. Where would the next ball come flying from? He didn't want to make the call, he just wanted to run away.

He finally dialed the number Yoriko had given him. The phone rang twice before it was answered. Mamoru didn't know what to say. He held the phone so tightly his knuckles turned white.

A calm, husky voice spoke to him.

"It's you, young man. I know it's you." The voice paused and then went on in a cheerful tone. "I'm afraid I've given you a bit of a shock. I want to talk to you. Without Nobuhiko Hashimoto, of course. His work is done . . ."

The Invisible Light

Mamoru had a flash of déjà vu. It was the same voice that had thanked him for killing Yoko Sugano.

"You're a smart boy," the raspy voice went on. Mamoru decided that whoever it was was either very ill or a chain smoker. "And quick to act, too. I'm looking forward to meeting you in person."

"You!" Mamoru finally forced the words out from between clenched teeth. "Who are you? You're the one behind all of this."

"All of this?"

"You know what I mean! The explosion that killed Hashimoto, the deaths of three of the women in the *Information Channel* article."

"I see!" The voice sounded genuinely surprised. "You've already looked into all of that? I called today to tell you that Hashimoto was dead and to explain about those women. I'm obviously too late though."

"But why?" Mamoru was unable to keep a hysterical edge out of his voice. "Why would you do all that and then go to the trouble to tell me about it? What do you want to accomplish?"

"It's too early to tell you that." Suddenly the voice switched to an almost gentle tone. "I'll tell you what you want to know when the time comes. Until then, just remember that those three women and Nobuhiko Hashimoto all died following my orders."

"Orders? That's ridiculous. What sort of person would follow orders to kill himself?"

The voice laughed. It was the mirthless laugh a teacher might have for a student who said something funny in class, and the voice continued in the condescending tone of a teacher dealing with a particularly poor student.

"I know you might not be able to believe it yet. But the world is full of things you'll never understand. You're still just a child."

Two women pushed their bicycles past the telephone booth. One of them looked at Mamoru with a concerned but condescending expression that seemed to say, *What's the matter, young man? If you've got a problem, you should go talk to an adult about it.*

Maybe whoever was on the other end of the line wore the same expression. *You poor boy,* the voice seemed to say. *I know it's more than you can handle, but do your best.* It made Mamoru angry, and the anger kept his fear in check.

The voice went on. "Every one of those women committed suicide. It's the only conclusion to be drawn. Even Yoko Sugano—I didn't get it quite right and that meant trouble for you, but I can tell you with certainty that she ran into that intersection of her own free will."

"But it was on your orders?" Mamoru persisted

"That's right. I got rid of each of them."

Got rid of? It sounded as though he had tossed them on the trash heap.

"And I don't regret a single one. I intend to get rid of the last one the same way."

The last one? Mamoru struggled to remember the name of the other woman—Kazuko Takagi. She had been seated on the far left of the photograph in the magazine. A beautiful woman with long hair.

"I'm not afraid," the voice went on. "Nobody will ever discover what I've done. But I can't take any chances. That's why Hashimoto had to go. He was down on his luck, but he wasn't a fool. After your visit, he started checking up on what had happened to the women. If he had found out three of the four were dead, he certainly would have suspected me."

"So you knew Hashimoto. Hashimoto knew who you were."

"That's right. Let me give you a hint. I'm the one that went to the *Information Channel* publisher to buy up all the copies they had left. I'm also the one who lied to Hashimoto about suing them, and asked him to show me his notes from the interview."

Mamoru remembered what Akemi Mizuno had told him about the man who had bought the magazines, and how she thought he had been trying to protect a daughter or granddaughter.

"I hear you're an old guy."

"Yes, I've lived at least half a century longer than you."

"But why are you doing this?"

"My convictions."

Now that was a declaration! Mamoru almost laughed out loud.

"My convictions. That's all I've got left to keep this old body moving. Let's you and I make a promise to each other. I'll let you know when it's time to get rid of the fourth one, Kazuko Takagi. I'll prove it all to you then. Then you'll understand what I'm capable of."

"And you expect me to sit around waiting until then?" Mamoru had lost every shred of fear. Now he was just mad. "I don't care what you can do. I don't want to know. I don't *need* to know! There's nothing you can do to keep me from hanging up this phone and running to the nearest police station." Mamoru was about to hang up there and then, but was stopped by the energy in the voice at the end of the line.

"Oh, I can stop you all right!" It was full of confidence. "Think about it. Hashimoto had nothing to lose but his stingy pride, but you have plenty. I had no choice but to deal with him as I did. You are different."

Mamoru froze on the spot. The voice waited to make sure he was listening, and then continued. "You understand now, don't you? I don't care what you know about me. There's nothing you can do. I can bend people's will to my own. And that includes your family and friends. It wouldn't be hard at all."

Fear returned to Mamoru's heart as quickly as if it had been attached to a tracer bullet. He could see the faces of everyone he loved in the light it shed.

"You're a coward." It was all Mamoru could get out. "It shouldn't be too hard for you to find me and kill me. What's keeping you?"

"I like you, boy. You're brave and you've got intelligence that you know how to use. There are a lot of things the two of us share."

"There's nothing—"

"How about a small demonstration?" The voice cut him off. "Tonight at nine. I'll use someone in your family to prove to you that I can make people do what I want. Then you can decide whether or not to believe me. It won't be too late for you to take action." The voice added in a teasing tone, "That is, if you still feel like taking any action . . ."

"You're crazy! Do you know what you're doing?"

"Why don't we discuss that when we meet in person? It's something I'm looking forward to. We have lots in common and there are many things I want to teach you. Until then, just forget all about me. I'll be in touch with you."

"I'm going to look for Kazuko Takagi," Mamoru began. "I'll make sure you can't hurt her."

"Do as you please." The voice laughed. "Tokyo is a big place. How do you plan to find her? I don't think she's anywhere you'll think of. She won't answer if you go calling her name. She's already scared to death."

He must mean that Kazuko Takagi knew she was the only one of the four left alive.

"I've got one last thing to say to you. Don't waste your time looking for me. All the clues are gone, and I won't be at this number again. You'll just have to wait until I contact you." The voice put an end to the conversation with a line that sounded as though it had been borrowed from somewhere else, before hanging up. "I won't answer, and I won't come home again. Not until the time has come."

<hr>

Kazuko Takagi also learned about Nobuhiko Hashimoto's death when she found herself in front of the burned-out shell of his house. She had decided to visit him when she was unable to bear it all any longer. She spent her days selling makeup, a smile pasted on her face, but inside something was eating her alive. It was like a stain on a carpet, impossible to hide or ignore.

She couldn't ignore the fact that she was the only one of the four of them left alive. Hashimoto might know something. Once she got the notion into her head, she hadn't been able to wait. After meeting him at the interview, she had sworn never to have anything to do with him again. Now he was her only key. He was the one person who knew all four of them and how to find them.

But now Hashimoto was dead.

Standing in front of what was left of the gate to his house, she realized that the fear she had been feeling thus far was nothing compared to what she felt now.

"You! Excuse me." Kazuko realized she was being addressed by a woman in a red apron, her eyebrows furrowed in displeasure. "Are you a relative of Hashimoto's?"

"No, just an acquaintance."

The woman squinted her eyes and lifted her chin in disbelief. "All he has is acquaintances, and they're showing up one after the other."

"Has someone else been here?" Kazuko couldn't imagine Hashimoto having any friends concerned for his well-being.

"About an hour ago. A boy—looked like he might be in high school. He stood there just like you. Looked like he was about to lose his lunch."

"A boy?" That was puzzling.

When Fumie Kato and Atusko Mita had died, Yoko had been certain it couldn't be a coincidence. Kazuko, however, had refused to take her seriously. *It must be one of our clients,* Yoko had declared. *He's looking for revenge and he's killing us off one by one.*

None of those men have got the nerve to do that, Kazuko had snorted.

And why would any of them have to kill all of us? None of us have had the same clients. If one of those jerks is looking for revenge, he'd only need to kill one of us.

Maybe he saw that magazine article?

There's not much chance any of them saw it!

There was someone, Yoko had murmured. *He read the article and he won't stop bothering me. I'm so scared.*

Is that why you moved?

Yoko nodded. *But he's already found me. He'll come after me.*

Pull yourself together! Kazuko had tried to act offhand, but inside she was shaking at the thought that the same thing could happen to her. *There's nothing that man can do. He can't even sue us. We were hired to do what we did. If there was any sort of scam, it was by the company. It wasn't our responsibility.*

That's why he's killing us. Kazuko could hardly hear Yoko's voice, it was so soft. *There's no other way to get to us.*

Stop talking like an idiot! Atsuko and Fumie weren't killed. They both committed suicide. How many times do I have to tell you? What exactly did we do wrong? It wasn't pretty, but it was our job—nothing worth being killed over.

Yoko had been silent. She just stared at Kazuko for a while.

What is it?

Kazuko, do you really believe what you're saying? Can you really say we didn't do anything wrong? How can you say that nobody hates us, nobody would want to get revenge on us?

Because it's true!

Yoko wasn't fooled. That day, just before they parted, she had said, *Kazuko, there is someone, isn't there? There's someone you know that would do this to us. You're just as scared as I am.*

Yoko had been right about someone knowing. But the only client of Kazuko's who had seen the *Information Channel* article was dead; he had died in May, four months before Fumie Kato had jumped from the roof of her apartment building. When Kazuko had begun to worry that the women in the article were the targets of a heartbroken client, she had looked him up at the last number she'd had for him, and the person who had answered the phone told her he had died of an overdose. Kazuko remembered that he had worked in a university laboratory. She couldn't remember what his field was; some kind of medical research.

Kazuko had mailed him the one copy of *Information Channel* that Nobuhiko Hashimoto had given her, jokingly calling it a "souvenir." The client had been disgustingly naive. He had spent his life in academics. He took everything at face value; all of Kazuko's tactics, all of her insinuations. She had had lots of clients, but he was the only one who had refused to believe she was capable of swindling him like that, even when he had received notices that she was defaulting on the repayments of loans he had guaranteed for her.

You're a fool! she had told him when he kept calling. *Haven't you figured it out yet? It was all an act! You're nothing to me!*

But he had refused to believe her, and had blindly chased after her. He didn't hate her—he still loved her. And that was why she had sent him the magazine. She wanted to make sure he understood how she felt about him and all the rest of them. It had done the trick. She'd never heard from him again. Kenichi Tazawa—that was his name. There was no way she could have known that he would kill himself.

"Tell me more about the boy," Kazuko asked the woman in the red apron.

"Hmm? He looked like any other boy you'd see. His hair wasn't permed, there was nothing unusual about his clothes. He didn't look like a delinquent."

"Did he look like Hashimoto?"

"No, much better looking."

As for Mamoru, he was already on the train home. If Kazuko had arrived ten minutes earlier, he might have caught sight of her on the opposite platform and come running over to talk to her.

"So, do you think you can get in touch with Hashimoto's family?" the woman persisted. "Someone's got to pay for the damage to my house."

"You should be glad it's something money can take care of," Kazuko replied and stalked off. When she got back to her apartment, she got a few things together and left at a run. She didn't tell her landlady or any of the neighbors that she was leaving. She had to find somewhere else to live. She'd find an apartment that you could rent by the week. Nobody would be able to find her. At least for a while.

———•———

Mamoru tried everything he could think of to forget about the time. He ran until he was ready to drop. He locked the door of his room, got out his lock-picking tools, and polished them. He called Anego and Yoichi Miyashita. He called the hospital to ask how Takano was doing. Maki came home at about seven, and he listened as she talked about the movie she had been to see.

"I fell asleep," she confessed. "I said I wanted to see an action movie, but the rest of them wanted to see this period drama. I lost the vote."

"You fell asleep because you're out so late every night," Yoriko said firmly.

Maki stuck out her tongue. "It's all those year-end parties I have to go to," she grumbled.

Mamoru knew, though, that at least half of the time she was out drinking to forget her troubles. She was out past midnight most nights, and she always came home alone. Taizo's accident had cast a shadow over her relationship with her boyfriend, Maekawa. Mamoru had heard her crying on the phone late at night. He could tell that she didn't want to tell her family about the breakup and put up with their pity.

"I know I'm having a little too much fun. Last night I couldn't even remember where I'd been part of the time. That is definitely *too* drunk."

"Now you're scaring me! You might as well put a sign on your back asking to be mugged."

"Don't worry, Mom. Ninety percent of all violent incidents are inflicted by someone the victim knows. I was only walking around looking for a taxi, so I wasn't in any danger."

"You can talk all you like."

Mamoru absently looked at the clock as he listened to his aunt and cousin argue. His mind went blank and he felt like a soldier crawling toward a landmine.

"Mamoru, why do you keep staring at the clock?"

They had just finished their simple Sunday evening supper. It was almost eight.

"Am I?"

"Yes, you are. Are you going out?"

"No, I was just wondering whether it was slow."

Taizo answered, "No, I just wound and reset it today."

The Asanos had an old wind-up clock that an antique dealer would probably give his eyeteeth to get hold of. It had been a wedding present and had survived earthquakes and moves, but it had never stopped ticking away. Taizo wound it once a week and oiled it occasionally. That's all it took to keep that pleasant ticking sound in the house, keeping time for the family. Now even that clock looked like a landmine to Mamoru.

At eight-thirty, Mamoru went up into his room and closed the door. He told himself nothing would happen if he stayed in there by himself. He turned off the light and sat in the dark staring at the digital clock next to his bed.

At eight-forty there was a knock on his door.

"It's me. Do you mind if I come in?" Maki opened the door and peeked around it, then slipped in without waiting for an answer. "What's the matter with you? Are you feeling sick?"

Mamoru couldn't kick her out. He smiled vaguely and shook his head.

"So, what do you think? It sounds good to me."

"What? What sounds good?"

"You know what I'm talking about. Weren't you listening just now? Mom was talking about Mr. Yoshitake's visit."

Now Mamoru remembered. Koichi Yoshitake from Shin Nippon Enterprises had been around while he and Maki were out. He had brought one of his employees with him, and had offered Taizo a job.

"Dad can't drive a taxi anymore, so he'll have to find some other work somewhere. Not too many places are looking for men his age. We might as well take Mr. Yoshitake up on his offer."

"But why would Mr. Yoshitake . . . ?"

"You know, Dad got thrown in jail because he ran away from the scene of the accident. He's trying to make amends. I don't know why Mom and Dad are making him wait for an answer. Shin Nippon is bound to pay well. I'm going to try to convince them. You should mention it too, if you get a chance. It'll be our joint project."

Maki wouldn't stop talking, and now it was almost nine. Mamoru was so tense he could hardly move and his mouth was dry.

Who in his family was the man on the phone after?

". . . Okay? Promise?" So saying, Maki got up and left. Mamoru exhaled slowly and stared at the clock.

It was eight-fifty.

"Mamoru, come fold the laundry!" Yoriko was calling loudly from downstairs. "Mamoru? Can you hear me?"

Eight fifty-five and thirty seconds. Mamoru sighed.

There was another loud knock on the door and Yoriko came in with both arms full of dried laundry.

"Your uncle is taking his bath. Do this for me until I call you for your turn." Yoriko stood for a second looking at Mamoru. "Are you sick?"

Mamoru just shook his head. Eight fifty-nine.

"Really? You're pale as a ghost. Oh, that reminds me—what were you talking about when you called home today?" When Mamoru refused to look up and answer her, Yoriko turned to leave the room. She frowned and looked briefly back over her shoulder at him before closing the door behind her. At that instant Mamoru's digital clock flashed on nine o'clock, and the wind-up clock downstairs began to chime the hour. Mamoru sat there with his arms around his knees.

The clock chimed over and over, and the digital clock showed the seconds. One, two . . .

The clock stopped chiming. It was nine o'clock and ten seconds.

Fifteen seconds.

Twenty seconds.

Mamoru's door slowly opened again, and Maki poked her head in. Her eyes were pointed in Mamoru's direction, but they didn't see him. She was looking off into the distance as she spoke in measured tones.

"Listen to me, boy. I called Nobuyuki Hashimoto. That's when he died."

The door closed as she left.

Mamoru jumped up and ran into the hall. He threw open Maki's door. She was sitting in front of her stereo.

"Hey! What do you mean running in here like that!" she screeched, jumping up with a CD still in her hands. "What's the matter with you?"

"Maki, what did you . . . just come in and say to me?"

"You mean about Mr. Yoshitake?"

She didn't remember.

"Mamoru, you're acting weird."

Mamoru made up an excuse and left the room. He sat on the edge of the bed with his head in his hands.

"Maki, telephone!" called Aunt Yoriko from downstairs.

"Who is it?" Mamoru heard Maki trotting quickly and lightly down the stairs. Just the same as usual.

Mamoru was left feeling alone and frightened out of his wits.

Mamoru's days began to feel like a series of recurring nightmares. He stayed away from everyone he was close to, fearful of what would happen to them if they got involved. He had to put a stop to it all. And he had to do it alone.

It was mid-December, and the streets were full of activity. Shops were decorated for Christmas and New Year's, and the Salvation Army trumpet could be heard. The community association began making its annual night patrols warning residents to be on the alert for fires. During his long, sleepless nights, Mamoru could hear the members greeting each other as they passed each other on their rounds.

"There are three Days of the Cock this year, so there are bound to be lots of fires," said Yoriko. She put up stickers throughout the house admonishing everyone to "Watch Out For Fire," including one in Mamoru's room. The sticker reminded Mamoru uncomfortably of how Nobuhiko Hashimoto had died. He recalled the melted filing cabinet and the horrible charred smell.

For the past few days, Mamoru had been having a recurring dream in which he heard the sound of gas leaking. It was not such an unusual sound, but it was happening in Mamoru's house, which for some reason was also Hashimoto's house. Mamoru could see the black silhouette of Hashimoto sleeping. The telephone was ringing. Once, twice, three times. Mamoru kept screaming, warning him not to answer it. But Hashimoto woke up and answered the phone. Then there was a muffled explosion. Flames blew out the windows.

Mamoru awoke, as he always did at this point in the dream. He was covered in sweat and curled tight into a fetal position, as if trying to protect himself from the impact of the explosion.

What if he told someone? What if he came clean about the whole thing? But no one would believe him. They'd laugh him off, and tell him he needed a vacation. He might even end up laughing at himself. But he was sure that anyone he told would be dead in a matter of days after jumping off a roof or running in front of a speeding car. Then the phone would ring for Mamoru: *Boy, you broke our promise . . .*

No, he couldn't tell anyone. And since he couldn't talk about it, he stopped saying much of anything. Maki was not pleased, and she kept asking him why he was so cranky. Yoichi Miyashita would sidle up to him for a chat, take one look at his face, and then move off again. Anego had stopped being worried and was just plain annoyed. Mamoru wouldn't even talk to Takano, who had discharged himself from the hospital so he could take care of year-end business in Books at Laurel.

A week after his first visit, Koichi Yoshitake came back, this time by himself, to hear Taizo's decision. Taizo and Yoriko had talked the matter over endlessly between themselves, and on occasion with Maki and Mamoru, too. They discussed the money they needed to live on and the difficulties Taizo would have finding another job at his age. Shin Nippon had recently gone into the rental furniture business, and the job Yoshitake had for Taizo would have him loading trucks according to the order forms he was handed. They had finally decided to accept the offer.

Yoshitake was delighted with the decision.

When they heard his car pull up, Maki tiptoed to the window to see what kind of car he had come in. She whistled in admiration.

"Is it an import?"

"No, he's definitely not a snob. I read an article he wrote about cars. Japanese cars are second to none, he said, and that's why he always drives domestic models."

Mamoru's first impression was that Yoshitake looked much younger and healthier than he did in photographs. His skin was deeply tanned, set off perfectly by the color of his shirt.

The Asano family was painfully aware of the difficult position he had put himself in by testifying about Taizo's accident. They knew that he had had to endure ridicule. Mamoru and Maki were unsure what sort of an expression they should present when Taizo introduced them to Yoshitake as his son and daughter.

Yoshitake, however, appeared to have no qualms at all. He praised the meal Yoriko had fretted over making for him; he expressed joy at Taizo's decision; and he answered Maki's questions with details of business trips he had taken overseas, trends in interior decoration, and information on the latest fashions.

Maki was spellbound as he described his first visit to Sotheby's, where he submitted the winning bid for a beautiful long pipe the Dowager Empress had used in the Forbidden City during the late Qing Dynasty. Maki hadn't looked so relaxed and happy since her father's accident.

"The Dowager Empress loved her luxuries, didn't she?"

"That's what they say. She was probably one of the reasons why the Qing Dynasty was overthrown. She supposedly had two thousand robes to wear. Have you ever seen the movie *The Last Emperor*?"

"Yes, it was wonderful!"

Mamoru had been to see it with Maki, and he distinctly remembered that she had slept through half of it, but he decided not to mention that. The whole time Yoshitake was in the house, Mamoru had the nagging sense that he had met him somewhere before. But where?

Before Yoshitake left, Mamoru sneaked a look out the window. That silver gray car—now he remembered. The night he had gone to Yoko Sugano's apartment, Yoshitake had been standing at the intersection where she had died.

After the family said their farewell at the front door and Yoshitake left the house, Mamoru slipped outside. Yoshitake had his hand in his pocket searching for his key.

Even rich men lose track of their keys, thought Mamoru.

Yoshitake noticed him standing there and called out, "Sorry for staying so long. Did I leave something behind?" He favored Mamoru with a well-rehearsed make-the-sale smile.

"Do you mind if I ask you a strange question?" Mamoru began.

"What's on your mind?"

"Mr. Yoshitake, I saw you at the intersection where Miss Sugano got hit. It was the Sunday after the accident, at two or two-thirty in the morning."

Yoshitake gave Mamoru a long, hard look. His eyes finally softened and he smiled.

"I guess I've been found out. How did you know?"

"I saw you. I go running, and that night I ran out to see where it had happened."

"I see." Yoshitake reached into his shirt pocket, pulled out a pack of cigarettes, and lit up.

"I remember the smell of your cigarettes, too. They're unusual."

Yoshitake laughed. "I'll be more careful the next time I go out on covert activities."

The purple smoke was lovely.

"I want to thank you," said Mamoru. "A lot was at stake for you, and you still came forward."

"That was a big fuss put on by the mass media. You don't have to worry about my private life. My wife won't divorce me, and I won't lose my position in the company. Just because I was adopted into my wife's family doesn't mean I can't take care of myself. I've learned my lesson. I've decided I need to be more upfront about the role I play in the company, and I'm ready to do just that."

Mamoru smiled in relief, and Yoshitake went on. "It's you and your sister I need to apologize to. I left the scene and waited to see if some other witness would come forward. I'm sorry for the grief that must have caused you."

"But you went to the police in the end."

"Of course I did. It was only right." Yoshitake's expression changed to one of concern. "Haven't you lost some weight?"

"Me?" Mamoru was surprised.

"That's right. Now it's my turn to catch you off guard! I came around here even before the police did. I thought of talking to your family before deciding what to do. In the end I didn't, but I did see you."

Mamoru tried to think when that could have been. "Were you in this car?"

"That's right."

Now he remembered. "You were parked by the riverbank."

Yoshitake nodded. "You were running. Your cheeks weren't quite so sunken in."

"Is that so?" Mamoru realized Yoshitake could well be right. He hadn't had a moment's rest since that mysterious phone conversation.

"Look," Yoshitake began slowly. "This was an unfortunate situation. But I'm glad that I got a chance to get to know you and your family. My wife and I don't have any children of our own."

He smiled gently. It was the sort of smile that could touch your heart. "I'm glad to have met you and your sister. If you ever have any problems, I hope you'll feel free to come see me. If it's in my power, I'll do my best to help you out."

"Thank you," said Mamoru. "Thanks for everything."

Yoshitake looked Mamoru straight in the eye as he spoke again. "I owe it to your father. I'm only doing what's right."

As the days went by, Mamoru began to forget where things stood. Every once in a while, he began to think that the mysterious caller would never contact him again. Maybe it was all over and there was nothing to be afraid of. But then, in the next instant, he remembered what the caller had said: *I'll let you know when it's time to get rid of the fourth one*, and he knew that this was the reality of the situation.

There were no reports on the news or in the newspapers about the death of anyone named Kazuko Takagi. Mamoru had been looking for a way to contact her. But just as the caller had said, there was no way for him to find her.

It wasn't an unusual name. He had looked it up in the phone book and started calling all of them, but none were the Kazuko Takagi he was looking for. She might not even live in Tokyo, and Kazuko Takagi might not even be her real name. Mamoru finally gave up on that idea. All he'd got out of it was a sore throat from so much talking.

He would just have to wait. But when the time came, he would stop the murder. He would not let Kazuko Takagi die, he told himself.

The only question was why the mysterious caller had contacted Mamoru in the first place. What had he meant when he said *we have lots in common*? He had told Mamoru that he'd explain it all when the time came. For now, all Mamoru could do was wait. He clenched his teeth in an effort to keep up his courage.

One night when he got back from running, there was an unfamiliar car in front of the house. The passenger door opened and Maki stepped out. The man in the driver's seat was talking to her, but Maki got out and started to walk away without a backward glance.

The man got out, walked around to the other side of the car to intercept her, and grabbed her arm. Mamoru was ready to run to her side, but Maki shook the man's hand off and slapped him in the face.

Then she ran into the house and slammed the door. Mamoru walked past the man, who was standing there in shock, and followed his cousin inside.

Maki wasn't crying. On the contrary, she looked almost cheerful.

"Well, that was impressive," Mamoru said, and Maki started laughing. "So that was Maekawa?"

"That was him. He started acting strange as soon as Dad had that accident. I'm sure he thought that anyone as elite as himself could never be bothered with a girl whose father was in prison."

"But he didn't go to prison." Thanks to the efforts of the lawyer Sayama, Taizo's own unblemished record, and the settlement with Yoko Sugano's family, the final sentence would most likely be a summary claim, the bare minimum for a driver hitting a pedestrian. He would only have to pay a fine.

"I was lucky to find out what he was really like, but it took me a while to finally give up on him. I don't like him anymore, but I didn't want people to think I'd been jilted. I was proud because so many of the other girls liked him. I guess I wasn't any less of a snob than he was."

"You'll find a better guy."

"Yup. The next one won't be so concerned with appearances."

"I know someone who would never pay attention to what people think."

"You'll have to introduce me to him."

Mamoru was referring to Takano, but he was not in a position to introduce his boss to his cousin at the moment, since their relationship was strained. And Mamoru knew it was his fault, but he believed Takano could be targeted because Mamoru depended on him. He was also worried that he might end up telling Takano about the mysterious caller. He was keeping his distance from him to avoid just that.

In the end, it was Takano who came to see Mamoru, on December thirtieth.

———•———

"I know it's a busy time of the year," said Takano. "I hope I'm not disturbing you." He looked much better, and you couldn't even see his bandages under the large sweater he was wearing.

"You're all better! I guess that'll put your fan club at ease."

"My fan club?"

Maki came discreetly into the room with a tray of refreshments. She gracefully set the coffee cups in front of the young men, gave Takano the subtle yet enticing smile that was the hallmark of an ace hostess, and quietly left the room.

"That was probably the newest member," Mamoru laughed. "But you'd better watch out, she's not nearly as meek as she looks."

The two chatted for a while longer about nothing in particular. Mamoru still didn't know why Takano had come. Or maybe he was pretending not to know.

"I came today for a reason," Takano said finally, setting down his empty coffee cup. "You've been acting strangely, Mamoru. I came to see how you were doing. We can't really talk at the store. You're almost rude when I talk to you on the phone."

"I'm sorry." It was painful to see that Takano was not so much upset as worried about him.

"Nothing bothering you?"

"No, and I'm sorry I gave you that impression." Mamoru wondered whether the lie was written across his face.

"Well then, I'm relieved to hear it. As long as that's taken care of, let me ask you for your opinion on something."

"My opinion?"

"First let me explain. It's about that girl who tried to jump off the roof. I've thought about it long and hard, but I just can't come up with a satisfactory explanation."

Mamoru remembered Takano talking about the girl while he was in the hospital. "You said she was an honor student, and not the type to cause trouble, right?"

"Yes, and that's what bothers me. Also the way her mother acted when it happened; I can't figure it out. Let me explain a little more." All of a sudden Takano got very serious. "Have you ever heard of kleptomania?"

"What's that?"

"It means someone who has a pathological need to steal. A person who has an irresistible impulse to take things even when they don't need them, and even if they have the money to pay for them. They steal and shoplift. It's a form of obsessive behavior."

Since he was at a public high school, Mamoru had not had the benefit of taking classes in psychology, and could only answer, "So are you saying that this girl had . . . that?"

"Yes, both she and her parents are at a loss as to how to deal with it. She's seeing a specialist."

"That must be tough."

So when she kept saying how frightened she was, she must have been afraid of her own lack of control.

"And then there's that Kakiyama guy who attacked Makino and me."

"I haven't heard any more about him. Is it true he was high on drugs?"

Takano shook his head. "He's got a record of using drugs, but he was clean when it all happened. His blood test afterward was negative."

"Wow! But you know I read somewhere that once you're hooked on drugs, you can still see things and lose control even after you stop taking them."

"Flashbacks. Yes, the police said that, too."

"Something tells me you're not convinced."

Takano had a distinctly skeptical look on his face. He finally answered, "These two incidents happened within ten days of each other, but nothing like them had ever happened at Laurel before. Don't you think that's strange?"

"It's just a coincidence. They're completely unrelated."

"Do you really think so? All of this started after we started that contract with the Ad Academy."

"Ad Academy?"

"That video display, remember? They're the company that runs it."

Mamoru remembered the logo he had seen on the screen. He was sure he had seen it somewhere before.

"The official name has 'marketing' or some word like that in it, but it's generally just known as Ad Academy. They're getting more and more large retail clients—family restaurants and other chains."

"Are they an advertising agency?"

"I don't think so. It's not that straightforward. They consult on sales promotions, training personnel, marketing research—whatever you want. I've read their brochure. They sound like snake oil salesmen to me. But it's a fact that their clients are showing increased sales. That's why Laurel signed up with them."

"So is there something like intimidation or bribes involved?"

Takano laughed. "No, that's not it. It would be a lot easier if it were."

It turned out that the bad rumors about Ad Academy were of a more technical nature.

"One of my friends from college—he was a few years ahead of me, and he now works at the research center of a major corporation—told me that Ad Academy had used a new, very subtle stimulant drug at a department store. It didn't have to be swallowed or injected; all a person had to do was inhale it. They spread it throughout the store through the air conditioning system. There's no actual proof that this happened, but the information I got was reliable."

"What good would a stimulant do? Make the customers come running or something?"

"Stimulate their desire to buy things."

Mamoru listened open-mouthed.

"You've heard of impulse purchasing, haven't you? People buy things they don't need and that cost more than they can afford. Afterward they regret it. If a store could artificially induce such an impulse, all they would have to do is sit back and watch their stock fly off the shelves."

"So it's like when customers get all excited when things go on sale?"

"Exactly! Laurel always plays uptempo music during the sales. More soothing music is played in the furniture and jewelry sections—we don't want the customers walking quickly past them. We're controlling their impulses to a certain degree. Ad Academy takes it all several steps further."

"It sounds creepy."

"And it's different again at restaurants. It's not your stomach that tells you you're hungry, it's your brain. There's a part of the brain that controls appetite. It commands you to eat when your stomach is empty and stop when it's full. Would you believe me if I told you that part of your brain could be tricked into commanding you to eat when you're full by using drugs, music, or low-frequency sound waves?"

"You mean you'd want to eat even though you were stuffed full?"

"Right! And sales would skyrocket. For a while, it was popular to lose weight using hypnosis. It's using the same principles to induce the opposite."

Mamoru tried to put it all together. "So what you're saying is that Ad Academy is doing something like that at Laurel?"

"I'm sure of it."

"But how did the two accidents prove that?"

"Side effects," Takano said without a hint of doubt. "The victims suffered side effects. It's the same with any medicine. I'm allergic to penicillin—I'd die of shock if I was given a shot. Some people can't use detergent because it irritates their skin. The sales promotion methods developed by Ad Academy are bound to be unsuitable for some people.

"The girl who tried to commit suicide and the man who attacked me had something in common. Both used or had used medication. I found out that the girl took tranquilizers for chronic depression. Kakiyama had been on drugs. Flashbacks can be caused by something as innocuous as a glass of beer or a dose of flu medicine."

It all sounded alarming.

"So you believe that Ad Academy is using something like a stimulant to get people to spend more money, and that stimulant reacted with the medicine those two took and made them lose control? Is that what you're saying?"

"That's what I thought at first, but then I got stuck." Takano sighed. "I asked the staff in charge of building management, but they said there was no sign of any tampering. To disperse drugs into the air would take large, invasive equipment. It's not just a matter of tossing drugs out here and there. And that Kakiyama—he was clean when the police tested him for drugs, and I don't think Ad Academy is capable of producing chemicals that can't be detected."

"So you're back at square one?"

"That's what I want—"

There was a knock at the door, and Maki peeked in. "You two have a lot to talk about. Would you like some more coffee?" She walked in with a pot of coffee and slices of cheesecake. "I just whipped this up. I hope you like sweets?"

Maki had completely recovered from her broken heart, Mamoru realized as he watched his cousin cheerfully pouring them coffee.

"What were you saying about Ad Academy?" asked Maki, as she discreetly settled onto a chair.

"Hmm?"

"Isn't that what you were talking about? I couldn't help but overhear. I had a really bad experience with them."

Now Takano was interested. "What happened?"

"Oh, I remember!" interrupted Mamoru. He hadn't meant to, but he suddenly recalled what she was talking about. "That sneak preview!"

Maki gave Mamoru a subtle look that clearly warned him to stay out of her way, and turned back to Takano.

"That's right. There was a sneak preview of a movie sponsored by Ad Academy and a cosmetics company. The movie was all right, but afterward in the hall outside the theater, the cosmetics company had set up a huge display of their new products and was selling them to the audience as they left. I bought a pile of things I didn't need. I regretted it as soon as I got home, but I couldn't just throw them out, right?"

"I suppose not."

Takano's brief response encouraged Maki on. "So I used them and broke out in a horrible rash. They still send me invitations to movies, but I've never been since."

"Yeah, but you gave me a ticket once." That was where Mamoru had seen the logo before.

"But you didn't go, did you?"

"I can't remember. Anyway, you were the one who spent all that money. You should be blaming yourself and not them."

"I just got caught up in the moment. I never usually buy things like that. I'm careful about the makeup I use."

All of a sudden Takano whistled. "That's it!"

"What do you mean?"

"Maki, you didn't get caught up in the moment. They used subliminal advertising on you."

Maki and Mamoru looked at each other blankly. "Submarine advertising?"

"No! *Subliminal*. Subliminal advertising."

Takano thought a second and then asked Mamoru. "Do you have a dictionary?"

Maki stood up and ran to her room. She came back with a dictionary the size of a phone book.

While Takano was looking the word up, Mamoru whispered to Maki, "What are *you* doing with such a huge dictionary?"

"It was a bingo prize at one of the parties I went to. It was awful—I had to lug it all the way home."

"Here it is!" Takano showed them the page. It was under "advertising."

> Subliminal advertising: Advertising that appeals to the unconscious. An image flashed on a screen or a sound aired over the radio that is too quick to be registered consciously, but has sufficient stimulus to convey a message to the viewer to use or go out and buy a certain product. This method of advertising was presented simultaneously in 1957 by the American J. Vicary and a company by the name of Precon Process and Equipment. They claimed that when commercials one-three-thousandth to one-twentieth of a second long were spliced into films at five-second intervals, the audience would not be conscious of them but the impressions would remain in their unconscious. The result was a fifty-percent increase in theater popcorn sales and a thirty-percent increase in sales of Coca-Cola. Such ads were subsequently banned by the Federal Trade Commission for ethical reasons.

"That means that while you were watching the movie, Maki, you were watching ads for cosmetics without being aware of it," said Takano.

Mamoru was finally beginning to understand. "There was a *Columbo* episode called 'Double Exposure,' and that was the trick behind the murder."

"Right, that's what I'm talking about!"

"It's not right!" Maki was fuming.

"Japan has yet to outlaw subliminal advertising because there are doubts about whether it really works. I'm sure Ad Academy would use it if they could. Anyway, this was what I came up with when I realized no stimulants were involved."

"You mean the video display!" shouted Mamoru.

"Yes. Ad Academy wanted to score with a major client, so they came to us with their latest system—that video display."

The three were quiet for a few seconds until Maki spoke in an uncharacteristically serious tone.

"But didn't you say they weren't sure whether it really worked?"

"Yes, it hasn't been proven, but that doesn't mean it *doesn't* work. And Ad Academy might have figured out how to make subliminal effects actually work in ways nobody else has even thought of yet. They might be using sounds and colors, not just the visuals themselves."

Mamoru shifted in his seat. "We've got to stop them! We can't have any more accidents."

Takano slowly shook his head. "I looked it up, and there are no articles about subliminal ads causing psychotic episodes. Theoretically it's not possible. No matter how they're doing it, it's only advertising."

So that's why Takano had said he was stuck.

"Have sales suddenly gone up for no apparent reason?" Maki tried to help out.

"No. Sales are always high at the end of the year. We're seeing exactly the curve we predicted."

"It's been forty days since they installed that display. The worst might be yet to come."

"But the problem is still the same. No matter how much money we make, who wants advertising that causes dangerous behavior in the customers? Even the guys in charge can't be that greedy."

Takano took a sip of his coffee, which had now gone cold. Mamoru crossed his arms across his chest and leaned against the wall.

"Have there been any other changes?" Maki was doing everything she could to help Takano out. "Have there been any customers who have been overly pleasant?"

"Customers? Or employees?"

"Customers. Have any of them praised the products excessively? Some other kind of brain short-circuit that could have been caused by stimulants?"

"People get excited about different things. Some people adore money, while others like our Sato get turned on by photos of mountains and deserts."

"What do you get excited about, Mamoru?" Maki playfully tapped him on the head with the tray she had in her hand. Takano laughed.

"Wait a minute," said Mamoru as he ducked another knock on the head. "There was someone who was overly excited recently. Makino."

Takano raised his eyebrows in disbelief. "Him? He's from the Self-Defense Forces. He'd hum to himself while he watched a coup d'état being carried out before his very eyes.

"And then pick up pieces of the grenades to take home as souvenirs. But he was high that one time when he caught that shoplifter who already had eight arrests on his record. He caught two high-school students right before that. He was on a roll. Not only that, but when I asked him about it later, he said he was bored. Not just him but the other security guards. He said that shoplifting had dropped dramatically."

"In other sales areas, too?" Takano repeated himself almost as if thinking out loud. "Shoplifting is down?"

"You must have that data, Takano."

"We never know how much we've lost from shoplifting until we do the inventory. But now that you mention it . . ."

Mamoru and Maki watched him in concern.

Gradually his expression began to brighten. "That's it!" he exclaimed. "Shoplifting! Ad Academy developed the ads not to increase sales but to cut losses from shoplifting!"

The Books section alone lost over four million yen a year. Madame Anzai had grumbled about how they were working for free one month out of the year.

"But would they go to the trouble of installing an enormous piece of equipment just for that? It has to be cheaper to hire more security guards."

"Listen for a minute," said Takano as he turned to Mamoru. "First of all, that display has a decorative effect in the store. It airs information about different products, so it's used for advertising, too. Now, splice in some shots that would keep customers from shoplifting—two birds with one stone! You're right, Mamoru. Shoplifting prevention alone would never be enough to cover costs—it would be easier to take the losses from stolen goods. But what if subliminal effects were an extra benefit added to something used mainly for advertising? It would be a lot more effective than depending on security guards with varying abilities."

But you know, he was sloppy today. That's what Makino had said about one of the shoplifters he had caught. *It's not the way he usually operates.* Mamoru distinctly recalled Makino's surprise at how easy it had been to catch him.

"They must show scenes of shoplifters being caught or security guards running after them that send a subliminal message. Thefts fall and thieves are easier to catch. While they're slipping things into their bags, the video convinces them they will almost certainly be caught for doing it.

"The girl and the man who had those psychotic episodes had something in common. They both had mental vulnerabilities. One was neurotic about her inclination to steal things, and the other was a drug addict with a criminal record. Now send messages to their unconscious that they are on the verge of being caught by the police. It's like stepping on landmines in their brains."

"It's awful," shivered Maki. "We humans like to believe we are acting on our own free will."

I can bend people's will to my own. Once again Mamoru heard the voice of the mysterious caller. *I know you might not be able to believe it yet. But I can do it.*

"Let's check it out," Mamoru said with decision. "The tape must be in the Laurel security control room. We should see what we can find on it."

Takano slapped his knee. "You're right, but how? The door's locked and nobody can get in unless they have business there. The tapes are locked away in a cabinet inside. And I'm sorry to say that I don't have either of those keys."

Here we go again, thought Mamoru. He wondered what he ought to do at times like this.

Maki seemed to sense that Mamoru had something to say, so she stood up to give the two some privacy. "I've got to get these dishes washed. You two take your time."

After she left, Takano turned to face Mamoru. Mamoru was still at a loss. He had never told anyone what he had learned from Gramps. He had planned to keep it to himself, but he was wondering whether Takano would believe him otherwise.

"You know, Takano," he began. "I think I can probably get into that room and get the tapes out."

"You?"

"It's hard to explain, and I really don't want to try, so I'm asking you to just take my word for it."

Takano thought for a few moments. "That time you got out onto the roof to save the girl—you said the door was unlocked . . ." He had a serious look on his face. "But when I checked later, there was a lock on it. Are you planning to do something . . . like that, again?"

Mamoru nodded.

Takano thought for a good two minutes. Finally he spoke.

"Okay then, how do we do it?"

———•———

They decided to go into action the next evening, New Year's Eve. Once the store closed that night, it wouldn't open again until January third, so they would have some time. After closing, employees were treated to a brief party in which they formally celebrated the end of work for the calendar year. When it was over, Mamoru pretended to leave, but instead hid himself in the restroom. After a half hour or so, the halls went silent and all the lights were turned off except for the emergency lights and those in the room for the security guards. Mamoru took a penlight out of his pocket, and stepped out into the darkened store.

He had checked out his route during the day, so he had no trouble finding his way. He avoided security cameras by staying low and close to the walls. From time to time he pulled out a small can of deodorant and sprayed it so he could make out the infrared security rays in the tiny particles of deodorant that filled the air.

Mamoru had spent the afternoon talking to the security guards and walking around the store. He even read the brochure of the security firm contracted by Laurel. As far as he could tell, nobody had been the least bit suspicious. One of the guards had been so pleased at the show of interest in his occupation that he had gone to great lengths to explain how it all worked.

Mamoru knew that most of the people he worked with considered him cooperative and diligent. He also knew that he had learned from his mother how to wear a look of blank innocence, and, walking through the store halls that night, he was grateful for both.

Opening the security control room door was the work of a few moments. The lock was operated by inputting a password on a panel of buttons with the numbers one to twelve and the letters A, B, and C.

Mamoru knelt down and shone his penlight onto the buttons. Of the fifteen, five reflected slightly less of a shine than the others due to the oil from fingers pressing them.

Out came Mamoru's baking powder. He carefully brushed it onto the five buttons. Of the five, four bore the perfect fingerprints of the person who had been here last. The numbers were 3, 7, and 9, and the letter A. Mamoru pulled out a pocket computer on which he planned to implement a program that would work out all the possible combinations of these. This was something neither Mamoru nor Gramps had developed—it was advertised as boldly as you pleased in a computer magazine.

So far so good. Then Mamoru realized something. The Joto district store was number 379 of the Laurel chain. All he had to do was figure out where the A came in, and that meant there were only four possible combinations. The winner was 3A79. That hadn't been too hard.

Once Mamoru was inside he had to open the locked cabinet that contained the tapes for the video display. Somehow "cabinet" didn't seem like the right word. It was more like a safe with a combination lock. This alone seemed to prove that Ad Academy had something to hide.

Before he got started on the lock, Mamoru looked around the tiny room. If the combination to the door lock was any indication, the person in charge here was not particularly cautious. Mamoru thought he might find a memo with the combination in a drawer, under the telephone, in a flower vase, or under the carpet.

Nothing. Maybe the security guard carried the memo with him. Mamoru gave up and got down to work.

First of all he put one end of a thin pencil lead into the center rotating part of the dial, and attached a piece of white paper to the other end. It looked like the needle and roll of paper used to record the strength of an earthquake.

Mamoru then put his left ear against the cold wall of the cabinet and began turning the dial. At certain points, there was a faint sound of pins lining up and the entire lock responding. These were the movements that the pencil lead would pick up and record on the paper. Mamoru then examined the record and counted the peaks, then turned the dial according to his calculations.

It took about thirty minutes. Covered in sweat, Mamoru grabbed the three tapes, retraced his steps back through the hallways, and exited the building through the restroom window. The in-store alarms were only activated if the window was opened from the outside.

Takano was waiting for him in the parking lot. He opened the door of his car and motioned Mamoru into it. "A friend of mine is waiting for us at his editing studio. Come on, let's go!"

The studio engineer was a college friend of Takano's. His name was Kamoshida, and he was a large man who looked like a gentle-natured bear in a children's cartoon.

The studio was still new, with sparkling white linoleum floors and clean, soundproofed walls. The entire operation was computer-operated, and it was equipped with a keyboard and footage counter.

Kamoshida got right to work. He fed the first video Mamoru had "borrowed" into the computer by inputting the address signal of each frame to get it to show up on the screen. Each second of tape had thirty frames, so it was a time-consuming process. The tape revealed its first secret in the twenty-fifth frame: a still of a security guard grabbing the arms of a male customer in a store that looked like Laurel. The customer had a look of abject disbelief on his face.

The next imbedded shot showed three policemen with their hands on the nightsticks attached to their belts, running toward the camera so fast that their sleeves billowed out.

A man being held down by two officers, his arm twisted behind him.

A woman being chased by a security guard, her head turned to look behind her and her mouth open in a silent scream.

Shot after shot buried like ugly stains among the scenes of the red fall leaves, the south sea paradise, and the fashion show featured on the video display.

Kamoshida gave a low whistle. "So this is the prescription for shop-lifting . . ."

Takano groaned. "Nobody knows why people are driven to shoplift. This is no more than intimidation."

"And it's what triggered those psychotic episodes," said Mamoru, peering at the screen.

"What this must do to people with mental bombs inside them!" Takano added.

Kamoshida swiveled his chair around and looked at Mamoru and Takano. "The effects of subliminal advertising are not widely acknowledged, are they? Could you really use this to prove cause and effect?"

"Well, they were using this tape when those incidents occurred."

"That's true, you saw the footage of the leaves. There's no problem there. But you can't prove that these shots were in the video when you saw it or when the incidents took place." Kamoshida shrugged. "I'll tell you what. I'll spend the night removing all of those shots from all three tapes. But Ad Academy is sure to come back with new ones. You can't stop them indefinitely."

Takano sat for a while staring at the empty screen and thinking. Eventually he spoke. "Could you copy these for me?"

In the silence of the studio, they heard the sound of the thermostat clicking on. Mamoru shivered.

———•———

Kazuko Takagi spent the last days of the year in a coffee shop called Cerberus in a town far away from both her apartment and her parent's home.

Cerberus was a tiny place that would be packed with ten customers. It was run by a man named Mitamura who was the same age as Kazuko. About a week after she had left her apartment and found a place that rented by the week, she was sitting on a park bench when Mitamura approached her.

"What are you doing here every day?"

Kazuko looked up, but did not answer. She was pretty sure what he would say next. *Haven't I met you somewhere before?* Or, *If you're not doing anything, why don't we go do something together?*

Just as she'd thought, he'd said "How about a cup of coffee at that place over there?" He pointed to Cerberus on the other side of the street. "I can guarantee that it's good because it's my shop."

Kazuko blinked slowly in surprise. She looked at him and then at the Cerberus sign.

He laughed. "I murdered the owner and took it over. There's a dead body under the floorboards. Come on, it's just a joke. It's really mine. At least one of the columns must be. The rest still belongs to the bank."

"Why are you inviting me?" Kazuko asked shortly.

"Some of my regular customers are mothers of children who go to that kindergarten over there. There seems to be a misunderstanding between them and you."

Kazuko glanced over at the kindergarten that was next to the park. Children wearing navy blue uniforms played happily on the tiny grounds.

"The mothers are worried because I sit here every day looking in that direction?"

"That's right. There have been a lot of crimes against children lately. They're all nervous."

Now Kazuko had to laugh. She hadn't been staring at the kindergarten on purpose. Here she was feeling that she was the one in danger as she sat alone with a desperate look on her face. No wonder they were afraid she'd kidnap one of their kids!

"Now there's a smile!" The man grinned. "Anyone who can laugh like that must be all right. I'll talk to the mothers. So how about that coffee to apologize for being rude?"

That was how Kazuko had found herself in Cerberus. It had a strange name but it was a comfortable place to be. The coffee was strong and hot. Mitamura had introduced himself and told her all about his travails in getting the shop on its feet. He talked about it as if it had been nothing at all. The one thing he didn't do was ask her name.

"Who named your shop?" she asked as she perched on a stool.

"I named it myself. It's different, don't you think?"

"Yes, it sounds like a monster or something."

"That's exactly what it is. It's the name of the dog that guards the gates of Hell in Greek mythology."

"Why did you name it that?"

"This shop *is* the gate to Hell. When customers go back out the door they will be leaving Hell behind them. No matter how bad things get, they'll never get any worse than this."

Kazuko smiled and gratefully accepted Mitamura's offer. After that she went to Cerberus every day. Mitamura was always too busy to talk when there were other customers, but Kazuko enjoyed just watching him.

"What are your plans for New Year's? Are you taking a trip?" Mitamura broached the subject on the afternoon of New Year's Eve.

Kazuko shook her head. "I've got no plans. I'll be at home alone."

She had already told her parents not to expect her. She didn't want to make it any easier for her pursuer to follow her.

Pursuer. Kazuko clearly saw herself as someone who was being chased.

"I'll close this evening and then open up after midnight when the date changes to New Year's Day. Customers stop in on their way back from visiting the local shrine. How about coming to the shrine with me before I open up? It'll be cold so late at night, but it feels good."

Kazuko agreed. She realized she was scared when she was alone, but it wasn't so bad when someone was with her. "Can I ask you to do something for me?" she asked.

"What's that?"

"Would you go with me to my apartment? It's kind of far, and there's something I want to pick up."

Mitamura looked at her seriously for a moment. She could see in his eyes that he was wondering what sort of life she was living. He finally answered, "Sure, no problem."

Mitamura drove her to her apartment in his old Mini Cooper, apologizing for the state it was in. "I spend all my money paying back the loan on my shop, so there's nothing left for a new car."

"A car is fine as long as it runs, I'd say."

There were five or six envelopes in her mailbox. They were ads for catalogs and credit cards, nothing that concerned her. There was one, though, that had nothing written on it. Kazuko opened it. There was a brief note.

```
I think I can help you, the last one left. Come to Ginza
Mullion at 3 p.m. on January 7. I'll talk to you. Don't
say a thing to anyone, and be careful. You're in danger.
```

Kazuko stood stock still with the letter in her hand. Mitamura walked up to her.

"What's the matter? Is someone after you because you haven't paid your rent?" Then he noticed that she'd gone pale right down to her fingertips. "What's the matter?" he asked again, and this time he meant it.

Kazuko handed him the letter. Mitamura read it and looked up. "What is it?"

Kazuko began to shake and couldn't stop. She stood there for a long time gripping Mitamura's arm. Finally, she spoke. "Will you believe that I'm not crazy? I've been telling nothing but lies, and everyone has believed them. If I tell the truth now, I don't think anyone would believe me."

She began talking, and told him everything.

Mitamura suggested that she follow the instructions in the letter. "I'll go with you. There will be lots of people there. It should be all right. We've got to find out what this person has to say."

"I'll be murdered."

"Of course you won't. You're not alone anymore."

That night, Kazuko paid up what she owed on the apartment, took her things, and moved into Cerberus. That was when she finally allowed herself to cry.

Later on the way back from the shrine, there was a young girl passing out leaflets by the road. She stood in front of a sign that said The Teachings of the Lord. She was singing hymns with another woman who appeared to be her mother. The two had beautiful, clear voices.

"It's a mini New Year's mass," Mitamura smiled.

The girl came up to Kazuko and handed her a leaflet. "This is a Bible verse. Please read it. God bless you."

Kazuko took the leaflet. She suddenly felt that it was something valuable and holy. She opened it up when she was back in Mitamura's car, and her gaze fell on a verse from the Book of Revelations. Startled by the ominous tone of the words, she quickly balled up the leaflet and threw it in the ashtray on the dashboard.

"What did it say?" asked Mitamura.

"I didn't understand it," she muttered.

Kazuko looked outside. Before long the sun would rise and the night would be over. It was a new year in a new town. But a phrase from that leaflet was engraved indelibly on her heart.

There, as I looked, was another horse, sickly pale; its rider's name was Death and the darkness obeyed him.

If Mamoru Kusaka didn't hurry, Kazuko was fated to die in a week.

CHAPTER

6

The Sorcerer

When Laurel reopened on January third, Mamoru and Takano were the only ones not in the holiday spirit.

"They acted like they didn't know what was going on." Mamoru had asked how his discussion with the management had gone, and Takano clenched his fist in frustration as he spoke. "I showed them the copy of the tape, and they didn't even flinch. When I pressed them, they asked if I could prove that the two incidents had been caused by it—and then they told me that if I continued to snoop around, it would be bad for the people who worked under me."

"You mean me and the others?"

"They're smart. They knew I'd put my own job on the line, but I wouldn't risk hurting any of the rest of you." Mamoru and Takano looked over at the video display. "I'll find a way to get that thing out of here," Takano vowed.

There were other reasons why Mamoru was having problems getting excited about the New Year. The anonymous caller still hadn't got in touch with him, and the stress of waiting was stretching him to the breaking point.

The Books section was full of children clutching their New Year's gift money. Mamoru helped out at the cash register, and had his hands full ringing up games, books, and manga for them. Mamoru envied Sato, far away from Japan, probably covered in the dust of some desert.

Standing at the cash register was a child who had obviously been strong-armed by his mother into purchasing a collection of classic literature. As he held out his money, his eyes turned wistfully in the direction of the section filled with colorful manga characters. Mamoru felt sorry for the kid, and handed him a sheet of stickers of one of the characters along with his change. The boy's eyes shone at the unexpected gift.

"Thanks!"

Mamoru motioned him to put it in his pocket. Just then he heard someone calling him.

"Kusaka!" It was Yoshitake, standing out from the smaller clientele.

"This is the best we can do at Laurel, sorry." Yoshitake had invited Mamoru to have lunch with him, and Mamoru had suggested the Chinese restaurant in the fifth floor food court. Mamoru knew that Yoshitake had probably eaten in much better restaurants around the world, but this was about as far as he could go on his break.

Yoshitake wiped his hands with the hot towel the waitress held out to him, and smiled. "Don't worry about it. I wish you could see what I have for lunch most days. It's usually fast food."

"Really?"

"Yes, really. Hot rice and miso soup is the most delicious food I can think of. It was what I dreamed of when I was living in flophouses."

Yoshitake ordered some of the pricier menu items, with lychee fruit for dessert. The waiter cocked his head doubtfully as he headed back into the kitchen with their order. Mamoru was suddenly worried that they might not actually have lychee in stock.

"I stopped by your house and found out you were working here during the vacation." Taizo and Yoriko were having a "New Year's in bed." Taizo especially was not used to the lifting involved in his new job and had hurt his back. Mamoru could just imagine them rushing around when Yoshitake appeared unexpectedly on their doorstep.

When their food came, the older man encouraged his young companion to dig in. "You'd better eat. It looks like you'll have your hands full again this afternoon."

"My family's going to be jealous of me eating so well so early in the day!"

"Next time, let's all go out together. At home it's just me and my wife, and we never have noisy meals together."

"Are you working today, Mr. Yoshitake?" Mamoru had imagined that company executives took longer and more leisurely vacations.

"I've got lots of things to sort out. I'd rather be working. If I went back to Hawaii, it'd only be crawling with Japanese and I'd end up running into someone I didn't want to see."

"Hawaii?" Now Mamoru noticed that Yoshitake was even more deeply tanned than before.

"All I did was play golf. My wife's still there and she's probably bored."

"Sounds good to me."

"You'll have to come visit me there. I bought a condominium with a view of Waikiki Beach. I'll feed you better than anything you'd get at a hotel." Yoshitake pulled out a box of chocolates, a typical souvenir from an overseas trip. "Share this with your friends in the Books section. They'll be needing the sugar to help with the fatigue."

He was definitely what Maki would call an "American uncle." Mamoru remembered a story that she'd told him, about a man from a poor family who'd gone to make his fortune in the States. He got rich and the money he sent back to his family enabled them to live happily, but he was alone and craved their love. It was the sort of story Maki loved. Mamoru smiled in spite of himself and Yoshitake asked him what he was thinking about.

"Whoops, sorry. It's really nothing. I was just thinking about an uncle."

"An uncle?"

Mamoru had to think fast. "I mean my uncle! He's getting used to his new job, and he looks pretty cheerful these days. It's all thanks to you." Mamoru suddenly remembered that Yoshitake didn't know about his background, and he grimaced in embarrassment.

Yoshitake laughed at his expression.

"The Asanos have adopted me. It's not official; I have a different surname. Maki and I are cousins."

"What about your parents?" Yoshitake asked slowly.

"My mother died. As for my father—" Mamoru hesitated. "I guess you could say he's dead; he's long gone."

Right when he started working for Shin Nippon Enterprises, Taizo had heard that Yoshitake was from Hirakawa. Mamoru thought he might have known about Toshio Kusaka and waited for a reaction, but there was none.

There followed a few awkward moments until their dessert arrived. Mamoru decided that maybe he could talk to Yoshitake about what was bothering him. "Mr. Yoshitake, do you think that it's possible to make someone do something against their will?"

Yoshitake stopped peeling the lychee fruit that had been set before him. "What do you mean?"

"I mean, if someone gave another person orders, they would follow those orders whether or not they wanted to."

Yoshitake laughed. "If you figure out how to do that, please let me know. I'd like to try it on my secretary. I'm the one she's got under control. Sometimes I feel like I can't even visit the men's room without getting her permission."

Even I can't believe it's possible, thought Mamoru, *even though I've seen it with my own eyes*. He wasn't surprised that Yoshitake hadn't taken him seriously.

"Have you ever heard of a company called Ad Academy?" Mamoru tried again.

"Hmm, no, can't say I have. Is it an advertising agency?"

The waiter arrived with jasmine tea. They had finished off all the food, and there was nothing left of the lychee fruit but skin and seeds and some melted ice cubes.

"That was delicious. I'll be sleepy all afternoon."

Mamoru and Yoshitake parted at the restaurant entrance. Yoshitake headed for the escalator saying he had some shopping to do and that the crowd would just add to the fun of it.

Thirty minutes later Takano came rushing over to Mamoru, who was back at the cash register. "Mamoru, that man who came to see you, do you know him?"

"Yeah, he took me to lunch."

"He collapsed in the first floor foyer just now; an ambulance is on the way. He was behaving weirdly, almost like that other guy."

"You mean Kakiyama? You've got to be joking!" Mamoru didn't wait for an answer, but went running down the stairs.

———•———

He was happy. He was wrapped in happiness the likes of which he hadn't known for twelve years.

He's a good boy. When I went to see his family, he came running after me to thank me. I would never have imagined that he'd seen me at that intersection.

A good boy . . . he's grown up to be honest and open. I've got to make sure he has a rosy future. It's my duty. I've got to do it right so I can support him and get him into college. I'll send him overseas if he wants.

After that he can work for me. I'll groom him to be a leader. He'll inherit the company I've built. I mean if he's interested in what I do. Anything he wants to do, I'll make sure he has the connections to do it. No, no, that won't do. I need him beside me. That's the way it will have to be.

He was almost drunk with pleasure, so much so that he hadn't noticed the queasiness right away.

It has to be the crowd. There's not enough fresh air. Why don't they ventilate these places? How can Mamoru spend so much time here? There's got to be a better job for him—

There's no reason to wait, I'll set him up to work part-time for me. They're looking for an assistant in Accounts. That way I can see him more often. Everything's going well. There is nothing to worry about.

Now he had a headache and couldn't breathe. His heart was beating out of control; he could almost hear it. It reverberated throughout his body—just like the phone on mornings when he was hung over.

He looked out at the swarms of customers as his eyes clouded over. He saw the bright video screen. He'd noticed it when he walked in; it was a nice display . . . Now it was bright, much too bright. It hurt his eyes it was so bright.

A female sales clerk came up to him. *Are you all right, sir?*

He tried to answer, *I'm all right. It's nothing*—then he realized. It wasn't a sales clerk and he wasn't in a store. He was in a place that terrified him. A place he'd only seen in nightmares. The kind of place you could never leave once you'd been shut up inside.

Sir, the voice called. No, it was just pretending to be kind. It was the voice of someone pursuing him.

Sir! A persistent hand reached out. It was trying to touch him. It was trying to catch him and drag him back.

He had to escape, but his legs wouldn't move. Everyone was staring at him now. They were pointing and whispering. It was his worst nightmare come true.

He had to get outside. He had to escape. There was still time. He could get away. *I'm trying to make up for what I did, why does this have to happen now? It's not fair!*

He wasn't conscious of losing his footing. First his knees bent, and then the upper half of his body followed. He was falling. He tried to press his hand to his chest, but there was nothing there. He had to protect something precious that he was carrying on him. He fell on top of his arm.

The floor was cold. He smelled something like the rubber of shoe soles. The last thing he felt before he lost consciousness was his lip splitting. The blood tasted like copper in his mouth.

———•———

Yoshitake regained consciousness about an hour later in a bed in a general hospital. Mamoru was sitting in a chair he'd pulled up to the foot of the bed.

Yoshitake had turned blue and had been clutching the left side of his chest as he collapsed, so the doctors had initially thought he'd had a heart attack. Mamoru feared the worst, and waited in the hallway with his eyes on the door of the room where Yoshitake was being treated. Within a half hour, though, Yoshitake's pulse and blood pressure had stabilized and his breathing was even again. The doctor was puzzled, and decided to keep him overnight for observation.

"What happened?" These were Yoshitake's first words.

"That was my line! How are you feeling?" Mamoru responded while reaching for the button to call the nurse, just as he had been instructed.

Mamoru mulled things over while he listened to the conversation between Yoshitake and his doctor. *He was behaving weirdly, almost like that other guy.* That's what Takano had said. That meant that Yoshitake might have become ill because of those subliminal videos.

"When did you have your last check-up?" asked the doctor.

"Last spring. I spent a week getting tests for everything," Yoshitake answered. "Did I have a heart attack?"

"No, nothing like that," the doctor responded. "Everything was normal, but it doesn't sit right. Has anything like this ever happened before?"

"Never. I can't believe it myself. Did I really faint?"

"I'd like to run some tests, so you'll need to stay here for a few days."

"But I feel fine." Yoshitake tried to argue with him, but the doctor and nurse both left the room.

"You've got to put your health first," Mamoru smiled and tried to mollify him.

"He's overdoing it," Yoshitake sighed. "It was just a little stress. It happens. Especially since December. I wake up in the morning and can't always remember what I did the night before. I must be drinking too much. Did you ride in the ambulance with me?" He looked at Mamoru, who was still wearing his Laurel uniform.

Mamoru nodded. "I called your house. The maid said she'd bring some things for you."

"Well, thanks, I appreciate it."

The hospital room was clean but stark. Medicinally scented air and a white bed. Other than that, there was just a chair and a small chest of drawers. Yoshitake's clothes were on a wire hanger hung on a hook at the side of the bed.

The maid finally arrived at about six.

"I won't need anything. Leave my clothes there for me. It's nothing, I'll be home soon." Yoshitake spoke brusquely, and his complexion was back to its normal color.

"But the doctor said you'd be staying for a few days," objected the maid, who then added with obvious reluctance, "Will you be needing me to stay the night here?"

Mamoru had been planning to leave as soon as the maid arrived, but he suddenly felt sorry for Yoshitake.

"There'll be no need for that," Yoshitake answered. "You can go now."

The maid smiled in relief. "Shall I notify your wife?"

"No need for that either. I'll be out of here by the time she gets home."

Mamoru spoke up after the maid left. "What if I stay tonight?"

Yoshitake sat up. "I couldn't ask you to do that—"

"But what if you have another attack?"

"Where would you sleep? I can't have you on the floor."

"They'll lend me a fold-up cot. There's enough space for that. I'll call home—they won't mind. There's not much I can do, I know . . ."

"That's not true. Well, I just might take you up on that."

Before lights out, the nurse came by once to take Yoshitake's temperature. She asked him if Mamoru was his son. Yoshitake looked perplexed, so Mamoru stepped in. "Illegitimate, of course," he replied with mock pride, and the nurse laughed.

"You're funny, but you're a good kid."

The nurse left but was back again in a few minutes. "Here, you can have these until we turn the lights out," she said handing him a few magazines. "You'll be bored before long."

It was a long night, but Mamoru wasn't bored. He had lots to think about. For the first time he had doubts about Takano's theory. Could the effects of the video display be proved? He was sure Yoshitake was different from Kakiyama or that girl. He might have had some residual unease from having had to deal with the police about Taizo's accident. But Mamoru couldn't believe he had any reason to be tortured by a subliminal message of *We'll get you!*

He hoped that Shin Nippon Enterprises hadn't been evading taxes, and with that in mind, he fell asleep.

In the middle of the night he felt something light falling on his covers. He heard a soft sound, too. He hadn't been in a deep sleep. He could hear Yoshitake's quiet, measured breathing.

Mamoru looked around the dark room and saw that Yoshitake's shirt and jacket had fallen from their hanger into a wrinkled heap.

He didn't want to get up, but managed to rouse himself and make a trip to the toilet while he was at it. When he picked up the jacket and shirt, something fell out. Something small and hard hit the linoleum floor.

By the faint light of the moon that came through the curtains, Mamoru tried to feel around for whatever it was. He finally found it in the shadow of one of the legs of the bed.

It was a platinum ring. It was so simple that he realized it must be a wedding ring. Why would he have a wedding ring in his pocket? Could this really be what had dropped? Mamoru took it to the window for a closer look. A date and some initials were engraved on the underside. *K to T.*

And the date—it was the same date as that engraved on his mother Keiko's wedding ring. The one he had kept after she died.

K to T. From Keiko to Toshio.

Mamoru recalled a time when he was small and had cut himself while riding his bicycle. He had got off and looked at it, shocked by the blood that came spurting out. That was how he felt when he realized he was holding his father's wedding ring. This man must be his father. His aunt had never met him, and Mamoru had been too young to remember what he looked like.

No wonder he had reacted to the subliminal shots. Toshio Kusaka had come back as Koichi Yoshitake. *His father was back!*

When Yoshitake woke up early the next morning, Mamoru was gone. He had gone to see Anego. Nobody else was awake at that hour. There was a hint of a sunrise in the east, but the sky was still full of stars. A newspaper delivery boy passed by on a bicycle.

There was a light on in the kitchen of Anego's house. Both her parents worked until late at night at a publishing house, so Anego got up, as she put it, "frighteningly early" instead of them.

Mamoru stood in front of her house, his cold hands in his pockets. Anego opened the front door and came out to check for the newspaper. She noticed Mamoru as she turned to go back inside.

"Kusaka?" She was startled. "What are you doing here so early?"

Mamoru couldn't speak. He could barely shrug his shoulders. Anego came over to him.

"You're freezing cold. How long have you been here?"

He still couldn't speak. What he wanted to say was, *You were right. My father really was close by. It's incredible, isn't it?*

"What happened?"

Mamoru put his hands on her shoulders and pulled her to him. He didn't want to hold her so much as he wanted her to hold him. He needed someone to cling to.

"What's the matter?" Anego continued to ask quietly, instinctively doing just as he had hoped, wrapping her arms around him to keep him warm.

———————•———————

"Hello, boy." Mamoru finally heard the raspy voice again on the morning of January seventh. "Glad you've been well. How were your holidays?"

Mamoru had not recovered, nor had he tried to. It was if he had suddenly been handed something infinitely fragile and he was too frightened to make a move.

Toshio Kusaka's wedding ring had fallen out of the pocket of Yoshitake's clothing. That was really all it had been, but it was too heavy a burden for Mamoru to even speak of. He hadn't told anyone, and he didn't know how he was ever going to be able to.

In the end, he had told Anego that he had just wanted to see her, that was all. She hadn't questioned him further and she continued to act exactly the same with him. "Come over to see me anytime if that'll do it for you," she had said with a laugh.

On the morning of January seventh, Mamoru's head was still in a fog. The voice wiped away the fog and had him sitting up straight.

"This afternoon at three. At the Sukiyabashi intersection. You know it, don't you?"

"I know it."

"Feel free to come. It will be the end of Kazuko Takagi. I'll see you there. I'll be waiting."

Mamoru got off the train at Yurakucho at noon on the dot, and walked the short distance to the Ginza Sukiyabashi intersection. The weather was clear. There was nothing he could do but wait. He gripped his copy of *Information Channel* and tried to commit Kazuko Takagi's face to memory.

He knew women could alter their appearance by changing their hairstyles or wearing different clothes. Maki had once told him that all it took was a new boyfriend, but Mamoru didn't want to even consider the possibility he wouldn't recognize her.

The area was crowded with people. It was as though everyone in Tokyo had showed up at once. Shopping, dates, movies. There were families, too. In the middle of this peaceful scene, Mamoru felt like an explorer lost in the jungle or a mountaineer on a snowy plain without a map. He wandered around by himself. He peered into the faces of young women, followed them from behind, and then got tired and stood still again for a few moments before he spotted another face in the intersection and went chasing after it.

He tried to remember Maki's face when she had been used as a demonstration of the voice's powers. Up until the minute it happened there had been nothing strange about her, but when she said *Listen to me, boy,* her eyes had been out of focus.

The face he was looking for in the crowd would probably be laughing and talking and shining just like all the others. She might not even be here before three.

What should he do? Go around to all the department stores, movie theaters, and restaurants in Ginza and have her paged? Mamoru continued his fruitless search.

It was two thirty.

Kazuko clung to Mitamura's arm as they walked up the stairs from the subway at the Yurakucho Mullion exit. It was two forty.

"The letter told me to come by myself. I might not find him if we're together."

"But I'll lose you in this crowd if we're separated."

Just then Mitamura spotted a vendor selling balloons. "I'll buy you a balloon. That way I'll know where you are."

He paid the vendor and handed Kazuko a red balloon.

"I feel like a child!"

"Think of it as an amulet to protect you."

It was two forty-five.

Mamoru sat on the edge of a flowerbed looking out at the intersection and rested for a few minutes. He would just have to wait here and be ready to leap out and stop anyone who suddenly started to act strangely at three o'clock.

It was a major pedestrian intersection. At regular intervals, the traffic signals stopped the traffic in all directions and allowed people on all four corners to cross at once. A police officer with a white armband helped direct traffic, blowing his whistle at cars that stayed in the intersection too long or pedestrians who insisted on crossing after the lights changed.

Why had this particular spot been chosen?

Two fifty-three and twenty seconds.

Someone tapped Mamoru's shoulder from behind. He whipped around to see a young woman with an eager smile and a clipboard.

"That was fast! Are you alone?" she asked with an air of familiarity.

Salespeople were lurking around every day of the year, Mamoru guessed. He glared at her and stood up menacingly.

"What's up with you, you creepy kid!" said the woman as she backed off.

Two fifty-six.

Kazuko Takagi stood in the covered Mullion walkway that separated the Seibu and Hankyu department stores and led to Yurakucho Station. It seemed to get crowded all of a sudden and she lost sight of Mitamura. She gripped the string of the balloon tightly and tried to maneuver into spots with fewer people, moving forward bit by bit, but there was a wall of humanity around her. Kazuko was irritated. *Why didn't they just keep moving?*

"Excuse me, I need to get through." A young couple that were looking up at something opened up a path.

"Excuse me . . . pardon me . . . I need to get through!"

Two fifty-nine.

Someone came up behind Kazuko and grabbed her wrist. Then whispered in her ear, "Excuse me, do you have the time?"

Kazuko let go of the balloon.

Three o'clock on the nose.

Mamoru heard the sound of a music box. It was the Mullion clock chiming the hour. He turned around to look at it. The crowd on the corner began to move as the signal at the intersection turned green for pedestrians.

The music box continued playing its familiar tune. Every day at certain times, colorful mechanical figurines would come out of the opening in the wall, moving along with the music. It was three o'clock, one of the set times. Everyone stopped to watch. So that was why it was so crowded!

Was that why this place had been chosen? There'd be so many faces, it would be impossible to pick someone out in the crowd. It was to make sure Mamoru couldn't find Kazuko Takagi.

"Look, a balloon!" A little girl passing by called out and pointed to the red balloon floating over the crowd. Mamoru automatically looked up at it.

The pedestrian signal turned red. Cars started up and began to roar past.

Just at that moment, someone came running out of the crowd under the clock and flew past him. It was a woman in a black coat. She showed no sign of stopping and was heading over the guardrail and directly into the traffic on Harumi Avenue.

Mamoru sprang up and yelled, "Stop! Someone stop her!"

Time came to a halt. He saw her white calf as she lifted her leg and the hem of her black coat flipped up. As Mamoru rushed through the crowd he was repelled by the impact of what felt like hundreds of fists. He stumbled back.

Someone else dashed out of the crowd. It was a young man, his face startled as he desperately made his way toward the woman. Mamoru got to the guardrail just as the other man grabbed onto the hem of her coat. A few people in the crowd finally noticed and screamed as the two pulled with all their might, and all three of them fell backward into a pile.

The woman, deathly pale, opened her eyes. It was Kazuko Takagi. There was no mistaking the resemblance to the photo in the magazine. Mamoru gave a silent prayer of thanks, the first time in his life he had ever felt lucky enough to do so.

"What just happened?" The other young man looked from Kazuko to Mamoru and back again. His face was as pale as hers.

The music box stopped and the crowd began to disperse. A few people looked at them with obvious distaste as they sat in a heap on the side of the road, but most just kept on moving.

The voice of the young man seemed to have roused Kazuko and she began to stir, then blinked and looked up at him.

"You just tried to run out into the middle of the street," the man said, his teeth still clenched.

"Me?"

"You're Kazuko Takagi, right?" Mamoru finally managed to catch his breath and ask.

She turned her head to look at Mamoru and nodded. "What happened to me?"

"You're safe now. You let the balloon go and I couldn't find you," the man said. "But I heard this guy yell and we both ran after you."

"You saved me?" she asked Mamoru.

"And him too. So you know each other?"

The other man nodded.

"A boy . . . are you the one who went to see Nobuhiko Hashimoto?" Kazuko asked as she reached out to grab Mamoru's sleeve. "After he was killed in that explosion. You were the one, weren't you?"

"Yes, I went there, and I've been trying to find you ever since."

"I wanted to meet you, too. Who are you? What connection do you have to Hashimoto? Do you know something? Did you write the letter telling me to come here today?"

"A letter?" Mamoru quickly asked. "Did someone tell you to come here?"

"That's right," the man said. "Whoever wrote the letter said they would help her."

Mamoru stood up, and pulled Kazuko to her feet. He looked at the man. "Take Miss Takagi and get out of here now! Do you have somewhere you can go? How will I be able to contact you later?"

The man held Kazuko closely and answered, "Come to my shop." He gave Mamoru instructions on how to get to Cerberus.

"We can talk later. You've got to get her away from here now."

When they had left, Mamoru looked around. Whoever it was, he had to be close by. He had to have seen it all.

Mamoru felt someone's hand on his right arm.

———————•———————

He was sick. It was strange, but that was Mamoru's first impression. The person that had kept him in such constant fear was a sick old man.

"Boy, we finally meet."

It was that same hoarse voice. He was about Mamoru's height. His head seemed too large for his body, but his body might have shrunk from his illness. The baggy silver gray suit he wore was the same color as his hair. The skin under his eyes sagged. He had the wrinkles of age, and the unhealthy pallor of someone wasting away with disease. Only the eyes that were pinned on Mamoru had any life in them.

"Boy, you know who I am, don't you?"

Mamoru nodded guardedly. "You didn't succeed with number four, did you?"

The man smiled faintly. "You did your job, I knew you would. I don't care anymore about Kazuko Takagi. Shall we go?"

"Go? Go where?"

"Don't be afraid. I like you, and I have lots of things I want to talk to you about. Come along with me."

Mamoru followed the old man into a taxi, and they rode for about thirty minutes. They got out in an area that was a mix of office and apartment buildings, with the Tokyo expressway rumbling overhead. The winter sunset painted the walls of the buildings an almost sinfully beautiful shade of reddish pink.

As the taxi drove away, Mamoru's heart once again clenched in fear. The taxi seemed to take with it the last piece of the sane world. The old man led him to a white-walled apartment building that was set off the main road. Mamoru took a good look around him, trying to memorize the appearance of the location. On the opposite side of the street, he caught a glimpse of a canal from behind some buildings. Directly ahead of him was a multistory parking lot. There was a utility pole with an address on it. No matter what happened, he wanted to have an idea of where he was.

They went up to the fifth floor, and the old man stopped in front of apartment 503. "This is it."

The sign over the door said Shinjiro Harasawa. Mamoru was somehow astonished that the mystery man would have such an ordinary name.

"Harasawa?" he mumbled.

The old man answered, "That's my name. It was rude of me not to have introduced myself before."

They entered the apartment and walked through a room that anyone might live in. Then the old man pushed open the door to the room in the back. He let Mamoru in first, and turned on the light before closing the door behind himself.

Mamoru was overwhelmed by what he saw.

One wall was completely covered in what looked like audio equipment. Mamoru was able to identify the three tape decks in the center, and the speakers and tuners on either side. Was that an oscillometer? He saw something that looked like an amplifier. There were other machines that looked like the ones used to record his mother's pulse and heartbeat when she had been in the hospital intensive care unit.

A heavy curtain covered the window and kept light out of the room. The opposite wall was covered by a built-in bookcase packed full of books. The short-weave carpet on the floor absorbed the sound of Mamoru's footsteps, and in the center of the room was a single easy chair.

"So, what do you think?" Harasawa asked. In the quiet of the closed-off room, his voice sounded terribly human.

"What do you do in here?"

The old man took off his jacket and laid it on a nearby machine. "It's a long story. Why don't you sit down?"

"No thank you." Mamoru leaned against the window. "You can sit down. You're the sick one."

"Is that what you think?"

"Anybody could tell."

"I see. So it means I don't have much time. Where should I begin?" He put his hands on his hips and walked slowly in front of the wall of equipment, stopping in front of the tape decks. "First of all, let me give you a name."

He turned on the tape deck and a red light went on. The sound of a tape running came out of the speakers, followed by the sound of Harasawa reading off the date and the time. "The subject is Maki Asano. Female aged twenty-one."

Mamoru jerked himself upright, away from the window.

"What is your name?"

"Maki Asano."

She sounded sleepy and calm, but Mamoru recognized Maki's voice. Maki answered the old man's questions clearly: date of birth, family, occupation, current state of health . . .

"Your sister, actually your cousin, is highly susceptible to suggestion. She's flexible and cooperative—the perfect subject for hypnotism."

"Hypnotism?" Mamoru jumped up and grabbed the old man's shirt. "Did you hypnotize my sister?"

"That's right, boy." Harasawa remained calm. "Let go of me if you want to hear the rest."

Still breathing hard, Mamoru let go. Harasawa turned up the volume on the tape deck.

"Where do you like to go?"

"To the sea. I love the blue sea."

"Where on the sea? A beach? Or out on a boat?"

"Umm, I'd like to be on a sailboat. Sit on the deck and feel the salty breeze."

The man's voice continued. He told Maki that she was on the deck of a sailboat, it was a sunny day, and she was relaxed . . . so relaxed . . .

"Listen carefully to what I say. Can you hear me?"

"Yes, I can hear you clearly."

"Is there a clock in your house?"

"Yes."

"Does it chime or make some other sound on the hour?"

"Yes, it's a big wall clock."

"Tomorrow evening, when that clock strikes nine o'clock, I want you to say this to Mamoru Kusaka."

"Tomorrow evening, when the wall clock strikes nine, I'll tell Mamoru . . ."

"Listen to me, boy. I called Nobuyuki Hashimoto. That's when he died."

Maki repeated the words in a monotone.

"That's right. Now I'm going to count to three and you are going to wake up and leave this building. As soon as you get outside you'll forget everything that happened here. You'll forget that you met me and that I gave you a command. It will come back to you at nine o'clock tomorrow night. After you relay the message, you'll forget that you did so."

"I'll forget . . ."

"Do you understand? All right then, I'm going to count. One, two, three."

The tape ended there.

"It's called post-hypnotic phenomenon," began Harasawa. "The subject is put into a hypnotic state and a command is planted in her brain. That command can be called up at any time using a keyword or a sound, or even some sort of action. At the signal, the subject will carry out the command. After that the subject forgets both the signal and what she has done. The only thing that remains is a small blank spot in her memory."

Mamoru recalled that the night before Harasawa's "demonstration," Maki had been drunk and couldn't remember what she had done or where she had been.

Harasawa motioned to the equipment against the wall. "I use this equipment to record the physical condition of subjects under hypnosis. If you're interested I can show you just how fascinating people are when they've been hypnotized."

Mamoru shifted his eyes away from Harasawa.

"I'm sure this is something you'd like to hear." Harasawa switched tapes. It was the voice of another woman. "This is Fumie Kato. She was remarkably unreserved. She explained to me all of the tiniest details of how she managed to earn her dirty money. She was proud of herself. You can communicate with the subconscious to find out the dark secrets of people, even the thoughts their conscious mind wants never to see the light of day."

"What do you mean, the 'subconscious'?"

"It's up here," said Harasawa tapping his temple. "It stands guard every hour of the day. Some scholars consider the subconscious to be the soul. The conscious mind is like a blackboard—you can erase anything written on it. But the subconscious is more like an etching—things are carved into it, and they don't get wiped out. Imagine a boy falling and breaking his front tooth at the age of five—the fear and pain of that event will stay in his subconscious until he dies at age eighty. Post-hypnotic phenomenon is triggered by making contact with the subconscious."

The old man turned down the tape so they could talk more easily. "I've got tapes of all four of those women. I made contact with them, hypnotized them, and gave them a keyword—"

"But what if somebody else accidentally said the keyword?"

Harasawa smiled. "Kazuko Takagi was the only one with whom timing was an issue. The other four had been hypnotized less than twelve hours before they heard the keyword. Only three hours for Nobuhiko Hashimoto."

A shrewd look suddenly appeared in Harasawa's eyes. "I monitored their movements. I didn't want to make any mistakes. After the other three died, there was a risk that Kazuko Takagi would catch on to me and disappear, so I approached her at the first opportunity. It was the night of Yoko Sugano's wake."

"But—"

"And I used a combination keyword to make sure nobody else got to her before I was ready. I told her I would give her the keyword and grab her right hand. Both would have to happen simultaneously for her to react."

"So you commanded her to die?"

"No," Harasawa shook his head. "I gave all four women the command to flee. Living beings have a natural instinct to protect themselves—if you told them to commit suicide, they wouldn't do it. The subconscious cannot separate itself from the person it belongs to."

"Flee?"

"That's it. Flee. Run away. Don't get caught by the person chasing you, or you'll be killed. Shake off any obstacles, run through doors, break windows, jump out of them, run, run, *run*! Otherwise you'll die. The subconscious then puts that command into action. Those women were killed by their own instinct to save themselves."

Mamoru stood speechless.

The doubt that had been swirling around in his mind finally cleared. "So you killed them. Why?"

"So they got what they deserved," Harasawa instantly replied, the smile now wiped from his face. "Until a year ago I was doing research at a university. I worked there with five researchers I'd trained myself. We studied hypnotism, bio-feedback, and traditional Chinese qigong. When our efforts bore fruit, I was sure we would be able to help people, especially those with depression or relationship problems."

He raised both his arms, and then lowered them sadly. "It was about that time that I learned I had cancer. I had been so wrapped up in my research that it was too late by the time I got medical attention. But we all have to die sometime."

He shrugged and went on. "I knew that even if I died, my researchers would carry on my work. They had so much more time than I did, and I knew they would do as I asked."

The old man went over to the bookshelf and took out a scrapbook. He flipped through the pages and found something to show Mamoru. "Look at this. Of the five researchers I had, this one was my pride and joy." On the left-hand page was a young man with heavy black-framed spectacles and a smile full of straight, white teeth. He had a broad forehead. A straight nose. And his eyes sparkled from behind the glasses. "His name was Kenichi Tazawa. He was a born scholar and full of natural curiosity."

"You're talking about him in the past tense."

"He killed himself. He took the sleeping medicine I kept in the lab. It was last May."

Mamoru looked up.

The old man looked at him and nodded. "He was in love. But it was an unhappy affair. I had hoped that the girl he loved so much would be suitable for him."

"So who was it?" asked Mamoru.

"Kazuko Takagi." After a few moments of silence, the old man continued. "I thought I would go mad when I lost him. I had to bury the young man who was supposed to be my successor."

"How did you know that his lover was Kazuko Takagi?"

"Tazawa left me a letter, describing how she had hurt him."

"But he didn't have to die. He had a future."

"Is that what you think—he was much too naive? He didn't have sufficient immunity?" The man shook his head at the idea. "Boy, what do you think romantic love is? Why do we love one person alone and not everyone? It's a mystery—even we scholars still don't understand it. But Kazuko Takagi used that passion for her own profit." Harasawa's voice had gotten stronger. "Boy, she didn't merely swindle someone out of their money. It was an act of desecration."

Mamoru couldn't respond.

"Even after she was through with him, Tazawa continued to believe in her and refused to accept that she had intentionally tricked him out of his savings. So she sent him a copy of *Information Channel*."

Mamoru remembered what Hashimoto had told him about that article. *I didn't add anything to what those bitches said in that interview. I didn't have to add any dirty words or any slutty turns of phrase. They said it all themselves. All of it—every single bit of it.*

"He left the magazine with the letter he wrote me. I read the article. Over and over. I read it so many times I memorized it. Then I made my decision."

"You decided to kill them all," Mamoru said. "But why all four? Why not just Kazuko Takagi?"

"It was more than just personal revenge. I used them as guinea pigs."

"*Guinea pigs*? Was it just another experiment to you? But you *murdered* them!"

"Mean-spirited, yes. Just like those 'lovers for hire' were mean-spirited. I wanted those four women to pay the price for their callous actions. That's all."

"You're crazy." Mamoru finally found his voice. "I don't care what you say. Murder is murder."

"That's for society to judge. I don't have long; I might not even last out the month. I have instructed the executor of my estate to send all of the material I have here along with my confession to the police."

There was nothing left for Mamoru to say. He wanted to get out of there as quickly as possible. All he had to do was stand up and leave.

"You're proud of yourself, aren't you? You're nothing but an evil old sorcerer."

"Sorcerer?" the old man laughed. "Scholarship is sacred. There is nothing wasted or frivolous about it. I'm a scientist. I'm searching for the truth. To prove it, I'll give you a piece of information I think you'll be interested in. You'll find it useful."

Mamoru stopped and turned back. "Useful?"

"That's right. Yoshitake, that man who testified on behalf of your uncle—I'll tell you who he really is."

Mamoru stared at Harasawa without blinking. "What do you know about him?"

"He's lying to you. He wasn't there when Yoko Sugano died. I'm sure of that. It has to do with the keyword." He held up one finger. "I used the phone with Fumie Kato. I talked to Atsuko Mita on the train platform. I hypnotized Nobuhiko Hashimoto at home, then opened the gas lines and spread gasoline throughout his house. Then I waited for a couple of hours until I was sure the house was full of gas, called him up, and gave him the keyword that made him light a cigarette."

"How about Yoko Sugano?"

"I used her watch as part of the keyword. The alarm was set to go off at twelve midnight. That's why she was running full speed right into the path of your uncle's car. I wasn't there when it happened. By that time, I was too tired to go after her myself, and my oversight ended up making trouble for your uncle."

Harasawa shifted his gaze to one side, almost as if he was really sorry about it. "After she died, I read all the articles I could find on the accident and watched the news on TV. When I learned that Yoshitake had come forward to say he'd been there, I knew he was lying. He said he'd asked Yoko Sugano the time and she told him it was five past twelve. That was a lie. It was impossible."

"Why?"

"She was already in the hypnotic state. She would have been running away from whoever it was that she thought was chasing her, just as I had commanded. She would never have responded to outside stimulus. She wouldn't have been capable.

"Yoshitake is a bald-faced liar. If he'd been there, he would have seen Yoko Sugano running for her life, chased by nobody. But why did he go to the trouble of lying?"

Mamoru closed his eyes and leaned against the door. "Because he's my father."

"You think he's your father?"

"I know it. He's the father that abandoned me twelve years ago. Now he goes by the name of Koichi Yoshitake. He lied about witnessing the accident to help me and the Asano family."

"How did you figure that out?"

Mamoru explained about the wedding ring, and how Yoshitake had been caught by the subliminal shots in the video. And there was something else, too.

"He called me by my name when he came to see me. How could he have known my name was Kusaka? The Asanos introduced me as their son. I don't know why I didn't notice it at the time."

Harasawa stared at the floor for a few moments. "Boy, the police looked into his past when he testified. They know who he is. They know where he was born, where he has worked, and who his family is."

"I thought of that, but he told me that he had spent time in a flophouse. In a place like that, he would have been able to buy a new name and family record. As long as he had money, someone like my father who wanted to erase his past would have been able to do it. He could have taken on the identity of some poor slob who died and was left to rot."

"I see. I suppose it is possible," the old man nodded. "But you're wrong, boy. He's not your father. The debt he owes to you and your mother is bigger than that." The old man stepped back toward the tape recorder. "I was intrigued when I learned he had lied. I wanted to know why. So I hypnotized him. Here's what he told me."

"You—hypnotized him?"

"That's right."

The old man started the tape. The long confession it contained took Mamoru back twelve years, to a point in time that had, for him, been surrounded by a deep, impenetrable fog.

———•———

Koichi Nomura was full of hope the spring he turned eighteen and left home to go to college in Tokyo.

His family in Hirakawa had run an inn for several generations, and was well-known and respected in the area. However, their home and business had been burned to the ground during World War II, and most of their assets lost. They had had to sell off what little remained just to stay alive in the aftermath of the war. By the time Koichi was eighteen, there was nothing left.

An unfortunate characteristic of old families is their reluctance to accept change. This was especially true of the Nomuras, and the lack of a flexible attitude and astute business sense vital to running a family business was affecting their ability to rebuild their livelihood.

Koichi was the only son, and the family's hopes were all pinned on him. By that spring, the only thing left to them was their family honor and the meager ground rents they earned. Umeko, Koichi's mother, was already a widow, and her son was her only remaining reason to live. She was determined to send him to college in Tokyo no matter what the financial repercussions were to her. Koichi understood better than anyone what that meant. To his mother, he was like a tiny green sprout on an already rotting stump.

He thrived in Tokyo and proved an excellent student. He and everyone else expected him to graduate and get a job worthy of the Nomura name.

Until he had his first clash with misfortune, that is.

It was an accident. A new building was going up in the neighborhood where Koichi was lodging. One day, as he was passing by the site deep in thought about a college assignment, construction workers were installing a window on the third floor, right over his head. The hand of one of the workers holding it slipped, and the window came crashing down on Koichi's head. His wounds took two months to heal.

Koichi received a generous insurance settlement, and recovered quickly thanks to his youth. He continued to read during his convalescence, determined not to let the time off impede his studies. He was just beginning to catch up when he was sent back to the hospital a month after being released.

He had been infected with hepatitis B.

These days the risk of infection from blood transfusions is well known. To Koichi, though, it was just another stroke of bad luck. The transfusion he'd received to save him from bleeding to death resulted in the loss of an entire school year.

Then, just as he was ready to go back to school, his mother Umeko had a mild stroke. Her life was not in danger, but the added financial burden left Koichi with no choice. In the spring of his twenty-first year, he was forced to drop out of college and go to work.

Umeko was superstitious, so she asked a friend to read her son's fortune based on his name, as is often the custom in Japan.

"His indications are strong," the fortune teller said, "but his name means he will continue to have misfortune. He ought to consider changing his name."

Koichi, however, did not feel inclined to listen to her advice.

His first foray into the working world was a job with a middle-sized real estate company in central Tokyo. It wasn't bad as jobs go, but Koichi considered himself too good for it, and he became bitter and difficult to deal with. He had trouble with customers and took an arrogant attitude with his coworkers. He made enemies and avoided people, and it ended up affecting his work.

He went from job to job. His résumé was filled with company names followed by "quit for personal reasons." He couldn't even remember the names of some of the places he had worked, so he just left them off the résumé the next time he had to write one. He eventually got sick of it all, and ended up, as he had told Mamoru, essentially homeless and living in flophouses.

The summer he was thirty-two, Koichi was hired at a transport company. He worked in the office taking care of general affairs, the only male clerical worker at the small company. One of his jobs was accompanying the company president on his visits to clients. One of these clients was Shin Nippon Enterprises.

When he met the woman who became his wife, Naomi Yoshitake, she was twenty-two and still a student. To the young woman, the cynical young man who stood firmly by his boss, sorting through papers to present in business negotiations during which the questions came at them rapid fire, was much more attractive than the coddled lads whose futures her father guaranteed. On top of that, Koichi Nomura, who lived in a world she was oblivious to, had the good looks he had inherited from his mother. It was the one thing his bad luck hadn't changed.

The president of Shin Nippon Enterprises gave into the demands of his daughter and began looking into Koichi's background as a first step toward grooming him as a son-in-law. His main concern was the long list of past employers on his résumé. After a while, though, that list intrigued him for another reason. Koichi's past employers were from all different fields, many of them industries that were beginning to show growth. Some of the companies he had worked for were small and insignificant when he came to them, but were now distinguished in their fields.

It couldn't be merely coincidence. This young man who his daughter was so taken with definitely had foresight. As the man who had single-handedly built Shin Nippon Enterprises from the ground up, Naomi's father knew that this kind of prescience was not something that could be taught or learned.

Koichi and Naomi Yoshitake were engaged that December, and Koichi was hired by Shin Nippon Enterprises. The boy who had planned to rebuild the Nomura family business agreed to be adopted into his wife's family without a second thought. They planned to be married as soon as Naomi graduated from college.

It was one week before he became Koichi Yoshitake that the greatest misfortune to date befell Koichi Nomura.

------------•------------

In that March of twelve years ago, Koichi had left Tokyo at night and driven straight to Hirakawa. The clock on the dashboard said 05:15 as he drove into the city limits. Rain beat on the windshield, and the whole town was enveloped in cold.

He had come to pick up his mother and drive her back to Tokyo for the wedding. He had taken a long detour, but was finally back on the path he was destined for in life. For once he had something to show his mother. He planned to stay one night, then head back to Tokyo with her the next day.

Rather than taking the highway straight through town, he decided to savor his triumphant return, taking the narrow roads past the station and then out to where he could see the mountains surrounding the city.

From the car window he saw on his right a mountain that used to belong to his family. A plot near the top had been cleared and leveled, and the steel girders of a resort hotel under construction stood black in the purple light of dawn. A huge sign announcing "Opening September 1!" was lit with footlights.

It was still too soon for Shin Nippon Enterprises to open a hotel, thought Koichi, but it wasn't an impossible dream. He would do it some-time in the not too distant future when he was president of the company. Until then he would learn everything he could. He was already thinking about expanding the company's operating policy to target the greater mass market. He was sure the day would come when "the masses" was no longer such a dirty word.

He drove halfway around the city, and was nearing an intersection where the road crossed the railroad tracks leading to the west side of town. The rain was coming down harder, and the windshield wipers slapping over the glass blurred his view.

He hadn't come across a single car during his early morning drive, and there were no pedestrians either. He picked up speed, and the car accelerated smoothly. It had been a gift from Naomi so he could go and collect his mother in style. The key had still been warm with her body heat when she had pressed it into his hand.

Later he couldn't remember whether he had seen the man or had braked first, but the dark shape that appeared in the mist disappeared the next instant. There was a dull impact, the car bounded sharply and then came to a halt. Koichi flew forward against the steering wheel.

All sound stopped. Koichi heard only his heart beating in his ears as he got out of the car. A pile of rags was heaped by the side of the road.

The pile had feet, but only one of them was wearing a shoe. The other shoe had come to rest where Koichi now stood.

Koichi edged closer, one hesitant step at a time.

The pile didn't move. Koichi knelt down and touched its neck: he couldn't feel a pulse. The man looked to be the same age as him. He had a tiny mole beneath his right eyebrow. He had fallen with his face half in a puddle, and blood trickled out of his left ear. Koichi reached down with shaking hands to lift the man's head, and it was limp.

Koichi pulled his hands away from the body and rubbed them over and over on his pants. His back was cold from the rain running down his neck.

The dead man's umbrella had fallen with its handle in the air. Rain was beginning to pool inside it, too. Koichi heard the shrill call of a bird from the grove of trees to his right.

He looked around.

He was out of town. The gentle curve of the railroad tracks disappeared on the other side of the trees, where it would eventually be drawn into a tunnel. There was a tilted traffic signal at the fullest part of the curve. It was an unmanned crossing. To Koichi's left was an old abandoned warehouse that still bore the words "Hirakawa Dying Works."

No one was there.

If he wanted to escape, he would have to do it now. He continued wiping his hands on his pants as the rain soaked him through.

Come on, if you want to get away from this, do it now! The rain would wash away the skid marks of the tires and the dead man's blood.

A voice from deep inside him began to speak to the man who was looking up at the sky in a position impossible for a living human. "I didn't know you were there." He wanted to speak up for himself. "I didn't see you."

You've got to run away! You'll lose everything!

From behind him came the sound of a warning bell. Koichi jumped in surprise. The signal at the railroad crossing was flashing. The bars came down. A train would be passing by any minute now.

Koichi stood staring at the signal as the warning bell clanged. The two red lights, one on top of the other, flashed on and off alternately. Top, bottom, top, bottom.

Would the engineer notice him? Would he see this car and the body? Would the passengers see?

Clang, clang, clang.

His blood ran cold. Koichi ran to the body and dragged it to the side of the car. He opened the door and began to shove the body into the back seat.

He ran back to look at the road. He grabbed the upside-down umbrella and put it in the car with the body. The blood in the puddles on the road was getting thinner and thinner. There would soon be nothing left.

As he got into the driver's seat, he tripped over a shoe. It was the one that had come off the dead man's foot. He hurriedly grabbed it and threw it in the back. Just as he shut the door, the train came speeding past.

Koichi didn't know how he managed to drive or what he thought about as he did so. When he arrived at his mother's home, he pulled into the garage where the bent fender and scratched paint would not be visible from the road.

His mother, Umeko, came out when she heard the noise. The "garage" was really no more than a plastic sheet on a frame in their tiny yard. She had withdrawn what little money she had in her savings and set it up for Koichi so it would be available now that he would be coming to see her more frequently. Koichi had promised his mother that he didn't need much; he'd soon be building her a much grander house anyway.

"Welcome ho—oh! What happened?" she asked looking at his face.

Koichi broke down in tears the instant he saw her. He bit on his fist to muffle the sound.

Umeko listened to the entire story. Instead of blaming him for the situation, she was matter of fact in her approach. "We'll have to get rid of the body."

In the back room, they laid it out on a piece of the plastic sheet left over from the makeshift garage. Umeko was calm and thorough. Her right hand was limp from her stroke, but her voice did not waver as she gave Koichi instructions.

He took off the dead man's clothes and stuffed them into a paper bag. There was a wallet in the jacket pocket with a driver's license and other identification. "Toshio Kusaka. Have you ever heard of him, Mom?"

Umeko said nothing, but grabbed the wallet out of her son's hands and put it with the clothes in the paper bag. She tied it up and finally answered, "He's assistant to the financial section chief at city hall."

They tied up the body in the plastic and hid it from view.

"What about the car?" Koichi asked.

"It's been scratched, hasn't it?"

That night on the seven o'clock local news it was reported that the assistant to the financial section chief at Hirakawa City Hall had gone missing. After seeing that, Koichi got his car out. He bashed it into the rock wall surrounding the neighbor's house, pretending that he had made a botched turn.

He called a tow truck and had it taken off for repairs. The loaner car arrived fifteen minutes later.

"I never liked that rock wall," Umeko said to her son.

They waited until after midnight before they put the body in the trunk of the loaner along with a shovel. Their trip out of Hirakawa went smoothly. They drove for about an hour after they left the city limits and stopped in a forest that formed part of a nature reserve. Koichi took the shovel and flashlight and hiked a short distance until he found a suitable spot on a slope. All he had to do was go back to the car, retrieve the body, and drag it there. He did it all himself. Umeko waited in the car in the dark, with neither a light nor the radio on to keep her company. She sat still, looking straight in front of her.

As Koichi was piling dirt on the plastic sheet to bury it and its contents, the rope came loose and the oddly bent left hand spilled out. He was almost afraid it would reach out and grab his ankle. He was even more dismayed when he saw the ring on the third finger. He'd missed it before, and he knew it could be used to identify the body. Koichi wiped the sweat off his brow. There was little chance the body would be found here, but he wasn't taking any chances.

He replaced all the dirt he had dug up and pounded it down before returning to the car. His arms shook with fear and fatigue.

When he was finally able to drive, Umeko declared in a low voice, "It wasn't your fault, so you just have to forget it all."

Koichi listened and nodded, but didn't imagine that he would ever be able to forget.

The wedding went off without a hitch. When the couple returned from their honeymoon, the first thing Koichi Yoshitake did was open the Hirakawa newspaper he had had sent to him. Toshio Kusaka's name was printed in large letters. Yoshitake could feel the blood drain from his head.

The article, however, only described how the financial section assistant was still at large, and that he was now the prime suspect in a case of missing public funds.

Life in Tokyo was fine. The incident in Hirakawa remained shrouded in mystery, and there was no reason for any suspicion to fall on Yoshitake. His safety was assured. The only guilt he felt, the extra weight he felt in his feet, had to do with the family Toshio Kusaka had left behind.

The family had had a husband and father who had embezzled public funds: that was a known fact. But he hadn't disappeared voluntarily. He hadn't run away. Yoshitake alone was responsible for the fact that Kusaka had not had the opportunity to explain his actions or offer any extenuating circumstances, nor had he been allowed to pay for his crime. Kusaka's wife and son had been left to fend for themselves, and Yoshitake was tortured by the guilt this caused him.

He picked up a bit of new information on the matter on his infrequent trips back to Hirakawa. He made it his business to know how the wife and child were faring.

He learned that Kusaka's wife Keiko and young son Mamoru had left the subsidized housing provided for city employees and were living in a tiny apartment. Yoshitake went to see it. It was one of the oldest buildings in the city and he wondered how much of a bribe the owner was paying to keep it from being condemned.

As he stood in the alley outside, the young boy and his mother appeared. Both of them were carrying paper shopping bags bearing the name of a store on the outskirts of town. Yoshitake imagined the two were not welcome in the local shops.

The child looked up to say something to his mother, and the two of them laughed quietly together. At the same time, one of the other residents in the building slammed a window shut.

The Kusaka family climbed the stairs of the dilapidated building. Yoshitake called out silently to them as they did so. *Why don't you leave town? Why are you staying? You know how things will be and yet you still refuse to go. Why?*

Keiko and Mamoru had lived in Yoshitake's heart ever since then. No matter how his own life in Tokyo changed, he had never forgotten them for even a moment.

Yoshitake had discreetly used his connections as a member of an old, established family in Hirakawa to find Keiko a job. Nobody was able to turn him down when he said that it wasn't the family's fault and that they really ought to be pitied. He continued making inquiries using different agencies to find out how the family was doing, and he was always prepared to make sure a hand was lent in their times of greatest need.

In direct contrast, Yoshitake's relationship with Naomi went sour. Naomi thought it was because she was unable to conceive a child, but he knew the truth. When he wasn't working, he was consumed by the Kusaka family. There was no space left in his heart for anyone else.

Five years after Toshio Kusaka disappeared, Keiko and Mamoru still showed no sign of leaving Hirakawa. Yoshitake had a growing collection of secretly taken photos of them. When he was alone in his study looking at the pictures he had a feeling of peace. He was wrapped, along with the guilt, in a mysterious sense of oneness. He felt as if Keiko was his own wife and Mamoru his son.

Keiko had a gentle face and sad-looking eyes. Her suffering had not robbed her of her innate softness. The boy had been raised in good health. The photos revealed a hint of understanding beyond his years, but he also had a bright smile that made even Yoshitake feel happy. He wanted to meet the boy. This desire gave him new hope.

Eight years after the accident, the spring of the year he had been promoted to the board of directors of Shin Nippon Enterprises, he made a special trip back to Hirakawa. The annual field day for all the city's public schools was held in April. It was a sort of festival to celebrate the end of the long winter. Yoshitake wanted to see the boy, now twelve, even if from a distance.

Yoshitake had stood behind the fence surrounding the schoolyard. He forgot how long he was there watching every move the boy made. The final event was, as it is in every school, the relay race among the sixth graders. The boy was running anchor for his team and stood waiting his turn, the red anchor sash across his chest.

When the boy took the baton and began to run, Yoshitake stood transfixed, his fingers holding on tight to the links in the fence. The boy had wings on his feet! He had begun the lap in fifth place, but took his strides with an admirable calm. He easily passed up three runners, and made the final turn. On the side of the track farthest from the fence where Yoshitake stood, the boy broke the tape at the finish line, winning by a nose. The students broke out in a cheer, and Yoshitake clapped along with them, yelling out his approval.

A woman standing on the edge of the crowd of parents turned to look at him. It was the boy's mother, Keiko Kusaka. A thickset older man stood next to her, and he too was clapping.

The cherry trees had been in full bloom, and petals fluttered down on Yoshitake's shoulder. It was not the cold, rainy day of the accident. It was a warm spring day. The air was full of cherry blossoms, and Keiko Kusaka had seen him. She broke into a smile and nodded in his direction. She was acknowledging a man she had never seen before who had applauded her son.

Yoshitake visited his mother's home that day, and was greeted with a startled look of accusation. "What are you doing here? Your home is in Tokyo."

Later, sitting alone in the dark, Yoshitake realized that there was nothing he could do but admit to himself that he loved the Kusaka family. Their brave resolve and their strength of will. He loved everything about the way they managed to live. They had refused to give up any of the things he himself had given up on the day of that accident, and he knew they never would.

His mother died six months later. After the funeral and before he sold the house, Yoshitake lifted the floorboards to pull out the paper bag hidden beneath, and burned it in the fire he built to dispose of some of his mother's possessions. He didn't know what to do with the one item that remained, and he eventually kept it—Toshio Kusaka's wedding ring.

He tried it on. It only went as far as the second joint of his ring finger; almost as if the original owner was objecting to his action.

It was the last trip Yoshitake ever made to Hirakawa, although he continued to monitor the Kusakas' life from Tokyo. His wife, Naomi, now considered him nothing more than another corporate executive at her father's company.

Keiko Kusaka died suddenly late in the year Yoshitake was promoted to vice-president. Yoshitake locked himself in his room and cried. He would never have the chance to pay her back for what he had done.

Mamoru was sixteen, and relatives had taken him in. Yoshitake hired a private detective to look into the life of the new family. He was briefly relieved to discover that it was a happy one, but that peace of mind was shattered by the accident resulting in the death of Yoko Sugano.

Yoshitake had a friend in the police department who looked into the matter for him. He learned that the lack of a witness to the accident had left Taizo Asano, Mamoru's uncle, in a position of serious disadvantage.

At the time, Yoshitake had a lover named Hiromi Ida. The relationship had grown, like a flowerless plant, from his strained marriage. One night, as he looked at Hiromi's face without makeup as she stepped out of the shower, he discovered something. Hiromi Ida looked like Keiko Kusaka. The apartment he had found for her had been not in the luxury neighborhoods of Azabu or Daikanyama, but in an old *shitamachi* district cluttered with narrow roads and old buildings. The reason he had done this, he realized, despite Hiromi's obvious displeasure, was so that he could spend time closer to Mamoru.

The time has come.

He had actually been with Hiromi on the night of the accident, but he had not passed through the intersection where it happened. And, of course, he had not witnessed anything. He hadn't even known about the accident until he read about it in the newspaper the next morning.

But he knew he could say that he had been through the intersection and that he had seen the accident. People living in the *shitamachi* area were notoriously interested in anything that happened there, and Yoshitake made good use of the business card of a newspaper reporter he knew to ask around for information on the victim—what she had been wearing, the color of the car, and anything else that would add credibility to his testimony. He committed the details to memory, and thought about the impression he needed to make when he talked to the police.

His position at Shin Nippon Enterprises was not so tenuous as to be rocked by the existence of a lover. Nor was he worried about a divorce. Naomi had been mistaken when she had boldly decided that he was the man for her, and since then she had stopped making bold decisions of any kind.

I'll testify, he decided. *This will get me closer to Mamoru Kusaka. It will give me the chance to insure his future. It will all be for his sake. If I can repay him for even a fraction of the pain I've caused, there's nothing I won't endure; no lie I would refuse to tell. After all, my life has been nothing but a lie so far.*

Everything will be for Mamoru. I'll stand by him. He'll have a better future ahead of him than he would have had if his father, the embezzler, were still alive. It would have made his mother happy, too.

I watched him grow up. He has been my only joy, my only hope . . .

———•———

The tape stopped there.

"It's a horrible story," Harasawa muttered. "Despicable."

Leaning against the door for support, Mamoru didn't even hear him. He felt nauseous.

"Can you believe it?" asked the old man. The only sound was of the tape rewinding. "Of course you believe it! You know what I'm capable of, whether you agree with it or not."

Mamoru nodded. "I believe it. Everything fits."

"What are you going to do?"

"Take it—to the police."

"You?"

"After you send your confession."

"I'm afraid that's not possible."

Mamoru lifted his head in surprise.

"Why? Isn't that why you've done all this?"

"That's where you're wrong, boy." The old man took a deep breath. All of this had apparently been a mere preface to what he had to say next. "Don't you remember what I told you? I told you we would understand each other. You and I have something in common. Can you guess what that is?"

Harasawa pushed the eject button and took out the tape. He walked toward the window with it. "I only recorded this for you to listen to. It has no other value." So saying, he opened the window and threw the tape out of it with surprising agility and speed.

Mamoru catapulted across the room. He watched, appalled, as the tape etched a slow curve and disappeared five stories below into the oily water of the canal.

"What did you do that for?"

"Forget all about it. It was a confession by a man under hypnosis. No court would ever accept it as evidence. Boy," the old man continued in a severe tone, "exposing Kazuko Takagi has not satisfied me. I wouldn't be satisfied with just handing the evidence over to the authorities. You're the same, aren't you? The courts of our country are much too lenient."

"So what do you think I should do?"

"He fooled you. You lived under false pretenses for twelve years. Then Yoshitake lied to help you, so now you have been fooled twice. Not only did he kill your father and escape from the crime, but he has been following you around for his own self-serving purposes. He wanted to get closer to you and for you to like him. He wanted your forgiveness the whole time he was deceiving you. He threw away his conscience twelve years ago, and now he's trying to buy it back. Can you really forgive him for that?

"It's your problem. Yours alone. I won't get involved; I'm leaving Yoshitake entirely out of my confession. There's only one solution left, boy." Harasawa looked Mamoru over with a cold eye. "You are the one who will have to deliver the verdict."

When Mamoru finally left, his ears were ringing and his mind was full to overflowing with the instructions the old man had given him.

I gave Yoshitake a keyword.

The traffic signal on the road blinked, and the taillights of the cars were bright.

It's a simple phrase. Very simple. This is all you will have to say. Wind pushed at Mamoru from behind. *It's foggy in Tokyo again tonight.*

"It's foggy in Tokyo again tonight." Mamoru repeated the words to himself.

That's all you have to say for Yoshitake to kill himself. You can even stay and watch.

Mamoru didn't feel like going home.

I hope you'll make the right choice.

He had been tricked from the very beginning. It had all been a lie.

I owe it to your father. I'm only doing what's right.

Yoshitake had wanted to make amends.

He went to the police in spite of all that. Yoriko had been thankful that Yoshitake had risked his position and his marriage, and Taizo had gone to work for him.

Mamoru thought about how Yoshitake had also got his mother a job, and he reflected bitterly that this was what had made it possible for them to stay in Hirakawa all those years. They would have been better off if they had left. Anger welled up inside him. Yoshitake had acted out of guilt and pity. And he planned to continue doing so.

Are you going to just let them all keep on making excuses for themselves? Harasawa had asked him.

No, Mamoru knew he couldn't. Because—

It would mean cutting away at your soul, boy!

The moon in the sky looked like a freshly sharpened blade.

———•———

Kazuko Takagi was waiting at Cerberus. There were no other customers in the shop when Mamoru came through the door. Kazuko looked as though she had aged ten years in a single day. As Mamoru talked, she sat quietly without interrupting, gripping Mitamura's hand the entire time.

Mamoru wanted to make sense of everything he had heard, so he told her everything that he knew about why Harasawa had tried to kill the four women. He spoke as though he were on the old man's side.

By the time he had finished, the warm shop had gone cold.

"I—" Kazuko put her hand to her cheek. "What I did, what we did was terrible."

There was silence.

"I mean, it was unforgivable, but—he didn't have to kill us!" Kazuko had begun crying. "It wasn't bad enough to die for!"

"That's enough now," Mitamura said soothingly.

Kazuko shook her head and looked up at Mamoru. "So what do *you* think? Do you believe I should have died? Do you know what happened to Atsuko Mita? She was decapitated! She was in pieces all over the track! At Fumie Kato's funeral, they couldn't open her casket so her parents could say good-bye. Her face was gone."

Kazuko grabbed onto Mamoru's jacket and sobbed. "I don't understand. Why did he have to go that far? Tell me! Was what we did so bad? I'm begging you to tell me! Was that the punishment we deserved?"

Mamoru averted his eyes from Kazuko's tear-streaked face.

"What we did was wrong. I felt guilty, but I had no choice. Once we'd started, it wasn't up to us to decide to quit. We had to continue. None of us did it because we liked it!"

Are you going to just let them all keep on making excuses for themselves?

Mamoru looked down and whispered, "He's not going to kill anyone else."

Mitamura put his arm around Kazuko's shoulders. "He's going to leave her alone? He's not going to kill her? But why?"

Mamoru slipped off the counter stool and headed for the door.

"He's gotten all the revenge he needs. What he wants now is a friend."

Epilogue

There was an unseasonable snowfall that day.

The Shin Nippon Enterprises headquarters was in the upscale Roppongi area. Just around the corner from the subway entrance on Roppongi Avenue was the Azabu Police Station. Mamoru stopped in front of it.

I'm on my way to murder someone.

A policeman stood at the entrance watching the cars going up and down the avenue. Mamoru watched the flakes of snow falling silently over the brightly lit city. The wet road reflected the car headlights, creating a Milky Way on earth.

Yoshitake had told Mamoru to meet him at an old-fashioned coffee shop named Hafukan. The door was heavy. Mamoru felt like the sheer weight of it was trying to tell him to turn back. There was still time.

But it was too late. Mamoru stepped inside.

The room was dimly lit and the air was full of the aroma of coffee. Even the customers who filled the shop had an amber hue to them.

Yoshitake had arrived first. He stood up in his booth and waved Mamoru over. Mamoru walked over to him, knowing that each step meant that Yoshitake was a step closer to death.

"Bad weather tonight. You must be cold." Yoshitake seemed concerned.

But all Mamoru could think of was how cold it must have been the morning Yoshitake had killed his father. "I'm fine. I like the snow."

"Yeah, I guess it's tame compared to snow in Hirakawa." Yoshitake was in good spirits. There was an empty espresso cup on the table. A waitress came over, and Yoshitake ordered another espresso. Mamoru asked for coffee.

"What's on your mind?" asked Yoshitake. Mamoru had called to say he had something to talk about, and asked if he could see him; he'd be glad to meet him near his office.

"Are you feeling better?" Mamoru asked.

"There was nothing wrong to begin with. The doctor couldn't figure it out either."

Mamoru was having trouble talking. He couldn't take his eyes off of Yoshitake's face and his smooth golf tan.

My father has been dead the whole time you've been playing golf, drinking, and even while you were at the police station testifying. He's nothing but a pile of bones buried in some mountain. You were living a happy life the whole time I hated my father, all those years my mother waited for him to come home. You're the only one who has had any happiness.

"Is something the matter?" Yoshitake's expression clouded. "Why are you looking at me like that?"

"Like what?" Mamoru reached out for his coffee cup, and missed the handle. The black liquid spilled out of the porcelain cup and onto his hand. Mamoru wondered absently whether it resembled the color of blood.

"Did you burn yourself?" Yoshitake put out his hand to touch Mamoru's, but Mamoru yanked it back.

You pitied and used us. Pitied . . . that's what I can't forgive. Do you understand what I'm saying?

"Are you sick? Your clothes are soaking and you're pale, too. Didn't you have an umbrella?"

I'm not shaking from the cold.

"You'd better go home. We can talk another time." Yoshitake pulled out his wallet. "Your family will be worried. Buy a shirt and a sweater somewhere around here and change before you go home."

Mamoru swept the ten-thousand yen bill onto the floor.

Say it, say it! It's foggy in Tokyo again tonight. Get it over with!

The man at the next table looked at the bill on the floor and the faces of the two men. He finally picked it up and put it back on their table. Neither Mamoru nor Yoshitake noticed.

Yoshitake finally spoke. "I'm sorry if I've offended you. I can't . . . I mean . . . it's hard to . . ." Yoshitake stared inside his cup as if it contained the lines he had in mind. "You . . . you seem like my own son sometimes. If I end up doing something rude, forgive me."

It's not hard! Say it! It's foggy in Tokyo again tonight.

Looking like he didn't know what else to do, Yoshitake took out a cigarette and played with it with his fingers. He looked like a child who had just been scolded.

Mamoru noticed how noisy it was in the coffee shop. With so many people in the city, who would miss one?

Thank you for taking care of Yoko Sugano.

Would my father say the same thing to me, Mamoru wondered. *Thanks for taking care of Yoshitake?* Then all of a sudden, he saw another face and heard a voice speaking to him. *Mamoru, never use your father as an excuse. Don't ever go looking for excuses.* It was Gramps.

I wanted to pay you back somehow. That was what Yoichi Miyashita said when he'd tried to commit suicide for Mamoru's sake. *My life wasn't worth living. I couldn't even hang myself.* Mamoru clenched his teeth. Just because you wanted to make amends didn't mean you could do just anything.

"Come on," said Yoshitake. "I think we should leave." He stood up and walked over to the cash register.

Mamoru went outside. It was snowing. It had begun to stick to the ground. The city was growing colder, and so was Mamoru. Yoshitake came out a few moments later. His breath was white. Mamoru's breath was white, too. Whiter even than the snow.

The two faced each other in the warm light that came out of Hafukan. Mamoru wondered if he'd be able to have confidence in himself thirty years from now. Fifty years from now. Would he be able to die without regrets?

"At least get yourself an umbrella," urged Yoshitake. "Go home and take a hot bath."

I'm here to murder you.

"I'll see you, then," Yoshitake turned to go on his way.

He has a broad back. If my father were alive, it's the sort of back he'd have, too.

Yoshitake turned to add, "I hope I can expect to see you again."

Mamoru didn't respond, so Yoshitake walked off.

One step, two steps. He was getting farther away.

You made a deal that wasn't fair. You used a dirty trick to try to buy back the conscience you threw away twelve years ago. And all for your own sake.

"Mr. Yoshitake!" Mamoru yelled out. Already well down the street, Yoshitake turned around.

There was time. There was a distance of twelve years. The snow, in its detached way, filled in that distance through which no voice could be heard.

"Mr. Yoshitake."

"What?"

"It's foggy—"

"What?" he had his hand to his ear.

Are you going to just let them all keep on making excuses for themselves?

"It's foggy in Tokyo—"

I wanted to pay you back somehow.

It's foggy in Tokyo again tonight.

Yoshitake walked back to Mamoru's side. "What did you say?"

Mamoru was tired of trying to make up his mind. "It's foggy in Tokyo again tonight."

Yoshitake cocked his head, and Mamoru held his breath. For an instant he thought the old man had taken him in. Nothing was happening.

But Yoshitake's eyes gradually began to lose their focus, and then they opened wide, looking all around him. He found the shadow of his invisible pursuer. Then he walked hastily away, leaving the snow, Mamoru, and the frozen city behind.

Are you okay with this? Something inside Mamoru was trying to reach him. Mom. His mother had believed in his father. She believed in the man who had left divorce papers for her to sign but had gone off still wearing his wedding ring. That's why she had waited. She knew that it was a sign of how he really felt.

It wasn't a smooth move, but it was the right one.

If I can repay him for even a fraction of the pain I've caused.

The snow came down on Mamoru's neck. A couple sharing an umbrella looked back at Mamoru, and then at each other, and hurried off.

Thank you for taking care of Yoko Sugano. Thanks for killing her. She had it coming.

But she had been terrified. She had felt remorse.

Tell me! Was what we did so bad?

All I did was give them what they had coming to them.

No!

Mamoru ran back the way he had come. Yoshitake was gone. The pedestrian signal was blinking as Mamoru dashed across the street and headed for the Shin Nippon headquarters.

The front doors were closed. Mamoru slipped and hit his knee, but quickly stood back up and began to look for the night entrance. He ran into a pedestrian whose umbrella unloaded its snow on him.

There was a light on in the security office. He tapped on the window.

"Where is the vice-president's office?"

A cautious voice replied.

"Who are you?"

"My name is Kusaka—where is it?"

"What business do you have?"

"What floor is it on?"

"The fifth floor, but—"

Mamoru ran for the elevator, the security guard close on his heels. He pushed the button, and saw that the elevator had stopped on the fifth floor. Now it was moving slowly downward. Mamoru decided to take the stairs.

The fifth floor. Doors were lined up along the hallway on both sides. He found a map on the wall. Yoshitake's office was at the end of the hall on the left. He ran, leaving wet footprints on the carpet and struggling under the weight of his wet jacket.

By the time he'd dashed through the secretary's office and rammed open the door to the inner office, Yoshitake was leaning out of the window on the other side of his desk.

"Mr. Yoshitake!" Yoshitake did not hear him. His knees were on the windowsill now.

Mamoru didn't think he could make it, but he leaped forward anyway and managed to grab the edge of Yoshitake's coat. He heard the sound of the fabric ripping. A button flew off. The two of them fell in a heap on the floor. Yoshitake's revolving chair slid across the room.

Mamoru sat up and leaned against the desk. Yoshitake blinked.

The security guard finally arrived, panting and out of breath.

"Mr. Yoshitake, what—what happened?" he asked.

The hypnotic state was broken. The keyword was no longer valid. Mamoru knew that when he looked into Yoshitake's eyes.

"I—I . . ." Yoshitake opened his mouth and looked at Mamoru. "Mamoru, what are you doing here?"

"Do you know him?" asked the security guard.

"Ah yes, but . . ." Yoshitake looked at Mamoru and then up at the window into which the snow was blowing.

"You can go," he waved the officer away. The man gave Mamoru a suspicious look and left the room.

The two of them were left alone.

Mamoru looked at Yoshitake's face. There were tiny wrinkles in the corners of his eyes, and his face had gone so pale that he had almost lost his tan. His open coat made him look as unkempt as a vagrant.

"There was something I forgot to tell you."

Mamoru grabbed onto the edge of the desk and pulled himself up. He went over to the window and looked down. The sidewalk was white, and a rainbow of umbrellas moved back and forth along it.

He closed the window and locked it shut. Then he turned his back on it and faced Yoshitake. "I won't be seeing you again. This is the last time." As he left the room, he caught a glimpse of Yoshitake still sitting on the floor. He seemed hunched over in remorse.

Mamoru slowly walked down the stairs. He had to sit down once and rest. By the time he got outside, it was snowing even harder. Both his jacket and his pants were soon white. He thought he'd like to stop and stand there forever, like a mailbox.

He began walking, and he could see his footprints in the snow. He was in a descent. He hadn't made it to the top.

He found a public telephone, dialed a number and let it ring. Was Harasawa too weak to reach the phone?

"Hello?" A hoarse voice finally answered.

"It's me."

There was a long silence.

"Hello? Can you hear me? It's not foggy tonight, it's snowing." Mamoru's chin began to shake. "Are you listening? It's snowing. I couldn't do it. I thought I could, but I failed. Do you understand? I couldn't do it like you did. I didn't let Yoshitake die." The snow on his cheek began to melt and run down his face. "I couldn't kill him. I couldn't kill the man who killed my father. What a joke!"

Mamoru began to laugh as he beat the inside of the phone booth with his fist. He couldn't stop. "You're a fine man! Crazy, but you did what you thought was right. I don't even know what's right. I didn't want to know any of it. I wanted to stay ignorant. Son of a bitch, I wish I could have killed you!"

Outside, the snow had turned into a blizzard and it beat against the phone booth. It made a muffled sound. Mamoru rested the phone against his head and closed his eyes.

"Good-bye, boy," the voice said. And then there was the sound of the phone being gently hung up.

On the long trip home, Mamoru had a hazy dream. He was standing on a crooked axis waving a wand, trying to conjure up a rabbit that showed no signs of appearing. It was the dream of a mad, decrepit sorcerer.

———— • ————

Mamoru made it home, collapsing the instant he was inside. His family helped him into bed, where he stayed for ten whole days.

He had pneumonia, and the doctor recommended hospitalization. His high fever gave him only shallow sleep. He occasionally mumbled something and turned over, but none of the Asanos could understand what he was saying.

He wasn't completely unconscious; he knew vaguely what was happening and could tell the different faces apart. There were Taizo and Yoriko, and Maki with her hand on his forehead. Sometimes he was sure his mother was next to him, and he tried to sit up when that happened.

He didn't see his father's face. He desperately tried to remember it, but couldn't. When he was awake, he could hear Yoriko and Maki talking.

"Why did he do something so stupid? He didn't even take an umbrella and it was snowing."

Maki sat next to him, staring at his face. "Mom?" she asked quietly. "Have you ever felt like he's keeping something from us?"

Yoriko took a few moments to respond. "Now that you mention it."

"I've often wondered why, but I can never figure it out. I can't imagine what it could be."

"Me neither."

"But I finally decided that if he was hiding something, it was probably something better left unsaid. He's decided that it's better that we don't know, and he's keeping it to himself. It makes me feel sad, but I'm sure that's what it is. You know, Mom," Maki continued, "he might be protecting us. So promise me you won't ask him anything until he decides to tell us himself. That's the only thing we can do for him."

"I promise," answered Yoriko.

Then Taizo came into the room.

"Where've you been, Dad?"

"I went to buy some ice."

When Mamoru began to recover he had some visitors.

Anego was in tears when she peeked in at his door.

"What's the matter with you?" Mamoru asked weakly. "It must be a sign of something ominous," he teased.

"Idiot!" She didn't even bother to wipe her face. "But since you've got that smart mouth back, I guess you're not going to die."

"Not me. I wouldn't be able to live with myself if I died of pneumonia."

"You know . . ."

"What?"

"I felt like you were somewhere far, far away."

"I was here the whole time."

"No, you were definitely gone."

"Well, I'm back now. I'll hear you when you call. I mean, you do have a loud voice."

When Yoichi Miyashita came by, Mamoru had a favor to ask him.

"Can you get me a copy of that picture, *The Disquieting Muses*?"

"Sure, I'll cut it out of a book."

"I really want it."

"Your wish is my command." Yoichi looked pleased but puzzled. "But why do you like it all of a sudden?"

"I don't know if I like it, but I think I finally understand it."

When Takano came to visit, the first thing Mamoru did was ask about the video display.

"I'm still at war with those in power," Takano replied. "But it's a just battle. And word is spreading among the other employees."

"Did you tell them all about the subliminal advertising?"

"Yup, I've got to get the numbers on my side. I'm working on the union right now. When I showed the union leaders the video, they jumped out of their seats. Since it almost killed me, I was pretty convincing.

"You've got to get back on your feet soon, we're all waiting for you. Sato's dying to tell you about his latest trek in the desert. Something about the wind being a living thing."

Mamoru's mind was like the pendulum on a grandfather clock that had stopped in mid-swing. He couldn't bring himself to think about either Yoshitake or Harasawa. He wanted to spend some time not thinking about anything at all.

At the end of February, the Kanto area had another heavy snowfall.

That morning, Taizo saw Mamoru and Maki off, telling them he wished he had his license back already so he could take them to work and school.

Taizo quit Shin Nippon Enterprises and went back to work for Tokai Taxi. He planned to start driving again as soon as his license was reinstated. Yoko Sugano's death had had such a strong impact on him that it had taken something even stronger to send him back to driving.

A single letter had done the trick.

The letter was written in beautiful penmanship, and it was from the woman Taizo had had as a passenger the night of the accident. He had already put up his Out of Service sign, but had decided to give her a lift anyway.

Her husband had had a stroke in another country and she had been hurrying to the airport to catch a plane to get to his side. When she had finally reached the hospital, the doctor told her there was nothing more that could be done for her husband. The last hope, he said, the only thing that might bring him back from the brink of death was hearing her call his name.

The woman had taken her husband's hand and called his name with all the feeling she could muster. She told him over and over that she was with him and waiting for him to regain consciousness. Her husband had heard her and responded. He had recovered.

> If I hadn't gotten there when I did—if you hadn't picked me up, and I had gotten to the airport later and taken a later flight, my husband would never have come back to me.
>
> I'm writing this letter to thank you. Please keep up your good work, taking care of the passengers who need you. Mr. Asano, your taxi carried with it my husband's life.

This was the letter that raised the flag in Taizo's heart from half mast until it was flying high again.

March came and there was still no sign that Harasawa's confession had been received.

Despite the concern expressed by the Asano family, Mamoru took a trip to Hirakawa on the first weekend of the month. He wanted to find out what had happened to his father on that early morning twelve years ago.

The plum blossoms were just beginning to open in Hirakawa, and the tops of the mountains were still blanketed in snow. Mamoru started out by visiting the city library, where he borrowed a map of the city from twelve years before. Using his finger to trace his way through town, Mamoru figured out what his father had been trying to do.

There was still snow in the public cemetery on a hill where both Keiko Kusaka and Gramps slept.

"I figured out where Dad was going," Mamoru reported to them.

Twelve years ago there had been a small building at the foot of the mountain. The road Toshio had been walking on had been a shortcut straight to it. He had left so early in the morning to avoid causing unnecessary confusion at work. It was the police station. The Hirakawa prefectural police station.

He had been going to turn himself in for taking the funds.

On the express train back to Tokyo, Mamoru finally understood what Gramps had said to him. *Your father wasn't a bad man; he was weak. Someday you'll understand your father's weakness and what was so sad about that.*

His father had been weak, but he wasn't a coward. He had tried to make amends for taking something that wasn't his. He had tried to pay it back in the proper way. That was what Mamoru felt.

I did what was right. Dad, do you believe it was right? I didn't kill Yoshitake. I couldn't. That was the right thing.

———————•———————

Harasawa's confession reached the police late in March. The sensation it created was a surprise even to Mamoru. The police arrived to investigate Harasawa's apartment, followed by the mass media and all of his neighbors.

Photos of the four women were in all the newspapers and magazines, and headlined the tabloid news shows on TV.

One day when Kazuko Takagi's photo was shown on the news, Yoriko pointed at it in surprise. "That woman was at Yoko Sugano's wake! She helped me when I was injured."

There were calls to outlaw fraudulent business practices, but Mamoru was vaguely uneasy that all this was merely an emotional outpouring and the urgency would quickly wear off. The storm was fierce, but it wouldn't be long before it subsided. In the meantime, everything in its path would be mowed down—Yoko Sugano's younger sister, for example. Mamoru thought about her often, but there was nothing he could do for her.

Just as Harasawa had promised, there was no mention in his confession of Yoshitake's testimony. Yoshitake was still widely known as a good Samaritan, and the mass media was back at his door as all of the incidents involving the four women were brought into the public eye. Mamoru turned off the radio and TV whenever his name was mentioned, so he never learned how Yoshitake responded to questions.

Interest in hypnosis exploded. Everything from the driest of scholarly works to the most basic how-to books flew off the shelves as fast as Laurel staff could load them on carts and restock them. Mamoru picked up one of the books. As he read through it he decided once and for all that Harasawa had been wrong.

He had claimed that he could hypnotize anyone into doing something that would result in self-destruction, but it wasn't true. The old man was able to manipulate them into fleeing to their death simply because deep in their hearts they felt that they had to keep running.

In other words, they regretted what they had done and were afraid. Results could not be pulled out of thin air. The trees these women had planted had borne the fruits of a guilty conscience. All Harasawa had done was shake the trees so violently that they were completely uprooted.

Harasawa had only punished criminals who were susceptible to punishment. Mamoru thought that there must be lots of other criminals who better deserved to be punished. Maybe the darkness in which the sorcerer lived made it impossible to distinguish between the two. Mamoru regretted that he hadn't sorted that out with Harasawa while he had had the chance.

Kazuko Takagi weathered the storm sequestered away at Cerberus. She had thought about leaving when Harasawa's confession hit the media. She didn't want to cause Mitamura any more trouble than she already had.

"There's no need to run," he had told her. "You've paid for what happened, and you understand what's going on better than anyone."

"Don't you blame me for this?"

Mitamura laughed. "You tripped and fell, and I held out a hand to help you up. There's no need to stand here apologizing. Don't you think it's time to move on?"

One day in April, when Kazuko returned from shopping, Mitamura had news for her.

"Mamoru Kusaka was here. He had a message for you."

"What was it?" Kazuko was prepared to accept the worst from Mamoru.

"He hoped you pulled through all this, and—"

"And what?"

"He said to thank you for protecting his aunt at Yoko Sugano's wake. That's what he said."

Kazuko leaned against the counter and covered her face.

"He's forgiven me," she finally said in a small voice.

How can I find my father? It was all Mamoru could think of. A forest reserve somewhere near Hirakawa. An hour's drive from the city. It would be impossible for him to find it alone without some kind of sign to look for. How could he get the police to help? He spent more and more time sitting on the bank of the canal thinking about it.

One day he received an unexpected letter from Harasawa. Mamoru took it to the canal bank to read. The letter opened in a way that almost made him feel nostalgic.

Boy,

I'll bet you're surprised. I'll be long gone by the time you get this. A strong will is a powerful thing. I can still write letters by myself. I'm taking twice as many painkillers as I was when I saw you, but I'm still alive.

This letter will arrive a while after my confession is delivered to the police. It's what I have instructed in my will. You can feel free to tear this up if it is no longer of any use to you.

Boy, you told me that you wanted to kill me. You said you didn't want to know anything. And you didn't kill Yoshitake.

But I still believe that you and I have something in common. Of course, we have many differences, but there is something we share, and I believe that you understand what I did and what I am going to do better than anyone else. Better than the mass media who must be making a huge outcry right about now, and better than all those social opinion experts.

The methods we chose were not the same. I believe what I did was right, and you probably do, too. I'm sure you don't regret sparing Yoshitake's life. But why did you decide to do it? Was it only because you were incapable of murder? I don't think so. Anyone can commit murder if the circumstances are right.

You must have realized, even if unconsciously, that in his own way Yoshitake loved you and your mother. You understood him. Understood and pitied him.

I've got something for you right before I die. A few days after you called me, I saw Yoshitake. I hypnotized

him and gave him another keyword. I'll write it here
for you. Don't forget that it's a combination keyword.
You'll have to be holding his right hand when you say
it, a nice touch, don't you think?

This is my final work, and I hope you decide to use
it. Do you remember when I gave Nobuhiko Hashimoto that
whiskey? I'm someone who always gives people what they
need most. This keyword is just like whiskey was to
Hashimoto, but it won't destroy you.

If you truly pity Yoshitake, give him the chance
to turn himself in. Don't let the past influence you.
You've got a wonderful life ahead of you.

Goodbye, boy. This will be the last time you'll hear
from me. When you're finished, you must forget all about
me. Are the cherry trees in your neighborhood in bloom?
My one regret is that I didn't get to see them once more.

The keyword was written at the end of the letter. When Mamoru read
it, he finally understood the old man. It was too late, but at least he
understood.

The keyword was simple to memorize.

The cherry trees were in full bloom. As Mamoru looked at the trees
over on the other side of the canal, he ripped the letter into tiny pieces
and let them fly out into the water.

He pushed open the door of Hafukan, where Yoshitake had promised
to meet him at seven o'clock. Yoshitake was sitting in the same booth as
last time. The two talked about matters of little consequence. Yoshitake
laughed a lot; he was glad to see Mamoru again. Mamoru talked and
talked. Neither of them mentioned Harasawa.

They left the coffee shop. The whole city seemed to shine in the warm
summer light. As Yoshitake lifted his hand to say good-bye, Mamoru
stopped him.

"I have a favor to ask of you."

"What's that?"

Mamoru held out his right hand. "Shake my hand."

Yoshitake hesitated for a second and then held out his large right hand and firmly gripped Mamoru's. His hand was cold but strong. At that moment, Mamoru leaned into Yoshitake as if to tell him a secret.

"The sorcerer's illusion."

Yoshitake began to walk slowly, and Mamoru followed behind him. Yoshitake stopped in front of the Azabu Police Station. He looked up at the building, and then calmly walked inside. Mamoru watched him go in, and then walked off.

Under a pink neon sign by the subway he ran into two girls about his own age. They were both beautiful with long hair and eyes shining with excitement. *The night has just begun!* It was written all over their faces.

When their eyes met Mamoru's, both of them began to giggle.

"Hi!" called out one of them. "Isn't it a great night? Where you going?"

"I'm on my way home," answered Mamoru.

Author's Acknowledgments

Kinko yaburi (published by Dojidai-sha) by Akizo Sugiyama was used as reference on techniques for safecracking.

*The description of subliminal advertising was quoted from *Jōhōchishiki imidasu*.

*Lyrics quoted on page are 90 from "The Stranger" by Billy Joel.

*All of the names of people and organizations in this book are fictitious.

The translator gratefully acknowledges the invaluable assistance of my reader, Anna Isozaki; my research assistant, Manna Iwabuchi; and my editor, Ginny Tapley, who, along with Ikuo, Hikari, Rebecca, Phil, Bobbie, and Wally, put up with me and keep me going through thick and thin.

Junko checked her surroundings quickly. She had to hide. Luckily the heavy darkness acted as a natural screen for her.

"What the hell are you doing?"

"Shh! Keep it down, stupid!"

The voices became clearer. The beams from two flashlights flew up and down, crisscrossing each other. She could make out heads moving in the light. It looked like there were three, maybe four of them. They were trying to get in through the same unhinged steel door that Junko herself had come through.

She ducked her head down and, in a crouch, slipped in behind the water tank, pressing herself against the wall. Junko's power, the lid slammed on just before release, had settled down quietly inside her, but her heart pounded at the sudden intrusion. Who the heck were these guys? What were they doing here? And at this hour?

The cluster of human shapes was still in a confused knot around the door. It looked like they were having some trouble getting in. Junko strained to see them. She could hear something thumping against the door.

Soon the black silhouette of the first figure became fully visible. In the light cast by an unsteady flashlight beam she could make out that his back was to her, and he seemed to be moving backwards. It looked like they were carrying something—

Junko's breath caught in her throat.

They were lugging in a human form. Dead or unconscious, it was stretched between them, hanging limply. The first guy grasped it under its arms, and another carried its feet. The thumping sound she'd just heard must have been its shoes hitting the door.

Behind them came another two figures carrying flashlights and nervously jerking their heads back and forth, checking the street outside, and hurrying the others along. The flashlights they were holding seemed to be much larger than Junko's, and the beams were stronger. Still crouching, she put her hands on the wall to guide herself as she inched along, retreating further into the shadow of the water tank.

"Hey! Hurry up and shut it!" someone ordered. In response, the unhinged door was closed with such a violent shove that it listed slightly to the side, opening a narrow crack through which light from the street outside poured in a thin diagonal line. The only other light in the abandoned factory was from the two flashlights held by the intruders.

Now that they'd gotten through the door, their progress was faster. One of the guys holding a flashlight led the way, coming in Junko's direction along the path she had cleared. His footsteps were getting closer.

As they got to the center of the factory, Junko could make them out a little more clearly. She couldn't see their full bodies in the capricious light of the flashlights, but she could discern their builds. And voices.

"About here okay?"

A young guy. Younger than Junko. Twenty? Were all of them so young?

"Let's put him down. He's heavy."

There was a thud as something heavy hit the ground. The way they'd been carrying the body was rough, but the way they set him down was awful. Even so, there was no grunt of pain as he landed and the wind was knocked out of him, no groan of protest. He seemed completely helpless. Was he dead?

Junko clenched her fists. Her palms were sweating. Whichever way she looked at it, this was clearly no friend of theirs. They didn't look like troublemaking high school students who'd been on a spree and were bringing in one of their friends who'd drunk too much and passed out, or a motorcycle gang who'd come in to lay low and hide a member injured during a police chase. This had more of a grim, ugly look to it.

Junko rigidly observed the proceedings. It seemed that none of the four youths had noticed her at all. One of the two holding flashlights yawned loudly.

"Man, I'm beat."

"What *is* this place? It stinks."

The beams of the two flashlights started flicking around the factory. Up, down, left, right. To avoid being caught in one of the circles of light, Junko crouched as low as she could, and kept her head down.

"Asaba, how'd you find out about this place?"

"My old man used to work here a long time ago."

"Oh, w-o-w," came from the other three, their voices a mixture of respect and derision.

"Hey, I thought you said your old man didn't have a job."

"Yeah. He was fired when this place closed down."

"But that must have been years ago, right? He hasn't had a job since?"

"*Whatever.* Who cares?"

They burst out laughing. Hearing their laughter confirmed for Junko that they really were young. They had to be teenagers. Unrestrained, youthful laughter. It was so totally out of place that it raised goose bumps on Junko's skin.

"Whadda we do? Bury him here?" asked one of them.

"Yeah, it's just bare ground, huh?" replied another, flashlight in hand. He was kicking at the ground with the toe of his shoe.

Bury? Then that guy was dead after all? They'd snuck in here to dispose of a body?

"But the ground's hard. You gonna make us dig a hole here?"

"Why don't we just dump him?"

"Yeah, and what if they find him?" came the voice of the one they'd called "Asaba" just now. "We've got to hide him right."

"Then why not throw him in the river like I said before?"

"Sooner or later, someone's gonna find him," said Asaba. His tone was admonishing. It sounded like he was the leader. "As long as they don't find a body, no one runs around screaming. That's the way it's worked so far. Just as long as we do it right, like I said."

"Shit. It'll take all night."

Asaba silenced the discontented muttering with a terse, "You've got a shovel, right?"

"Yeah, got it."

"Then dig around here. This is a good spot. Nobody'll come poking around behind these machines."

Junko thought that Asaba must be on the other side of the factory from her, somewhere by the conveyor belt. One of the flashlights was shining over there. But the second flashlight started moving around the interior of the factory again. Worse, it wasn't aimed at the ceiling at all anymore, but instead was carefully going over the area from about waist height down. Junko held her breath and shrank deeper into the crevice between the water tank and the factory wall.

She heard the crunch of the shovel hitting the ground.

"What the fuck is this? It's too hard for this shovel."

"Just shut up and do it."

The other flashlight was still shining here and there. The beam landed on the water tank Junko was hiding behind, the wall next to it, skimmed the rim of the holding pool, went to the conveyor belt—and suddenly flicked back in her direction.

"Hey," the guy called to the others. "Looks like a pool or something."

The round beam of light from the flashlight was on the holding pool, just a few steps from where Junko was hiding. Sandwiched in between the water tank and the factory wall, Junko's ribcage was squeezed painfully and breathing was difficult, but she controlled herself, remaining absolutely still. They might catch any inadvertent movement.

"What're you talking about?"

"Over here."

The sound of the shovel ceased. The guys came closer to the holding pool, and one of them leaned over the rim. Junko could see his silhouette reflected on the water's surface.

"This water's putrid!"

"It's oil, isn't it?"

"That's what I mean! It's perfect. If we toss him in here, no one will ever find him. Looks good and deep, too."

"It might work . . ."

There was a splashing sound, as if someone had plunged their hand into the water.

"It'd be better than burying him, right, Asaba?"

Asaba didn't reply right away. Junko thought he was the one who'd plunged his hand into the holding pool. After a few moments, he pulled his hand out of the water and answered.

"Water this filthy could be okay."

The other three cheered. Junko closed her eyes. What *was* this? They'd come searching for a place to hide a dead body, and now they were all excited to have found her holding pool. What *were* these guys? Were they human beings?

Human.

Junko opened her eyes, and shivered from a different kind of tension than she'd been feeling until now.

These four. These four creeps . . .

They left the side of the pool and headed back toward where they'd been digging. Moving with purpose. Were they seriously planning to throw a dead body in there? Dead body? Dead *person*?

Not just dead—these guys had killed him, she was certain. And they were planning to dispose of him here. And worse, from what she'd heard Asaba saying, this was not the first time they'd done this sort of thing.

That's the way it's worked so far. Yes, that's what he'd said. They must have killed before.

Could their type be called human? Or was it stretching the word too far? Well, they could be called anything—people were free to say what they wanted. They were human, they were wild and aimless youth, they were victims of society. . . they could be called whatever people wanted. But she, Junko Aoki, didn't think a group like these four were human. And furthermore—

She wouldn't mind getting rid of them . . .

(英文版) 魔術はささやく
The Devil's Whisper
───────────────────────────

2007 年 6 月 27 日　第 1 刷発行

著　者　　宮部みゆき
訳　者　　岩渕デボラ

発行者　　富田 充
発行所　　講談社インターナショナル株式会社
　　　　　〒112-8652 東京都文京区音羽 1-17-14
　　　　　電話　03-3944-6493（編集部）
　　　　　　　　03-3944-6492（マーケティング部・業務部）
　　　　　ホームページ　www.kodansha-intl.com

印刷・製本所　　大日本印刷株式会社

落丁本・乱丁本は購入書店名を明記のうえ、講談社インターナショナル業務部宛にお
送りください。送料小社負担にてお取替えします。なお、この本についてのお問い合
わせは、編集部宛にお願いいたします。本書の無断複写（コピー）、転載は著作権法
の例外を除き、禁じられています。

定価はカバーに表示してあります。